I Almost Do

Trust & Tequila Book One

Evangeline Williams

Copyright © 2023 by Evangeline Williams

Published by Evangeline Williams

All rights reserved.

This book or any portion thereof may not reproduced or used in any manner whatsoever without the express written permission of the publisher except for the use of brief quotations in a book review. No portion of this book may be reproduced in any form without written permission from the publisher or author, except as permitted by U.S. copyright law. This is a work of fiction and any resemblance to actual persons, living or dead, is solely coincidental. Names, businesses, characters, places, locales, and events are either used in a fictitious manner or the sole product of the author's imagination. They are intended solely for the purpose of entertainment and are in no way based on real events.

Edited by Kristin Scearce and Jamee Thumm/ Hot Tree Editing

cover by Getcovers

Contents

Dedication — VI

Content Notes — VII

Playlist — VIII

1. That's My Girl — 1
2. Cruel Summer — 8
3. Hurricane — 13
4. Easy On Me — 22
5. Stand By Me — 29
6. Raise Your Glass — 40
7. Kiss Me — 51
8. Say You Won't Let Go — 59
9. How Do I Say Goodbye — 64
10. Carry You — 71
11. Safe Place — 77

12.	When the Party's Over	82
13.	Good as Hell	88
14.	This Is Me Trying	98
15.	Brave	106
16.	Fall Into Me	112
17.	Dangerous Woman	124
18.	Don't Blame Me	130
19.	Say You Love Me	138
20.	Lost Without You	142
21.	Peer Pressure	154
22.	I See Red	166
23.	Waking up Slow	169
24.	Falling Like the Stars	171
25.	Incomplete	180
26.	Naked	187
27.	If You Need Me	194
28.	I Don't Want to Lose You	199
29.	Only Love Can Hurt Like This	209
30.	Hurts Like Hell	216
31.	If the World Was Ending	222
32.	I Will Be	229
33.	Roots	239
34.	River	246
Epilogue		251

| Afterword | 259 |
| Acknowledgments | 260 |

For Kurt.

You taught me what a real happily ever after feels like.

Content Notes

INCLUDES SPOILERS

This work of fiction contains adult themes and language that may be disturbing to some readers. They are as follows:

*Swearing *On-page consensual sexual intimacy using graphic language *Alcohol consumption and intoxication *Emesis *Terminal illness and on-page death of a parent due to cancer *Grief/mourning *Reference to past domestic violence, murder of a parent, and child abuse *PTSD, codependence, and mental health issues *Sexual Assault/Sexual Violence (does not occur between main characters) *Depiction of violence, blood, and injury *Off-page kidnapping of a child *Off-page gun violence *Medical emergency/surgery/hospitalization

Playlist

Dear Reader,

 Did you guess the chapter titles for this novel came directly from my playlist? Then you're absolutely right. Every chapter title is also a song title.

 Music has always helped me connect to characters and emotion, and I'm really excited about the songs I've included in this playlist. They provided the soundtrack to Clarissa and James's story as I wrote it.

 Listening to the playlist is not a requirement to enjoy the novel. However, if you're like me and enjoy music as an additional emotional connection, you can access an expanded playlist directly by logging into your Spotify account and entering "I Almost Do" into the search feature. Or you can enter each song title/artist individually into whatever music streaming service you prefer. You can listen to the playlist songs at any time: before, during, or after reading.

Lyrics should not be taken literally. Instead, they're about emotion. The playlist is a vibe. Enjoy.

Playlist

That's My Girl | Fifth Harmony
Cruel Summer | Taylor Swift
Hurricane | Tommee Profitt/Fleurie
Easy On Me | Adele
Stand by Me | Ben E. King
Raise Your Glass | P!nk
Kiss Me | Sixpence None The Richer
Say You Won't Let Go | James Arthur
How Do I Say Goodbye | Dean Lewis
Carry You | Ruelle/Fleurie
Safe Place | RuthAnne
When The Party's Over | Billie Eilish
Good as Hell | Lizzo
This Is Me Trying | Taylor Swift
Brave | Sara Bareilles
Fall Into Me | Forest Blakk
Dangerous Woman | Ariana Grande
Don't Blame Me | Taylor Swift
Say You Love Me | Jessie Ware
Lost Without You | Freya Ridings
Peer Pressure | James Bay/Julia Michaels
I See Red | MymTaleto

EVANGELINE WILLIAMS

Waking Up Slow | Gabrielle Aplin
Falling Like the Stars | James Arthur
Incomplete | James Bay
Naked | James Arthur
If You Need Me | Julia Michaels
I Don't Want to Lose You | Luca Fogale
Only Love Can Hurt Like This | Paloma Faith
Hurts Like Hell | Fleurie/Tommee Profitt
If the World Was Ending | JP Saxe/Julia Michaels
I Will Be | Florence + The Machine
Roots | Grace Davies
River | Bishop Briggs
You Make My Dreams | Tim Halperin

1

That's My Girl

CLARISSA

Present Day

In almost two and a half years of marriage, I've never been to my husband's apartment here in the city. And I have never been inside James's office in the gleaming high-rise that boasts my maiden name in polished letters twenty feet tall.

I stand on the sidewalk, craning my neck to look up, and up. As if I can somehow peer through concrete and steel to see what kind of reception I'll get. I rub sweaty palms on my pencil skirt and let the sea of pedestrians flow around me. I'm a boulder in a current, but I vibrate with a combination of nerves and hopeful excitement.

I wonder how he'll react when he sees the paperwork I've brought with me. I wonder if he'll smile and hold his arms out for a hug or if he'll give me that cold, hard stare he reserves for people he wants to step back in line.

Maybe he'll just give me that slow shake of his head and flat-out refuse. James has never been afraid to let "No" act as a complete sentence.

Maybe he won't be here at all, off on one of his international business meetings.

Wouldn't that be a kick in the pants after all my planning? To have simply forgotten to confirm that he'd be here today?

I didn't try to go to his penthouse first. Security would never have let me in. They don't know me from Eve.

But I'm counting on some of the same security officers being here at the office from *before*. Before I married my dad's CFO. Before my father died. Back when I was a freckle-faced teenager who sprawled in her dad's office after school, doing homework, scrolling IG, and waiting until he was ready to take me home.

I've spent a lot of time waiting, but we're finally done.

I push through the revolving doors into the echoing space of the foyer. Directly in front, beyond a wide expanse of marble floors, a double staircase of glass and steel looms. To the sides, groupings of modern furniture cluster, all hard lines and symmetry. The effect is softened by washes of warm light and living greenery. Soft music plays in the background. The air smells subtly expensive.

I asked my father about that once. Why some buildings, like ours, smell wonderful all the time. He told me small things matter. Visitors might not actively notice the way The Harcourt Tower smells, but they often act on their subconscious feelings and impressions without even realizing it.

For a while I thought there was a single employee traipsing from floor to floor, hiding until no one was watching, then stealth spritzing perfume around like some kind of smell ninja.

I was a little disappointed to learn the scent was pumped through the vents.

Of course, I was six at the time. Now I'm an adult. And everything has changed.

The structure of the building is the same, but the furniture, the huge curving front desk, the names on the sign next to the elevators, and yes, even the smell of the place are subtly different.

"Well, now! Here comes trouble!"

Ah, yes, that old joke. I'd never been "trouble." Once upon a time, I was the most docile, easy-to-please girl in the world. Until I wasn't.

I turn with a huge smile for my favorite security guard, Tony Moretti. His hair is now solidly gray, not the salt-and-pepper I remember.

"Mr. Moretti, are you working hard or hardly working?"

His eyes twinkle. "You know how it is. Have to keep Eleanor in dogs and oil paint."

He takes me in with that Proud Papa grin and says, "You sure are a sight for sore eyes. You haven't been back in a long time."

I give him a hug. "Too long. I don't have a key card for the elevator." I nod at the gleaming silver doors. "Care to do the honors?"

He shoots a glance at the reception desk. I know what he's thinking. I'm supposed to sign in. They'll call up for permission and give me a temporary keyed ID.

I bump him with my shoulder. "I want to surprise my husband."

That's the idea, anyway.

I see the quick calculations going on behind his eyes before he throws in the towel. I am Marcus Harcourt's daughter and James Mellinger's wife, after all.

He swipes his card.

When I breeze past the outer executive offices and head straight for James's door, Rebecca, visibly flustered, rises from behind her desk.

She's one of his executive assistants. *The* executive assistant, if you ask her. She's ruthlessly efficient, gorgeous, midthirties, and svelte, with long blonde hair that drops in a perfectly straight fall that could rival a ruler.

She has a golden tan, as if she's recently spent time in the sun. And if a freckle ever had the nerve to appear on her flawless face, she'd…. Honestly, I have no idea what she'd do. No freckle would ever have the audacity.

"Mrs. Mellinger, I thought you were—"

"In the Hamptons. I know. Surprise!" I say with a smile and waving hands.

"I didn't see you on the schedule—"

Her desk buzzes, and James's voice comes through loud and clear. "Have you made those calls to Lofton yet?"

She looks down, distracted, then presses a button on her desk. "Not yet. It's the middle of the night in his time zone."

James grunts. "If he'd done his job yesterday, we wouldn't need to interrupt his beauty sleep now. Call him."

"Of course. Um, your *wife* is—"

I don't give her a chance to finish. In the time it took for their brief conversation, I'd already slipped past her and pushed open James's door.

His chair is turned so he can admire the view from his enormous windows, tinted on the inside but mirrored from the outside. At the sound of the door opening, he swivels back toward me in surprise.

"I see that," he says into his Bluetooth headset. "No interruptions." He reaches for the headset, makes a show of removing it and turning it off, then leans forward and laces his fingers together tightly on his desk to form a single fist. His knuckles are white.

No smile. No hug. My stomach lurches because this isn't the reception I expected. I thought he might be angry later, but not yet. Not before he heard me out.

I shut the door, then take off my jacket and lay it over the back of a chair. Smoothing down my skirt, I fiddle nervously with my briefcase and pull out the manila folder inside.

I bought the briefcase specially for this occasion. Because briefcases are serious. Professional. *Competent*. It's still pretty and a bit feminine because *why not?* But it's also secure, because the last thing I need is the paperwork in this thing making it into the hands of the press before it's in my husband's.

I try to give James a tentative smile, but it stalls on my face at the hard, flat expression on his. I wasn't sure what to expect when I saw him for the first time in person in six months, but I know it wasn't this nonreaction.

He stands, and the sight of him has my heart in my throat and my knees weak. And suddenly, I can't believe I had the nerve to just show up like this without calling ahead first. Without telling him about the lawyer. It seemed like such a good idea when I planned this moment. I'd march in all Boss Babe Miss Independent. I'd show him how together I have my life. How I don't need him anymore.

But James isn't giving me any reaction at all to go on. Is he pleased to see me, or would he just like to get this interruption over with so he can go back to the things he does in this fancy office, in the fancy building, with my father's name lighting the New York City skyline? Did I misinterpret his letter?

James doesn't smile. He just sends his burning blue gaze in a slow slide from the top of my curly auburn head to my cute ruby ankle boots and back up again.

I should have worn black stilettos or at least a pair of pumps. But the slim gray pencil skirt, ivory button-down, and *briefcase* were as far as I was willing to go in my bid to convince my husband to take me seriously. I'd looked at those stupid stilettos and couldn't do it. They were a bridge too far.

Liking cute shoes that don't hurt my feet doesn't make me immature. It makes me fun and practical.

Looking at my husband, I'm struck again by just how utterly beautiful James is. I don't use that word lightly. He's tall and fit, with a swimmer's physique he keeps honed with hours spent in the pool. His hair is dark, with just a touch of a wave to it. I drink him in like I've been in the desert, and he's a tall drink of water.

Like Rebecca, he has a bit of a tan right now too.

James is dressed in a bespoke suit that cost more than some people pay for a car. His tie is off, though, and the top button of his shirt is undone. He moves to sit on the edge of his desk and beckons me closer.

My feet move before my brain gives them permission. And then I'm standing in front of him, close enough that if he reaches out, he can touch me. Close enough that I can smell the warm, familiar spice of his cologne. Close enough to see the little dent in the center of his full lower lip.

I stare at the tiny scar on his earlobe because that should be safe. No one lusts after earlobes. Except, apparently, me. *Damn it.* I want to touch him. My fingers practically vibrate with the need.

The silence is stretching painfully between us. Involuntarily, I sneak a peek at his eyes. He's watching my mouth. And there's something so tormented about him that it hurts to look at.

His lashes lift, and his gaze clashes with my own. He has on that severe expression he sometimes wears. His eyes burn like a blue flame, and a muscle twitches in his jaw.

He looks so angry. But why? He doesn't even know I've been to a lawyer.

James got a lot out of our arrangement in the end. He got a multi-billion-dollar corporation and a lot of money, at least. Though my father probably would have given him the company whether he married me or not. As James once told me in biting tones, "Your father didn't buy me." But I guess he also got a pretty big pain in the ass when he married me.

So I look at his ear again. Because that's so much easier than looking into those burning eyes.

I'm not the only one who's paid a price for this dubious marriage. I caused him pain when he married me. Mostly inadvertently, but I still did it.

He's waiting for me to speak. But this moment feels too fragile for the words I carried with me up that elevator of glass and steel.

He breaks the silence when it becomes painfully obvious that I'm just going to stand there, staring at his gorgeous earlobe.

"You traveled all this way, Clarissa. It must be important for an in-person meeting without even calling ahead. What can I do for you?"

I swallow hard, and then I hold out the folder. "You can sign these papers."

2

Cruel Summer

CLARISSA

Two and a Half Years Ago

"Say it like you mean it." Bronwyn narrows her blue eyes, glaring at me through FaceTime.

I glance around my Brooklyn Heights brownstone bedroom, checking for an audience I know isn't there.

"I...." I clear my throat.

"Clarissa, if you want to go away to school, you should go. Repeat after me: 'Dad, I'm a twenty-year-old woman, and I want to go to college in Pennsylvania.'"

It's true that I want to go away to school. Sometimes, as ungrateful as it sounds, I feel like I'm trapped here, living my life for another person. I want to make my own choices. Take some risks. Try something new.

But the idea of setting off my father's anxiety pulls me up short every time. He's an amazing man. It's not only me who thinks so. He's been on the cover of *Time*, after all. But he's also fragile in a way the rest of the world doesn't understand.

"I can go my senior year," I hedge. "I should keep commuting from home for now."

"Psssh. At the rate you're racking up credits, you're not even going to end up having a senior year. You'll graduate early."

"What else am I supposed to do with myself? You and Franki and Janessa are all gone. I have zero social life. Zero activities. School and writing are the only things I have besides my dad."

"That's all the more reason to get a life and grow a pair, Harcourt."

"I've already brought it up, and he can't handle it."

"You were kidnapped by your own nanny *seventeen* years ago. You were only gone for three hours before they got you back without a scratch on you."

"But then my mother died. It broke something in him. I can't scare him, Bronwyn. When I bring up going away, he looks so worried and heartbroken."

"He was worried, so you didn't go with my family to Europe. He was worried, so you didn't play sports. Not even swim team, and you're like a fish in the water. He worries, so you don't date, just in case the guy turns out to be Jack the Ripper or something. It's pathological.

"Mark my words—one of these days, you're going to flip a switch and end up on some viral video having a meltdown. It's better to ease into freedom now. Think of it as a controlled release."

I gurgle in laughter at the ridiculous thought, throw myself back onto my bed, and land in a fluffy cloud of comforter.

I hold the phone above me, looking up at my blonde firecracker friend. On the screen, my own image reflects back in the corner. And, for some reason, the contrast of my freckled complexion against the baby pink of the comforter makes me squirm. This entire bedroom is like sleeping in a vat of cotton candy.

"He's protective. He loves me, and I'm all he really has."

She scoffs. "He has friends. Stop making your father sound pathetic."

"Okay. I'll bring it up at dinner," I soothe, knowing full well I'll tiptoe around it and back off at the first sign of trouble.

"Your dad's fear rubbed off on you, too, even when your logical brain says it doesn't make sense. It's natural. You were raised by someone who's convinced the outside world is a constant threat. But you wouldn't be alone. I'd be there with you. And I know for damn sure he'd send your freaking security detail. Nothing bad is going to happen to you."

"It's not about something actually happening to me. He needs me. I can't be selfish and leave him alone."

"Who told you it would be selfish to live your own life?"

I'm saved from answering by a knock at the door.

Turning my head, I call, "Come in."

No one besides Dad or our housekeeper, Julia, ever comes up here. So, for a moment, my brain doesn't compute what I'm seeing when the door swings open.

The man standing there is the absolute last person I expect to see in my bedroom doorway. For a moment, I just lie there in stunned silence.

This feels like some one-of-a-kind event. I want to point a fan at him so his dark hair blows in the wind. Would he notice if I film him walking toward me in slow-mo?

Yes, of course he would. I've made the man uncomfortable enough over the years with my particular brand of hero worship. I've made a very big point of not giving away my ridiculous crush since his initial rejection and avoidance of me—for both our sakes.

But here he is. The subject of my previous high school heart doodles. The youngest CFO in Harcourt's history and my dad's best friend... James Mellinger is in my bedroom.

I drop the phone onto my face with a squawk, and he lurches farther into the room as if he's about to reach for me. He stops about a foot from the bed and stuffs his hands in his pockets.

"Are you all right, Clare?" His voice is a little gruff.

I rub my cheekbone and climb out of my bed to stand, smoothing down my shirt as I go. I'm still dressed from a day of classes at Columbia.

"Fine," I say, praying I don't sound as breathy as I feel.

Generally speaking, James rarely makes eye contact with me, choosing to focus somewhere around my hairline instead. At least that's been the case since I first tried to flirt with him at the age of sixteen.

I can hardly blame the guy for his reaction. He's never rude or dismissive, but he's also, until this moment, been meticulously careful about never being alone with me.

Good for him. I'm not even being sarcastic there. What else was he supposed to do when a teenager flirted with him? James isn't a creep.

But today he does look at me, if only briefly. His blue gaze darts to my cheekbone, then to my eyes in concern.

"Do you need some ice?"

I shrug sheepishly. "I fall asleep holding my phone and do it all the time. No harm, no foul."

He frowns, and I think for a moment he's about to deliver a lecture about not using my phone in bed.

Bronwyn howls through my phone, "Oh my God, is that *James Mellinger* in your bedroom?"

I snatch up the phone, my cheekbones burning, and hang up on her. I'll beg her forgiveness later.

James backs up toward the door, rubs the back of his neck, and says, "Your father sent me up to tell you dinner will be ready in half an hour."

I glance back down at my phone. Sure enough, dinner is about to be served at exactly the same time it always is. There's no logical reason for this message that I can understand.

I give him a confused but cheery thumbs-up. "I'll be there."

He stops for a moment. "Did you... already know about dinner?"

"I mean, it's our standard dinner hour, so yes."

He pauses, frowning, before shifting gears. "I see. I'm sorry to interrupt your phone call." He gives me a sharp nod. "I'll see you at dinner, Clare."

And then he's gone.

3

Hurricane

JAMES

MARCUS HARCOURT IS UP to something. Which is nothing new. He always is. Usually, however, it involves other people. Not me.

I'm sitting in one of his leather armchairs in his study, an ankle resting on the knee of the opposite leg, bourbon on ice held loosely in my hand. I haven't had a single drop. When Marcus Harcourt is up to something, it's best to keep your wits about you until his cards are all on the table.

He's standing near his fireplace mantle, a look on his craggy face that tells me he's struggling to determine the best way to start our conversation.

He looks... tired. I've never noticed that before. It's a mildly cool night in September, but he has the fireplace blazing and a cardigan thrown on over his button-down. Like it's February in Maine, and he's ready for an L.L. Bean photoshoot.

I've been to his brownstone more times than I can count. Often it's just the two of us having a drink and shooting the shit. Or it's a quiet dinner with Marcus and his daughter, Clare.

He's been a widower since she was four. He could have remarried at any point since then. Women still throw themselves at him.

I asked once why he'd never remarried, and he just shook his head and said, "If you ever loved a woman like my Ellie, you wouldn't ask that. It wouldn't be fair to anyone else. They'd always be in second place."

Marcus plays favorites. Always has. Always will.

It's just my dumb good luck that I caught his attention as a green and hungry intern seven years ago. At twenty-nine years old, with no family connections, I should still be hustling to fight my way up the ladder, not CFO of a multibillion-dollar company.

I don't belong here. I'm smart, sure. Driven? Definitely. Ambitious? Obviously.

But I'm not some guy who grew up listening to talk of tax shelters over his organic fresh-squeezed orange juice and chef-prepared English muffin.

Marcus saw something in me, regardless, and he said he didn't "waste opportunities" when God dropped them in his hands. He's been more of a father to me than my own old man ever was.

It's also obvious he's grooming me to take the helm at Harcourt when he retires. "Clare doesn't want it. She says she isn't mean enough," he'd said with a grin on his face.

There's no grin tonight. Just a cold, tired man staring into the flames and nursing a tumbler of the good stuff.

It's been a week since the first time Marcus made up an excuse to put me in direct contact with Clare. Since then, he's found some reason to leave us alone in a room together four times. One of which was in his own damn office at Harcourt.

Obviously, given that she had a bit of a puppy love situation for me, I avoided Clare when she was younger.

She'd tried out her fledgling flirting skills, and I'd shut her down as gently as I knew how to do—which was admittedly probably not all that gentle in hindsight. We both tended to avoid each other after that.

Apparently, Marcus has decided it's time for us to move past that history and act like the adults we all are. I suspect he's trying to ease the awkwardness between his daughter and me by sheer force of proximity.

But if his intention is to make me more comfortable with Clare, he's failing miserably. It seems I've recently developed an inconvenient *infatuation* with my best friend's daughter. *Comfortable* is not a word I'd use to describe our interactions.

Eventually, Marcus throws back his bourbon and moves to sit in the other chair, lowering himself like a creaky old man. When did that happen? Marcus is fit, energetic, a live wire. He's only fifty-one years old.

Some people think our friendship is strange, given he's more than twenty years my senior. But Marcus and I, we're alike in ways no one will ever understand. He gets me.

"I need to ask you for a favor," he says.

I don't need to think about it. "Of course. Anything you need."

He grimaces. "Not so fast. It's a big favor. I don't need an answer tonight. Take the weekend if you need it...." He trails off with a frown and a shake of his head.

I lower both feet to the floor and lean toward him. "Marcus, just ask."

"The thing is... I'm dying. Inoperable. I had that scare about eight years ago. Colon cancer. It's back. They warned me it might happen. Now it's metastasized. Doc figures I have maybe three months."

That makes no sense. The man takes care of himself. He's a complete health nut. "Did you get a second opinion? Maybe there are experimental treatments."

"Second opinion. Third. I know it's a shock, son."

Shock? He thinks the news that he's dying is a shock? It's not a shock, it's a devastation. A tsunami of fear and pain and loss and grief, and I'm standing in the window of a high-rise watching the wave crest the shore, knowing the entire damn building is about to be washed into the ocean.

I stare at my own hands for a long time before I finally manage to say something. "How is Clare taking the news?"

"I haven't told her yet. I wanted to talk to you first." He rubs his eyes. "She's so sweet. Just like her mother that way. Soft too. You know her. She's so innocent. So trusting. She's not ready to be out there unprotected in this world."

I nod because I know it's true. I don't know how he managed it, but Marcus has successfully sheltered his daughter from the worst of this awful world. He's loved and protected her the way a parent is supposed to.

After a horrific episode in her childhood, Marcus somehow turned that around for her.

He says she doesn't even remember that, while her mother was sick with cancer, a temporary nanny and her boyfriend attempted to kidnap her for ransom. She knows it happened as a matter of record, but she was only three and doesn't remember it or the bloody shoot-out that occurred as a result.

Thank God for that. Because no one needs memories of blood and death.

I'm only nine years older than she is, but it feels more like twenty. "Do you need me to look out for her? I can look in on her for you, manage her finances—"

"I need you to marry her."

I look at the tumbler in my hand, then knock back the entire glass of bourbon in one go. When I can breathe again, I say, "I don't look at her like that." Which is true. But also an outright lie.

"Oh, I know," Marcus says dryly. "I see how much you don't look at her. But I think the way you *don't* look at her now is a little different from the way you used to not look at her."

He's right that I don't look at her. I look anywhere but at her. I avoid her when I can. And when I can't, I keep my vision squarely focused on her forehead.

I keep a tight rein on my fantasies. I don't want to know where my mind could wander if I ever let it. Clare Harcourt is a goddamn dream.

Her freckles and wide green eyes give her a girl-next-door look that couldn't be further from reality. As Marcus Harcourt's daughter, if we had royalty in this country, she'd be a literal princess.

Marcus knows where I came from. And not because I ever told him or talked about it. It's because before he ever allowed me in his home, he had me investigated down to my preschool records. He dug into things he had no legal right to stick his nose in. He even knew I'd changed my name when I was fourteen.

And, for some insane reason that I cannot fathom, he decided he didn't care.

Now here he is, offering me his daughter. As if there was ever a scenario where Clarissa Harcourt could be my wife. Even imagining it feels like flying too close to the sun.

She's off-limits. Full stop. I owe everything to Marcus. Every bit of my career success, every bit of any sense of family and stability I have, he's provided those to me. The man has been a mentor, a friend, and a father to me, never mind that I was in my twenties when I met him.

But I don't come from the kind of life Clare has been raised in. My hands are covered in blood. They have been since I was seven years old. She needs someone gentle and soft and clean. Not someone like me.

"Why marriage? I don't need to be married to her to manage her money for her or make sure she has what she needs."

"She's never lived on her own in her life. She has a gentle heart, and people will take advantage of that. They'll *hurt* her. She's commuting to college where she's majoring in library science, of all things. She wants to work as an elementary school librarian. This world is going to eat her alive. The heiress librarian. When she loses me...." He closes his eyes in a long blink. "She will be sad and lonely and rich as fuck. Predators and con artists are going to be coming out of the woodwork and gunning straight for her."

Marcus isn't wrong.

"You're a good man, James," he continues.

At the unconscious shake of my head, Marcus fixes me with a stern look. "*You are a good man*. You understand loyalty. You'll be gentle with her and ruthless with anyone who tries to hurt her. You are the *only* person I trust to protect her.

"I'm leaving the majority of my assets to the two of you. I'd also like to transfer trustee status of her trust fund from me to you until she's twenty-five. It's not that far off, really.

"You could keep the vultures away. I'm not asking for more than that right now. Once she has her feet under her, the two of you can come to whatever arrangement you want. But she needs someone she can count on to be there for her.

"Without a spouse, she won't have a single next of kin. Imagine that. Imagine a health scare, like me or her mother, and not having a single person there to...." He closes his eyes briefly before shaking away the thought. He's giving in to his fear, and he knows it.

"You don't think Clare would object to this?" He can "offer" all he wants, but this is the twenty-first century. A man doesn't just get to decide who his daughter is going to marry. Moreover, he *shouldn't*.

Marcus gives me the signature expression he uses when he thinks someone is trying to blow smoke up his ass: one eyebrow raised, head slightly tilted. "My daughter has been in love with you since she was old enough to write 'James Mellinger' in a heart on the cover of her notebook. She won't object."

Heat curls up the back of my neck. "It was a little crush. She got over that."

Marcus waves his hand. "I know that. But I also think the two of you are a good fit. In time, you *will* love each other. Clare is imminently lovable."

I'm half in love with her already. It would take nothing for me to fall. The only thing I'd need to do is give myself permission—but I don't trust myself to lose control like that.

"In the meantime," he says, "while she's still getting her feet under her, you could be her safety net. Her soft place to fall. I can't leave her alone. I can't leave her with no one."

I don't think Marcus realizes the pleading note that's entered his voice. He's never begged for a damn thing in his life, but he's begging me to marry Clare.

The answer is yes, of course. I would never allow Clare to be alone or frightened if it's within my power to prevent it.

And I won't let Marcus die afraid for his daughter. If he dies—and I haven't quite accepted that yet, but if he does—it can't be in turmoil and fear that Clare won't be cared for.

"I'll do it."

"Thank you—"

"If Clare agrees."

"She will."

"But, Marcus," I warn, "you know what I'm like. I can only promise to be her friend."

Marcus reaches over and opens a box of Cuban cigars I hadn't noticed earlier. I've never seen him smoke before.

He offers one to me, and I shake my head. He proceeds to snip the end and light it up. At my raised eyebrow, he huffs, "What's it going to do? Give me cancer?"

I don't smile.

He looks back down at the cigar contemplatively for a moment. "She's what you need, too, James. You don't know that yet, but the two of you...." He holds the cigar between his index finger and thumb and brings the remaining fingers of both hands together, meshing them. "You're like pieces of a jigsaw puzzle that are made to snap together."

For the briefest moment, a familiar spark of mischief enters his eyes. "You're going to fall madly in love with my daughter."

Marcus has always had an eerie ability to predict connections. To choose the exact right fit, whether it's building a team or acquiring a company.

Just this once, for Clare's sake, I hope he's wrong.

4

Easy On Me

CLARISSA

I STAND IN MY father's study, my arms tight around his waist, and try to make sense of the things I've learned over the last two days.

Dad has been my entire world. I've built every piece of my life around him. And I've been his. And now... I'm losing him. To cancer. He's dying. And I can't even bear to say those two words out loud.

Dad wraps his arms around me, and I breathe in the familiar scent of his cologne.

He told me about the cancer two days ago. He didn't tell me James was going to show up with a diamond ring until half an hour ago.

It's an autopilot reaction for me to agree to anything my father could ask at this point. He wants me to marry James—so I'll marry James.

Since his diagnosis, my father's every thought has been for other people. How will the staff and employees manage? Has he done everything necessary for the people who rely on Harcourt? How can he prepare his friends? How can he make his own death easier on everyone? And, especially, how can he ensure that I'm safe and happy after he's left this world?

The truth—that I will never tell him—is that he can't ensure something like that.

But he's got this idea that he can stop worrying about me if I marry James. In his words, it's "the only way I'll find peace." He says James will "take care of me."

I know I've been sheltered. But I don't need or even want James to take care of me. That's not how I picture marriage.

When I said as much, Dad's response was that James will be lonely after he dies. Then he told me that James, who frankly has always seemed like the least needy or anxious person I have ever known, will need a friend as much as I will. That we'll take care of each other in our own ways.

I'm not sure I believe that. James will be sad, but I doubt he's in need of friendship with me.

Still, it pulled at my heartstrings, exactly as Dad intended. Not that he needed to do that. I will never allow my father to leave this world in fear if it's in my power to prevent it.

But I can't deny that the entire idea of marrying James is surreal. I've had some variation of a crush on him since I was fourteen years old, and this carries the potential for disaster. I could end up pining miserably for my own husband for years.

Oh, I know it's infatuation and not real love—no matter how much I've spouted about it for the last six years. How can it be real, lasting love when I'm too nervous to even act like myself around him? How can it be real when he doesn't act like himself around me? But there's no question that the potential for it is there.

And I hate that some silly part of me—the goofy sixteen-year-old who's still hiding inside—is secretly counting on the idea that one day this marriage will become real. Maybe we'll fall madly in love with each other.

For me, this is like another girl being told the lead singer of her favorite band needs to fake-marry her for some absurd PR reason. Of course it all works.

But what if this marriage isn't the beginning of my own personal romance novel? What if it's some literary fiction novel where I'm supposed to learn some horrible lesson?

Dad rubs my back and speaks cajolingly, almost teasingly. "It's the smartest idea I've ever had. Trust me on this."

I take a deep breath and nod. "You can send him back in."

He kisses the top of my head and leaves me standing there alone.

James returns less than a minute later. When he enters, he leaves the door partially cracked open—the better for Dad to hear if I have an attack of the vapors, I suppose. Just like a Victorian maiden with her suitor.

The thought nearly forces a bubble of inappropriate hysterical laughter out of me.

James lowers himself to one knee and opens a little blue box. The solitaire inside is perfect. Classy. Large but not obnoxiously so.

James is wearing a dark blue suit with a light blue button-down shirt that sets off his eyes.

I'm in a T-shirt and flannel pajama bottoms, my nose red and eyelids swollen from crying.

For once, James is looking straight at me.

"Are you sure you want to do this?" I ask.

He frowns. "I'm sure. Are you? There's no pressure."

Of course there's pressure. I don't say that, though. "Yes. It's just a lot to wrap my head around," I say instead.

He stands up, and I think he's realized the lunacy of this plan.

Instead, he leads me to the love seat and then sits beside me, his hard thigh brushing against my softer one.

The contrast between us couldn't be more obvious. But he reaches for my left hand and plays with my fingers. "I'll be kind to you. In fact, I expect it will turn out better than most marriages. I hope you know I care about you. I want to be here for you. As a friend."

Faint praise, indeed. "I'm... awkward with you."

"We'll get over that, Clare."

"Clarissa."

At his raised eyebrows, I shrug. "I know Dad calls me Clare, but my mother named me Clarissa, and I like it." I don't tell him I feel as though it's my adult name. It's the name that separates me from the child I used to be in his eyes. I don't want him to see me as that girl.

He acknowledges my request with a dip of his head. "Of course. Clarissa."

"People will say horrible things about us," I say. "There'll be rumors that you married me for my money."

He doesn't answer right away, just rubs his thumb over my palm almost absentmindedly. It causes a building heat to ignite low in my body. It's an unexpected sensation in the face of the situation. James has never, ever touched me like this.

Finally, he says, "The best thing to do is ignore them. It'll blow over. We'll know why we're getting married. That's all that matters. To the outside world, we'll be like every other married couple. Eventually, we'll be too boring for them to bother speculating about."

For a moment, I consider letting my next question go. I'm marrying him for Dad, not for me. But this is my future. And there are things I need to know. Things that are none of my father's business.

James's answers won't change whether I marry him... but they'll affect whether I stay married to him after Dad passes.

"Can we discuss this a little? Just so I understand what exactly to expect."

His brows come together a little, and then he dips his chin. "Of course. Did you have a chance to read the prenup?"

I nod my head, very aware of his strong fingers still wrapped around my own. "Yes. But I wanted to talk about more... personal things," I say haltingly.

"You want to manage expectations."

That wasn't exactly how I'd thought of it. But I like that wording. He makes the conversation we're about to have sound businesslike. It's not based on emotion. It's just *managing expectations.*

The idea steadies me a little. I've been in the background of enough of my father's phone calls and meetings that, surely, I can emulate him in my first ever round of negotiations. "Yes."

James is wearing his customary stern expression when he says, "It's a good idea."

I reach for my phone and pull up the notes app.

He lifts a single eyebrow, and I think I see a hint of approval in his eyes. "You are definitely your father's daughter."

At my wary look, he nods back down to my phone. "By all means, let's put this action plan in writing."

I type "Marriage Plan" at the top. "Okay." I clear my throat. "You said we would be friends. Can you clarify that for me a little?"

"Platonic. We'll spend time together. Provide a support system for each other. We can be each other's plus-one."

Exactly what I thought. It's not a bad idea to start out as friends first. We'll need time to transition into him seeing me as something other than his friend's daughter. I can accept that. I don't expect it to take long once we're living together. Unless...

"I just want to check that you aren't, um, seeing anyone else?"

He shakes his head, frowning. "No." The word is clipped.

I press my lips together and bob my head in a nervous nod. Heat washes up my neck and over my entire face. I'm pale and freckled. And now I'm blushing. Hard.

He's watching me intently. "I'm not the kind of man who would ever, under any circumstance, fuck around on my wife." he says.

James has never sworn in front of me before. He isn't someone who would have done it accidentally. And something in his language feels oddly reassuring. He's giving me a glimpse behind his polite mask, and he's doing it because he understands that I needed to see exactly the level of disrespect he feels for anyone who is disloyal.

"Okay," I manage a small smile as my shoulders loosen. "We're faithful."

I type in capital letters, NO CHEATING. "Do you have any requests for our plan?"

He stands up and wanders to the window, shoving his hands into his pockets. "We should speak to each other for at least half an hour every day, if possible. Ideally, we should attempt to have a meal together daily, as long as we're in the same city at the time."

"I agree." I tap the words into our plan.

He loosens his tie and leans back against the wall, casual and relaxed. All slick negotiator. "I have another demand."

"Demand away," I say, feeling more confident by the minute. This plan was a good idea. Everything he's said has turned out to be exactly what I needed to hear.

"I expect you to chase your dreams. You have your whole life ahead of you. This marriage isn't here to hold you back. My only expectation is for you to be reasonably safe when you do. Don't be reckless."

I type, DON'T BE RECKLESS and CHASE OUR DREAMS.

I nod and put my left hand out, waiting for him to place the ring on my finger.

There's approval on his face as he does so. "I wasn't sure whether you'd have some romantic fantasy about this. I should have known you'd be reasonable. You're a smart girl."

I shrug.

"As long as we keep things strictly friendly, we'll get along fine," he reassures me.

"What do you mean?"

He pulls back a little, brows furrowed. "I mean as long as we're careful not to develop romantic feelings for each other, we'll have a successful marriage."

"You think that's something a person can control? That you can just decide not to catch feelings for someone?"

His eyebrows lift. "Yes." He says the word the way someone would say, *"Obviously."*

At my look of consternation, his expression changes. He's looking at me like I'm an employee he just learned didn't meet a quota. Or a teenager who snuck out after curfew.

He nods over at my phone. "Write it down, Clarissa. Last rule: don't catch feelings."

5

Stand By Me

CLARISSA

I'm a miserable bride. Not that anyone realizes it. I've stuffed all my fear, grief, disappointment, and anxiety all the way down where, hopefully, no can see them.

Of course I'm marrying James. There was never a question that I'd do it. For Dad.

James is marrying me for the same reason.

But the way he's so confident that he'll never develop an attraction to me.... My initial embarrassment is giving way to reluctant resentment.

It's true that I've never dated. *But I'm not ugly.*

I look down at this dress and swallow that thought.

I feel ridiculous. This gown, or one very like it, was the one I insisted I wanted back when I was around fifteen years old. It's a confection of sparkling white organza and seed pearls, with a cathedral train and layers upon layers of mesh, tulle, bows, and flounces everywhere.

I look like a wedding cake.

But my father is staring at me with so much love and pride and hope. I just have to keep reminding myself that he is the *only* thing that matters at this moment.

Bronwyn, Janessa, and Franki are waiting near the altar. My bridesmaids are wearing hot-pink-and-black taffeta dresses, and the way they put them on without a word of complaint just goes to show how amazing they are. That pink is bright enough to fry my retinas.

They know exactly what kind of wedding this is. They've also been my best friends since elementary school, which means they'll never breathe a word of it to a single soul without my say-so.

The organ is playing, and I'm supposed to look at James as I walk down the aisle. But I can't. This feels wrong to me, as if I'm making a joke out of something that should be sacred.

So I look at my friends instead.

Franki is trying to smile, but she's all choked up. Her big brown eyes are wet, and she's sniffling loudly enough that I can already hear her. Janessa elbows her and passes her a tissue.

They all tried to talk me out of this before finally acknowledging it was a foregone conclusion. After that, they rallied around me with their unwavering support.

Of the three of them, Janessa was the most vocal of my friends to tell me this was a "horrible idea" and that I was "asking for a broken heart."

She's five foot ten, topping Franki's height by five inches and Bronwyn's by nine. She's right there in the middle of them, looking like an Italian model and trying to force herself to smile for my sake. It looks more like a worried grimace.

Bronwyn's blonde hair glints under the spotlights, and she points at me from the front of the church, wiggling her curvy little behind. She fans herself with a hand, licks her finger, and pretends to burn it on me, mouthing, "Hot."

She's trying to lighten the mood and turn my smile into something real. We both know I'm giving more Glinda the Good Witch vibes than sex kitten in this dress.

When the wedding planner had asked about my dream wedding, I'd just pointed her to my old Pinterest board—the one I'd made right around the time I'd started practicing my signature as "Mrs. James Mellinger." So... yeah. This wedding is a bit of a hot mess express. Though no one can say the planner didn't *try*.

We had a month to plan this thing from start to finish, so I'd sent her the Pinterest board and said, "Figure something out, and please don't bother me with the details."

Spending time with Dad was more important to me than picking out napkins and cake toppers.

Now, my bridal party, flowers, and dress are giving "A Very Barbie Wedding" vibes.

Not that I care. It's not a real wedding, anyway.

I finally get up the nerve to look at James as he stands there at the altar in a black tuxedo. His face is even more serious and stern than usual, his posture stiff.

We stop just in front of him, and Dad turns to me, whispering against my temple, "You will always be my baby girl. Don't you forget that."

I choke out a watery "I love you, Daddy."

When my father hands me over to James, they do that man-hug thing that practically looks like assault, with the mutual back slapping. It's intense. Then Dad kisses my cheek and puts my hand in James's.

James's expression is severe. He almost looks angry, so I fix my attention on the minister instead.

James's hand, however, is steady as a rock when he slips his ring on my finger. And his voice is strong and confident when he makes his vows to love, honor, and cherish me.

When the minister says, "You may kiss the bride," I shoot a startled glance up at my new husband and feel my nerves twang.

How did I not think about the fact that our first kiss was going to be in front of a cathedral full of witnesses? We didn't have a wedding rehearsal, or I might have thought of it then. But we were trying to minimize the number of activities Dad would feel he needed to participate in.

And it hits me all of a sudden that I've just married a man I've never even ki—

"Hey," he murmurs quietly in my ear while he trails his knuckles down my cheek. "Stop worrying. It's not that kind of marriage. I *also* vow not to attack your lips with mine," he says dryly.

He leans down and rubs the tip of his nose against mine, then kisses me on the cheek.

That's my wedding kiss? A peck on the cheek?

I know this marriage isn't normal, but did he have to make it so publicly *obvious*? Now the minister is introducing us as Mr. and Mrs. James Mellinger. I spent years doodling that name, but now that it's here, I'm not sure I want it.

I'm not giving up the name that defined me to this point in my life. I'll be *Harcourt*-Mellinger. I can't just become an entirely new person in the course of one afternoon, an extension of a man who isn't even in love with me.

Then Bronwyn is handing me back my flowers, arranging my train, and James and I walk back down the aisle. We prepare to take the short drive to the location for pictures, both of us sitting quietly in the car.

James clears his throat and says, "You look beautiful, Clarissa."

I want to sink into the leather seat because I don't feel beautiful. I feel pretty silly, and I'm still trying to wrap my brain around the idea that he wouldn't even kiss me the one darn time in front of an audience.

I tip my head at him, force a smile, and say, "Thank you."

He runs his thumb over his new wedding band and says, "The ceremony was nice."

A laugh bubbles out of me, but I squelch it quickly.

He frowns. "Are you okay?"

I lie like a Persian rug. "Just nervous. There were a lot of people there."

"I see."

And then the man who expects me not to catch feelings reaches out and squeezes my hand. "Can I make a confession?"

I look down at our hands twined together, then stiffen my spine. "What's that?"

"I was nervous as hell too."

Damn it. Is he seriously trying to comfort me by showing me his vulnerable side? How am I supposed to keep my heart hardened against that?

Then the photographer and his assistant are climbing in with us, and he's telling us how to sit and where to look. And I don't have to answer James.

The photographer, Rafe, is an energetic man with a shaved head. He is enthusiastic as hell and just as obnoxious.

He tried to get photos of the girls and me jumping on the hotel bed, to which I'd simply given him the Marcus Harcourt stare.

He'd backed off a bit after that. But he and his assistant were waving wand lights around and "orchestrating moments" every minute.

Then he intruded on my time with Dad. At which point, again, I'd channeled a little of my father, pointed an imperious finger, and demanded, "Wait outside." Which he did, all the while muttering anxiously about his "shot list."

Under different circumstances, the photographer would have amused me. Under different circumstances, I'd have welcomed his obsessive attempt to mold a vision of this day as the fun and happy young heiress marries her dream man. But these are not "different circumstances."

The planner gushed over Rafe. Apparently, he's world famous in wedding photography circles. He's won all kinds of prestigious awards, and they flew him in just for our wedding.

"Congratulations, you two! You did it," Rafe says in his New Zealand accent, a big grin on his face.

The less we smile, the harder he smiles back at us, as if he's willing us to respond in kind. His expression has become something of an unmoving rictus on his face.

I try to fake a polite expression, but I can't quite manage "happy."

When we arrive at the location the planner selected, he says, "Okay, guys, just stand right here. There you go. Now, hubby, just reach your arms around your new wife. No, not her waist, up here—"

He touches James and attempts to move his arm up around my collarbone area.

I can't see James's expression, but the photographer jumps back as if he's seen a snake, then starts bobbing his head. "Right. No touching.

Bad habit," he says. From a distance, he starts to mime the motion instead. "Bring your face right in."

James slides in close. Tension is vibrating from him. Or maybe that's me.

It's chilly out here, but James's body is warm around me, and he smells delicious. I want to turn around, burrow into his arms, and hide there. Let Rafe get shots of nothing but this poofy skirt and the top of my head.

"Excellent." Rafe is moving around, snapping shots. "Sweetheart, turn your face toward the sky and close your eyes. Gorgeous."

Sweet baby Jesus, this is awkward.

"Now, sweetheart, we're going to do the piggyback pose. James, can you lift her on your back without help?"

I whip my head toward the photographer in horror. *That dumbass Pinterest board.* That's where he's been getting his "shot list." The memory of some of the poses fifteen-year-old me had pinned... pure cringe.

James and I both speak in tandem and say one word. "No."

"Cool. Cool. Maybe the planner showed me the wrong Pinterest board."

She did not show him the wrong Pinterest board, but I nod furiously. "I think she must have," I say brightly.

Yes, I'm throwing the planner under the bus. She lost my loyalty when she said we were "lucky the groom cheated" regarding the wedding Rafe was originally scheduled to shoot this week.

Let the planner and Rafe hash it out between them.

James looks down at me, and whatever he sees on my face has him turning to Rafe and saying, "We're very private people."

I nod in agreement. "*Very* private."

"You'll appreciate having these memories later," Rafe argues.

James squeezes my hand but doesn't look away from the photographer. "You're making my wife uncomfortable, Rafe," he says coldly. "I don't like it when my wife is uncomfortable."

Those words shoot a thrill through me that I don't want to feel. It'll be that much harder to get over my crush if he goes around calling me his *wife*.

Rafe sputters. I get the impression that he's used to being in charge, which makes sense. He's telling couples how to pose and what to do all the time.

But I've never seen anyone stand up to James when he uses that voice. Rafe is certainly not going to be the first.

I feel a little bad for the man. He's just trying to do his job.

"I think what we need are some more classic poses. Does that sound all right to you?" Rafe finally asks.

I smile at him as brightly as I can manage. "That sounds wonderful. Thank you so much for being accommodating."

James grunts beside me, and I can almost hear the words he doesn't say: *"We're paying him to be accommodating."*

We do a number of classic couple poses on the steps, which are fine, if slightly awkward.

Then Rafe has James dipping me ever so slightly, my flowers hanging loose from one hand. My other hand is on the back of his head. It's the first time I've ever touched James's hair. It's silky soft and cool in the October air.

Flashes are firing around us as James looks into my eyes.

This pose is orchestrated. But the intensity is disarming, nonetheless.

James has had his CFO face on all day—distant and a little scary.

And I've been tense and nervous, giving fake smiles and forcing myself through the motions. It's been awkward and uncomfortable, and I just want this day to be over.

But the longer we look into each other's eyes, the more the tension starts to bleed out of me. The tightness around his mouth eases, and my own muscles relax.

I've known this man for *years*, but I've never had the pure freedom to just blatantly stare into his eyes.

I no sooner have the thought than, for no reason I can see, the corners of his mouth tip up just a little. I blink, surprised, and ask, "What?"

"I've never looked into your eyes like this," he says. "I thought they were green. But they're not just green. They're the color of moss with little flecks of gold in them and a halo of light brown around the outside. Your eyes are...."

When he doesn't continue, I prod a little. Because now I need to know. My eyes are... weird? Pretty? Odd? "What are they?"

"Magic."

The word seems so out of character for James, so... *fanciful*. It breaks something loose in me, and I have the strongest urge to just lift my head and close the distance until our lips meet.

James moves closer, and his gaze seems to catch on my mouth. I strain toward him, my breasts pressing forward, as he balances my weight with a single hand at my midback.

"That is gorgeous. You two are absolutely stunning. Give her a kiss." Rafe's grating voice interrupts the moment, and I'm startled to remember where we are and what we're doing.

James doesn't kiss me. Instead, he hitches midmove, then brings his mouth to my ear. His lips brush the outer shell as he mutters, "This guy is the most annoying little shit I've ever met."

I laugh, a full-on giggle-snort.

James pulls back from my ear. And when he's looking into my eyes again, his have those crinkles at the corner that I love so much.

He kisses my forehead, and Rafe "oohs" and "aaahs."

"Let's get a couple sexy shots now," Rafe says, completely ignoring our earlier comments about being private people.

And then he makes a critical mistake. "James, I want you to just run the back of your fingers across Clarissa's collarbone like this."

The photographer demonstrates by touching me, dragging his fingers across my clavicle and brushing my breast, probably accidentally, with his forearm. It's a stunningly intrusive thing for a stranger to do, and I jerk away from his touch.

I'm about to tell Rafe to keep his hands to himself, but before I even get a chance, James is *growling*, "Don't touch her."

Something about the way he says it feels as though he's an attack dog ready to rip the man's throat out.

He's using his body to intimidate and back Rafe away from me until they're far enough that I can't hear a word they're saying.

But I can tell James is laying into the man. And I don't think it's the usual threats of financial destruction that powerful men like James typically employ. I think he's threatening to tear the photographer's arms off.

I married James to give my father comfort and because I have dreamed of being loved by James for years. James married me as a favor to my dad. But I thought when he said we'd be friends that meant we'd be partners. I didn't realize James was signing up to be another one of my guard dogs.

I might never have rebelled against my father, but I can promise rebellion is coming for my husband if he tries to stuff me into the same role Dad did.

I'm not a stubborn or unreasonable person, I don't think. I will gladly and willingly accept James's help and support. And I hope he lets me support him in return.

But I don't need him fighting my battles.

I would have told Rafe to back off on my own. And if the man hadn't listened, then I would be all for this current display. But I could have handled this.

We end the shoot standing a foot apart, holding hands but looking off in different directions. It feels like an omen.

6
Raise Your Glass

CLARISSA

When we reach the hotel ballroom, I excuse myself to go hide in a restroom for a while.

One of my usual bodyguards, Sasha, enters first. She's a fit black woman in her midthirties. She's in plain clothes today, dressed as a wedding guest, albeit one wearing practical shoes. I follow inside when she gives the all-clear. Then she stands near the sinks.

What I need is a good cry, but I won't do that. Not even in the privacy of a restroom. I'd leave with red eyes, a shiny nose, and my makeup wrecked. Screw that. No one gets to see what a disaster this day feels like for me.

Besides, my father would see the evidence of my tears. I can't have him worrying about me on my wedding day. He seems so relieved and happy about it all.

I lock myself behind the paneled wooden door of the handicap stall—the only one big enough to fit my dress—then stand still and just take a moment for myself.

Two women have entered the restroom and are standing near the far end of the sinks, just this side of the lounge area. I can hear them loud and clear through the stall door.

"That ceremony has to be one of the most uncomfortable moments I've ever witnessed."

The other woman says, "It's clearly a business arrangement. Harcourt plans to give James his shares when he dies. Without that family connection, the inheritance tax alone would be brutal."

Water runs, and I miss some words. "...you would know, I guess. I hope they manage to work it out."

"Please. Can you imagine James with a girl like Clare Harcourt? This is about money. Knowing him, I'd be shocked if he ever lays a finger on her."

The other laughs. "He couldn't even bring himself to kiss her at the wedding."

"She's not just young—she's a spoiled little princess. She has to annoy the hell out of him."

Then I hear the clicking of their heels as they move toward the exit.

I rip the stall door open, peering out just in time to see the back of a svelte woman with pale blonde hair, styled straight as a ruler, as she sashays her way out the door. The sound of her stilettos echoes like gunfire.

I meet Sasha's sympathetic eyes in the mirror, and I burn with humiliation and rage.

When I told James that people would talk, I tried to convince myself I could grow a thick skin about it. I was determined to stay away from social media and stick my head in the sand. But I never expected to be confronted with it on my actual wedding day.

It would sting less if there weren't tendrils of truth woven through the malicious supposition.

He *couldn't* bear to kiss me. He doesn't ever *plan* to kiss me. And our marriage is most certainly an arrangement.

I want to go home. Right now. Just take a pair of scissors to this dress, climb into my cotton-candy bed, and pretend none of this is happening. Not Dad being sick. Not this wedding. Not these rumors.

Bronwyn, Janessa, and Franki are waiting outside in the corridor, along with James, his groomsmen, and Dad, who played the part of best man and father of the bride. James has a couple of friends I've never met before here too.

There's no time for anything except to be announced into the ballroom.

By the time the toasts roll around, I'm seriously ready for a drink.

I've only ever had a sip or two of alcohol in the past because, duh, good girl. But there's no time like your wedding to a man who married you as a favor to someone else and can't even bear to kiss you to get trashed on champagne, I always say.

When the server begins to pour my glass, however, my new husband slams a hand over the top and scowls. "She isn't twenty-one. Didn't the planner arrange for sparkling juice or something for her and the girls?"

Heat rises in my face.

"No need," I say, saccharine sweet. "I'm sure I've got some juice boxes in my bag."

He doesn't even hear me, too busy signaling the wedding planner, who quickly scurries over to retrieve the glasses of champagne my bridesmaids were served. She whips Bronwyn's drink right out from under her nose just as she's about to take a sip.

Bronwyn and I share a frustrated look. Then she makes a great show of looking around for witnesses. Reaching into the deep side pocket of her pink bridesmaid gown, she slides out a silver flask.

She shoots James a fulminating look, then leans over and whispers, "Later."

I nod. I will definitely take her up on that. A toast to my looming celibate marriage.

My friends are livid right now. Even Franki, who's always the first to see the bright side of anything, has her phone clutched in her hand like she's preparing to hurl it at James.

Bronwyn stretches across me and raps on the table with her knuckles until James turns his head back to her, raising one eyebrow in a stiff gesture of annoyance.

A mask falls over him like window blinds closing. His severe expression is the same one he wore when he watched Dad walk me down the aisle.

I remember what he said about being nervous and the way he looked when he hugged my dad. And right then, I realize what I don't think anybody else notices—my new husband is masking pain. He has been all day. Probably the same pain I'm feeling. He just handles it differently.

James stood there at the altar and married someone he doesn't love for purely unselfish reasons. And, damnit, this just sucks for both of us, doesn't it?

Bronwyn leans across my body, practically climbing in my lap as she hisses at James. "I just think it's funny how—"

I grab her into a full-body hug. She shuts up and hugs me back, clutching me fiercely.

She's so much shorter than I am that her face hits my neck when we hug, and her breath tickles as she loudly whispers, "Okay."

We've been friends for so long that she responded to my unspoken request before I'd even said the words. But I say them now, anyway. Just to be sure we're on the same page. I taste hairspray as I talk into her updo. "Be nice."

"You should file for divorce tomorrow," she mutters.

"I'm not thinking about divorce at my wedding. And he's done nothing wrong."

The hug is going on longer than anyone would consider normal. Another set of arms wraps around the two of us, long and thin and smelling of cocoa butter—Janessa. Then Franki squirms in and asks, "Is this an official meeting?"

Bronwyn says, "We're supposed to be nice to James."

Janessa reluctantly agrees. "For you. Not for him."

Bronwyn nods, face still crammed against me. "But if you ever need me to make him suffer...."

Bronwyn has no fear. She never has. But I can't have her making an enemy out of my husband.

Everything she knows about James is filtered through the lens of my girlhood crush. Over the years, I've waxed poetic over everything from the flex of his forearms to the rasp in his voice. His particular brand of gentle politeness with me has her thinking he's harmless—like a pit bull who looks scary but has a heart of gold.

That's a mistake. He has a reputation for being even more ruthless than my father. And I'd rather not test that theory on my friends.

I try to defuse her temper with a joke. "He's already suffering. He had to marry me."

"Don't make me force self-affirmations on you. You're an angel. Anyone who marries you is the luckiest man on Earth," Franki says.

She has a gentle, dreamy voice that makes her threat the equivalent of being pelted with cotton balls.

Bronwyn heaves a sigh, then stretches her arms to shove all of us away. "That's enough of that. It's getting maudlin. I've got a toast to give."

James clearly heard this last part and says, "Absolutely not—"

She turns back to him. "That was a dick move you made at the wedding," she says in a surprisingly quiet and measured voice.

"Bronwyn," I warn.

"I said I'd be nice. This is nice. I'm not threatening him. I'm discussing the situation," she says to me.

She turns back to James. "For the record, I don't care if you make yourself look like a dick." She pulls out her phone, opening her socials. "But I do care that you made a joke out of a wonderful person."

Bronwyn's voice wavers, and for one horrifying moment, I'm afraid she's going to cry. Instead, her words get harder. "Not only does Clarissa not deserve this, but you don't deserve her."

His voice is impatient. "What are you talking about?"

She shoves her phone toward him, and I shiver a little at the rage that descends over his expression at whatever he sees there.

Bronwyn says, "So you weren't deliberately attempting to humiliate her?" It's not a nice, polite question. It's a demand, full of disbelief.

He doesn't answer. Just reaches for her phone, tense with fury.

She stares at him. Evaluates his reaction. Then she puts her hand back out for her phone and says, "You can look at them later. Most of them are speculation about what's so awful about your wife that you wouldn't even kiss her at the altar. You're trending. #ialmostdo."

"God dammit." He pushes the phone back toward her.

My stomach, already in knots, now feels like a ball of lead has taken up residence there. I make a gurgling sound—one part defeat and one part hysteria.

Bronwyn gives me a side hug. "Enough of that. Now that we know James wasn't deliberately trying to embarrass you, we can work with this. I'll give a speech that paints you two as fucking *fated mates*. Full-on destiny shit. I'll make up a stupid story about the kiss on the cheek. Everyone will want to gag from how sweet it is when I'm done."

She levels a scolding look at James. "But you two have to hold hands, look into each other's eyes, and sell it." The ice in my water glass is warmer than her words.

James's blue eyes meet mine, and then he's up and at my seat. He's very careful as he offers me his hand and helps me arrange my skirt as I rise. With a hand on my lower back, he guides me from the ballroom. A few people try to stop us to chat, but James just keeps on walking.

The manager appears before us, concern written all over him. James barks a demand, and the man shows us to a luxurious lounge space—all velvet drapes and club chairs. The logs in the art deco fireplace beneath a marble mantle burn merrily against the far wall.

Sasha clears the room, speaking into her earpiece. Then she shuts the door quietly behind her, leaving us alone.

I can't look at him. I don't even want to. So I wander to the fireplace and watch the flames dance.

"I apologize." His voice is clipped. Sharp.

I nod and pick at a seed pearl on my gown. I don't say anything for a long time. I'm not trying to be a bitch—I just don't have words.

He starts again, his voice like gravel. "I didn't think about repercussions."

That strikes me as odd. "Why not? You think about repercussions all the time. It's part of your job."

He moves in front of me, and his hands go to my shoulders. They tighten against me, and then he drops them.

"I planned to kiss you at the altar, but then you looked so nervous. I was trying to reassure you."

Oh. "It was the audience. I wasn't nervous because of you," I say, and if that isn't the full truth... well, I wish it were.

He turns away and paces in front of the fireplace, rubbing the back of his neck. "I can do damage control. There'll always be gossip, but we can manage it."

"What happened to ignoring rumors and letting them blow over?"

He glares back at me. "I meant I didn't care if the world decided *I* was a mercenary prick. I don't like them talking about *you*."

I nod. "Do you think we should make a statement? A press release?"

"The only way to make people believe we're in love is to act like we're in love."

At my dumbfounded expression, he puts a finger under my chin and closes my mouth for me. "Just in public," he says. "Behind closed doors, we're friends. But Bronwyn is right. In front of others, we should be... affectionate."

I wonder if this is the best thing that's ever happened to me or the worst. Because seeing how James would act if he loved me, but knowing he doesn't... it will be a special kind of torture.

At my prolonged silence, James clears his throat and tugs at his bow tie. He turns away. "Never mind. You don't have to do it."

Something in me snaps. He can't offer something like that, then snatch it back. "Oh, I'll do it. I'm going to be so affectionate you won't know what hit you."

In my peripheral vision, I catch the flex of James's hand. He's turned away, but I'm almost sure I hear him breathe, "Thank *fuck*."

Then he moves back into my space, his eyes on my mouth. For the briefest moment, I think he might actually kiss me.

Instead, he reaches into his tuxedo and pulls out a clean, monogrammed handkerchief. I stop his hand as he reaches toward my face with the cloth. "What are you doing?"

"I'm mussing you up. So we look like newlyweds who snuck away for some fun."

"Ummm."

He swipes at my lips with the fabric, then shows me the lipstick on it before he shoves it back in his pocket. "That works."

I look at him speculatively. "What about you?"

His mouth twitches the tiniest, tiniest bit. "I don't wear lipstick."

I purse my lips. "I'm sure I can come up with something."

With a lift of his eyebrows, he says, "Do your worst."

I yank at his tie, fussing with it until it sits askew. Then I lift my chin in challenge.

He twists his lips to the side and looks me up and down slowly. Then he pulls one small strand of hair out of my updo to dangle by my shoulder before he spreads his hands in a motion that says "Your move."

I rake my eyes over him, thinking. Then I reach for his pocket square and mess it up.

There goes that lip twitch again.

I wait. There's not much else he can screw up on me, really. The dress is pretty much—

He runs a finger across my neckline until he stops at the ridiculous bow that rests low on my shoulder. Then he rips it right off and shoves it in his pocket.

I gape. He smirks.

Narrowing my eyes, I shove both hands into his hair and give it a good swish. God, he smells good. And that hair is so soft. But that's not what this is about. It's about making him look like he just got some at his wedding reception.

Snickering, I pull back to admire his brand-spanking-new case of bedhead. James looking disheveled is my new favorite thing. Ever.

My pulse picks up when I see the amused calculation in his eyes. There's retaliation coming for me, and he's about to deliver it. For a split second, I consider bolting just to see if I can get him to chase me.

Then James puts both of his hands in my hair, exactly the same way I did to him, and gently but firmly makes a freaking *mess* out of my updo.

I gasp in laughing outrage. And James—growly, grumpy James—*grins*. "Too far?"

So I bite him.

I don't do it *hard*—I'm not a monster—but I lean right up and close my teeth gently on his full bottom lip. Then I give a little tug, just enough to make his lip look swollen and loved on.

He goes perfectly still as I press the entire front of my body against his for those three seconds. Then I ease back.

He looks shocked, but I know I didn't hurt him.

I'm a little stunned myself, partially at my own audacity and partially from the sheer physical intensity of it. I've never done something like that in my life.

He blinks, swallows, and takes a step back. Then he runs a hand through his hair, honestly probably more from habit than remembering how I mussed him up. I'm a little disappointed that he manages to smooth most of it back into shape in one move. I thought I'd been more thorough than that.

Curse his perfect hair.

"I think that's probably enough," he says.

"Should I fix my hair a little?"

"No. It just looks like it's down out of the—" He waves a hand at my head. "—whatever that is. You have the most gorgeous hair I've ever seen. I don't think it could look bad if you tried."

It's clear that, as far as he's concerned, he's just stating a fact. And it makes me warm all over, like I just swallowed sunshine.

"So," I say. "We just go out there and…?"

"Sell it."

And James takes my hand.

7

Kiss Me

JAMES

My bride is trashed. I didn't see it happen, but I'm blaming it on the feisty one, Bronwyn, as being her supplier.

We're riding up the gleaming elevator to the honeymoon suite. One of Clarissa's security detail, a blonde named Beth, stands in the corner, pretending she isn't there. And Clarissa serenades her own reflection in the polished steel walls.

She's singing something about buying herself flowers and holding her own hand.

I keep an arm around her waist because she's not that steady on her feet.

And, yeah, if I'd realized Clarissa and her bridesmaids were going to be sneaking alcohol, I'd have been an ass about it. I don't have a choice. It's about PR.

But they were sly. By the time I noticed what they'd done, the party was nearly over.

Bronwyn's toast was ridiculous. The guests knew she was kidding about some of it, of course. She's a natural comedian.

But most of them bought the spirit of it, which is that Clarissa and I are not just in love with one another—we're *soul mates*.

The alcohol the guests were imbibing probably helped in their suspension of disbelief.

According to Bronwyn, I'm such a lovesick sap that I drive halfway across the city just to bring Clarissa a cup of her favorite coffee every morning. (To be fair, I actually would do that for her if she wanted me to. I really don't see why that one was such a big deal that it got a round of "aaahs" from the assembled guests).

Apparently, I also made her a layer cake from scratch for her birthday, which tasted worse than it looked.

In reality, I've never baked a cake in my life. I'll be buying Clarissa's birthday cakes from the best bakery in the city. Hell, I'll take her to Paris, if she wants me to. Why would I give her my shitty subpar efforts if I can pay someone to do it better?

Also, according to Bronwyn, I've been writing Clarissa terrible poetry.

She then read one of "my" poems aloud. She wrote it in five minutes and rhymed "auburn curls" with "my heart whirls."

I met every over-the-top, doe-eyed, fluttering-lashed look Clarissa sent my way with a ridiculous smolder of my own. The day started awkward as hell, but the one-up flirtation game was… fun.

I'm not the kind of person who has "fun." I'm someone who is occasionally entertained. Sometimes I'll classify something as having been "a good time." But Clarissa had me grinning like a kid who was sneaking cookies.

I didn't even do that when I *was* a kid sneaking cookies.

Knowing it wasn't real took the pressure off.

But when she said she'd be so affectionate I wouldn't know what hit me, she wasn't lying. It was a game, yes. But now I'm horny as hell and about to sleep on a pull-out sofa bed.

Clarissa is... stunning. Even tipsy and silly.

She's always beautiful. But today she looks like an angel. Her gleaming hair is arranged on top of her head, but a wealth of long, loose tendrils frames her face.

I'm the one who gave her that tumbled look, and I don't regret it.

Her unusual eyes sparkle under long lashes. She's wearing a small crown-looking thing, and between it and the shimmery gown, she looks like a fairy princess. Like she could grant all my wishes, if only I would ask.

I half expect to see her feet leave the floor and watch her float to the ceiling.

Clarissa changes tunes, turning in my arms and warbling a spectacularly off-key rendition of "Unchained Melody," full-on Elvis Presley performance style.

She maintains eye contact as she musically assures me she's been hungry for my touch a long, lonely time. Then she sings that she can't help falling in love with me.

She pokes her index fingers into my cheeks and grins. "You're smiling."

I try to fake a stern expression, and she laughs. "Don't pretend you're not. I refuse to live in a women's fiction novel."

"You're wasted," I say, pulling her poking fingers away from my face. "Where'd you get the alcohol?"

She mimes zipping her lips and throwing away the key. "I am a vault. Bronwyn's secrets are safe with me."

I narrow my eyes at her. "Clearly. Do you do this often?"

"Sing? Sometimes." She whispers very loudly, "But I'm kind of bad at it."

I bite back my smile. "I was referring to getting drunk."

She snorts inelegantly. "This is my first time. I have babysitters who tattle on me if I even talk to a guy, let alone try to sneak a nip of the hairy dog that bites you."

I take a second to understand where she was going with that. I'm pretty sure she means "hair of the dog," but she doesn't have the context right.

She looks over at Beth and says, "Tell him. How you all spy on me and report back to Dad if I sneezed, and what I ate for lunch, and if I vary from my schedule by over ten minutes."

Beth appears stone-faced and uncomfortable. "I do my job. We all do."

Clarissa makes a "pffft" sound and leans into me. "One time, in eleventh grade, I sent a guy I liked a text. I'm sorry he wasn't you," she says loftily, "but you weren't available. I tried to hold his hand the next day at school, and Sasha pulled a *firearm* on him."

She turns back to Beth and slurs, "Please don't bother my father with this whole slightly tipsy thing. He's sick. You'll stress him out."

Beth says nothing, and I turn incredulous eyes on her. *Is she for real?* The woman is going to give Marcus some report on Clarissa's behavior? That's... fucked-up.

It's not even that I think Marcus would care. He knows she's safe with me.

Clarissa thinks it would stress him out. I think he'd probably just laugh about it, but that's not the point. These people have no business reporting on her activities like she's a misbehaving child.

I bite out, "I took over all the household contracts three weeks ago. You're no longer employed by Marcus Harcourt. And you will report exactly jack shit on my wife's activities to her father. Do you understand me?"

The blonde's eyes widen before she dips her chin in an abrupt nod. "Understood."

When we reach our floor with the honeymoon suite, I swing Clarissa into my arms. "If anyone is liable to trip over the threshold, it's you tonight," I say.

She sighs and holds on, and after the guard confirms the room is clear and leaves, I carry her through the door.

I kick it closed, then take her to the bedroom to lay her on the bed.

She stares at me, a dent between her eyebrows, sudden determination written on her face. Then she launches herself at me, pressing her lips against mine. I freeze, then pull away, dragging her arms from around my neck.

"My whole life," she says mournfully, "I'm going to look back and remember how my own husband couldn't even stand to kiss me on my wedding day."

I sit down heavily on the side of the bed. *Is that what she thinks?* "Clarissa—"

"I don't want your pity." She sounds embarrassed. And, yes, definitely very drunk.

"Clarissa," I say more firmly. "I want to kiss you. I want it more than you can imagine, but it wouldn't be right. I'd feel like a dirty old man."

It's not her age. I know she's an adult. But she's never even dated, according to her father. And after that conversation with Beth in the elevator, I wonder if she's ever done anything at all.

Add in that she's stressed out over Marcus's health and also factor in her alcohol consumption? Yeah, the things I picture doing to her make me feel like a creep.

She recoils hard, and I realize my phrasing could have been better.

"So you never kissed anyone when you were twenty years old? Please. It's *ridiculous*," she says.

It's probably fewer people than she imagines. I despise when most people touch me. It makes my skin crawl. Or worse, it ignites a bone-deep anger in me. Clarissa is... an exception.

"If I kiss you the way I want to, then I'll want other things we aren't ready for."

"You'll want to fuck."

"Yes, Clarissa," I say through a clenched jaw. "I'll want to fuck."

"Good. I'm down." She throws herself back on the bed, arms out like some kind of virgin sacrifice, and I'm the dragon ready to devour her.

I jerk to standing and turn my back to her, trying to will my erection to go the hell down. It's not working.

My *wife* is lying in her wedding dress on the bed of our honeymoon suite. And she is "down to fuck."

She's also drunk as hell, and we agreed we wouldn't do this. I resent being put in a position where I have to reject her.

Especially when I don't *want* to reject her. I want to peel that sparkly cloud of a dress off her, taste every freckle on her body, and lose myself inside her. I want to do it again and again. At least three times.

She'd hate me for it later. And I'd hate myself. She isn't thinking about what a violation of trust this would be.

And she agreed to those boundaries. Yet she's pushing them on our very first night as man and wife.

"Aargh!" she cries in frustration. "I'll bet you were having tons of sex when you were my age."

I absolutely was not. But I just say, "This is different. We have to live with each other. If we cross that line, we can't take it back. We're trying to build a friendship here."

I expect more of an argument, but she turns away and asks in a resigned tone, "Are we going to be married without benefits forever?"

"We can have sex when you're twenty-five," I say. "If you still want me then."

I didn't plan to say it, but she's right. The idea of never sharing a bed with her is not only intolerable, it's impossible. There has to be an end in sight. Either I can trust myself with her by that time... or she divorces me when she's financially independent so she can move on.

Yes, it's a long time. But we need it.

I have a very driven personality. I focus my energy on my career. Sometimes I barely sleep when I'm in pursuit of a goal. I don't know what kind of monster I'd become if I turned that energy on a person.

My father claimed he loved my mother. But it was obsession. Violent obsession.

I have to practice maintaining emotional distance with Clarissa. In the past, I've just avoided all relationships. That's not an option with her. So by the time we have sex, she has to be so firmly established as a friend that it's nothing more than an act of physical relief. There can't be passion.

Twenty-five is the sensible choice. It's when she takes over all of her own finances. I can't be in charge of her assets and sleep with her. It feels too much like I'm controlling her. She needs money, and I *have* all her money.

I'm only just now thinking about how warped that is. How easily I could trap her and control her.

And Clarissa herself needs to gain some autonomy. The revelation that bodyguards have watched and controlled her even after she entered adulthood has left me uneasy.

She turns back, wobbly on her feet, and her jaw drops. It took her a moment to process my words. To do the math in her head. Her eyes are like saucers. "Twenty-five!" she squeals. "Are you crazy? Nobody waits to have sex until they're twenty-five!"

I shrug as if the idea of waiting five years doesn't sound like hell to me too. "Twenty-five is when I no longer control any of your finances. You'll be independent then. There's a power imbalance between us right now. It's not fair to you, and you'd hate me for it later."

"I would not," she says, scowling, words overenunciated in that way drunk people the world over do when they're trying to sound sober.

"You don't know that."

"Neither do you."

She moves into me and runs her hands up my chest to rest on my shoulders. Her warm body presses against mine. My hands land on her waist. I know she's only this bold because she's completely soused. Tequila, if I can trust my nose.

Her eyes glitter. "Kiss me on my wedding day, James. Just a kiss."

Tenderness pangs in my chest—along with a dose of guilt. When she says she'll never forget that I didn't kiss her on our wedding day, I believe her.

It can't hurt to kiss her. Not really.

A kiss on your wedding day is symbolic of a promise. Of a future. And I do plan to give her a future.

I cradle the back of her head with my hand and kiss my wife.

8

Say You Won't Let Go

Clarissa

James kisses like a god. This kiss is the kind I've read about in romance novels and thought were just fiction. I didn't believe anything like this existed in the real world, only in some writer's imagination.

My body doesn't quite feel like my own. And while some of that is on the tequila, most of it is the wild rush of sensation from James's mouth on mine.

His lips are firm but soft. His tongue moves against mine. And I feel it not just where he's touching me but inside, down low, in a spiral of heat and tension that makes me want to squirm and push closer to him.

He nips my bottom lip and pulls on it lightly with his teeth, exactly like I did to him downstairs. And now I realize why he looked so shocked—because the sensation is delicious.

I give an involuntary cry of pleasure, arching my back to press my body against his. His erection pushes against my belly, and a touch of nervous anticipation joins the spiral of heat inside me.

He pulls back, just enough to meet my gaze with eyes of blue flame. I slide my hand down to his chest, where his heart thunders under my palm.

My breathing is awful. I sound like I've just sprinted a mile uphill. I whimper and try to pull him back down for another kiss, but he stops me with that hand on my head. It's probably for the best, because the room has begun spinning around me. I don't feel well at all. I need him to keep me anchored.

He drops his forehead to mine and breathes, slow and deep. Reaching up, he presses the hand I have on his chest harder against his heart, his other hand holding my head to his. I feel the slow, deliberate rise and fall of his breaths beneath my palm, his pulse calming. After a moment, I mirror him. Breathing in when he does. Letting it out slowly. We stand that way for long moments.

Eventually, he pulls away. Takes his hands off me. Steps back.

"I'll get you some water and painkillers. You're going to need them," he says, heading for the door. "Call me if you need me."

"James, wait—"

"I'm sleeping on the couch."

"Of course," I say, irritated all over again. "But I need you to help me out of this dress first." I turn to show him the back. It's lined from the base of my spine to the back of my neck with tiny buttons. There's no way out of it without help unless I take a pair of scissors to it.

James makes a noise in his throat, but when I look back at him, his expression is blank. Like he's watching paint dry.

"It's not as bad as it looks," I say. "There's a zipper hidden under the buttons."

He mutters something under his breath. Then he's tugging on my zipper. It slides down my spine like a shiver, his knuckles brushing the exposed skin of my back. He stops when the zipper ends just at the crack of my butt. Then he backs away.

"Get settled for bed. I'll be back with the water and painkillers," he says as he shuts the door behind him.

I struggle out of the dress and shoes and garter, dizzy and nauseous now that some of the adrenaline has worn off.

Then I search through my suitcase in dawning horror, more frantic by the second.

Julia packed my suitcase for me... and she didn't add pajamas. What she did pack has me breaking out in a cold sweat.

I use my thumb and index finger to pick up the sheer white babydoll nightie and thong Bronwyn gave me as a joke. I never planned to wear it, but Julia didn't know that. All she knew was it was brand-new bridal lingerie shoved in my top drawer.

The only thing I have packed for tomorrow is a structured dress I can't sleep in either.

Naked or lingerie. Those are my choices. And James is going to be walking back in here with water and ibuprofen any minute.

I crack the door and call out, "I'm sorry to bother you, but I, um, forgot to pack something to sleep in. Do you have an extra T-shirt or something I could borrow?"

There's silence for a moment. Then he says, "Yes." There's some shuffling, and then he passes a white cotton undershirt through the crack in the door. It's warm in my hand and smells like him. Twenty seconds ago, this was on James's body. I hope he never wants it back because it's mine now.

I pull it on, then make my way to the bed. I don't get far when the nausea hits me.

I make it to the toilet. Just. I'm kneeling there, hugging the porcelain throne in a strange hotel room, wearing nothing but my white silk wedding panties and James's tank, puking my guts out, when he returns to the bedroom.

"Oh, shit." James joins me in the bathroom and puts a warm hand on my back. Then he gathers the strands of my hair that are hanging down toward the toilet and clinging to my sweaty face.

"Ugh," I sob. "I'm dying."

His voice is dry. "No, sweet girl. But you might wish you had in the morning."

I try to turn a scowl his way, but I can't hold it because I'm losing the contents of my stomach into the toilet. Again.

He holds my hair, then fidgets with it. He's removing my tiara. It was still on, loose and threatening to join the contents of my stomach in the toilet bowl. I lay my head on the rim, closing my eyes. James lifts me away from it and wipes my face, hands, and neck with a cool washcloth.

"All done for now?" he asks.

I nod, so he flushes the toilet, then lifts me up and sets me on the counter, handing me my toothbrush. I brush, and he holds a cup of water for me to rinse with. I spit awkwardly into the sink while he hovers to make sure I don't lose my balance.

James isn't wearing a shirt. He's barefoot, wearing only trousers, and he's as fit and beautiful as I expected him to be.

My eyes catch on swirling tattoos rendered in black ink that stretch across his upper arms and chest. They don't fit his CFO image at all. It's like thinking you're entering a room containing a cat and then realizing two steps in that the "cat" is actually a mountain lion.

I peer drunkenly at his half-naked body and notice something even more startling. The tattoos are covering scars, many of which are small and round.

"Now, take these." He hands me two pills and an open bottle of water. "And drink the whole thing."

I don't want to. But he sounds like the voice of experience, so I try. I'm so uncoordinated that I spill, and James ends up helping hold the bottle for me.

No wonder he's not interested in sleeping with me. I'm a hot freaking mess. So gross. I'll never be able to look him in the face again.

"Why," I ask as he guides me back to the bed, "does anybody ever drink alcohol? This is horrab... horrabll."

He pulls back the comforter and settles me there, tucking the blanket around me. The ceiling spins in a merry-go-round twirl.

"Some things you only learn by experience. Moderation is the key when it comes to alcohol. And plenty of water."

"Did you learn by experience?" I slur, eyes closed. "Or were you just born knowing everrrrryyything?"

I hear him huff in amusement. "Remind me to tell you about my twenty-first birthday sometime. I'm pretty sure there's a bar in Newark that has my picture posted with 'Do Not Serve This Asshole' written on it."

I think I laugh before I drift into unconsciousness. But I might have just dreamed it.

9
How Do I Say Goodbye

JAMES

I move into the brownstone the next day. I have my own room, on a different floor than Clarissa's.

Apparently I don't need to worry about her demanding any more kisses. She's embarrassed by the memories of our wedding night enough to avoid the subject.

Even if she weren't, our focus is on Marcus, not the two of us. Because Marcus is dying. It's happening now, not in some vague future timeline.

Over the next two weeks, it becomes horrifyingly obvious that Marcus isn't going to make it the full three months the doctors predicted.

Three months was such a short time. To have even that stolen from us creates a grasping, desperate sense of impending doom.

Within four days of the wedding, his hospital bed is set up in his study. Understandably, Marcus doesn't want to be shut up in his room for his last days.

Clarissa dropped out of school for the remainder of the semester. She spends every waking moment with her father or arranging for his care.

I thought I'd be the one making those arrangements, caring for the both of them. I am not a man who knows how to sit with his feelings. When life sucks, I get up, and I do something about it. I need to fix this. And since I can't, I need to do the things that need doing.

But Clarissa isn't having that. She won't be usurped. And I am useless and helpless in the face of it.

There is no stopping the clock. I accepted that weeks ago.

And now I'm supposed to be sad. That's allowed, understandable, even encouraged. And if I dig around under all the layers inside me, I know it's pain at the core of me.

But my overriding emotion right now is anger. A therapist from my childhood once called anger a "secondary emotion." He'd encouraged me to look beneath the anger, to find the pain and fear underneath.

Why would I want to do that? Why would anyone?

Losing Marcus so young and in such a horrible, unforgiving way is enraging. I struggle to hide that because it's the last thing Clarissa or Marcus needs from me. But it's there, nonetheless.

For these last seven years, I saw in Marcus the father I wish I'd had.

And I watched him with Clarissa, watched how he loved her and protected her. And in a weird way, seeing him with her was healing.

Marcus is not perfect. I can see now that he stifled Clarissa's growth and freedom in some ways. But it was never from a lack of control or a lack of love.

She told me yesterday that she has no memory, in her entire life, of Marcus ever raising his voice or his hand to her. I can barely imagine the childhood she described. Peace and safety inside a family? It seems impossible.

And now Marcus is leaving. He's abandoning Clarissa, *long* before she's ready.

It's a stupid thought. It's wrong, so I shove it down as deep as it will go. But it keeps creeping back up to scrape at me.

I don't know who I'm angry at. It's not Marcus, and it's not Clarissa. Maybe it's God. And there's definitely some of it that's self-directed. Because here I am again, watching someone I love die without a single thing I can do about it.

I hate all that psychoanalysis shit. When I was a kid, I had to go to a therapist to talk about my father after he murdered my mother. And all those people do is rip pieces out of you and put them on display, like some kind of mental autopsy.

Instead of butterflying my lungs, they want to rip out my nerves and heart and call them trauma. But I don't sit around and cry about feelings.

Sometimes anger is productive. Sometimes it's what keeps us from sinking into all that shit we would drown in otherwise.

Marcus has asked me to take care of Clarissa, to be there and protect her the way he would have. He wouldn't have ever had to ask. There is nothing that will stop me from doing it. She is not going to be alone and hurt and terrified. No one is touching her. No one is harming her. No one.

Clarissa is coping better than I am, at least on the surface.

She talks kindly to the nurses and the doctors. She patiently coaxes Marcus to sip just a little more soup. She tidies up around him and helps him with sponge baths. She teases him and reminisces. She falls asleep holding his hand in the chair next to his bed. And sometimes she doesn't wake up when I touch her shoulder, so I carry her up to her bed. Then I return to take her place.

I sit with Marcus and hold his hand. When he's asleep, and we're alone, I let the angry tears fall. And when he's awake, I make the promises: I will stand in his shoes. I will protect her. I will be a man who does not hurt and does not leave.

I always knew Clarissa was sweet and good-natured. What I didn't know was that she has a hell of a backbone. She has mental fortitude. I know she wants to cry, and she does, often. But she doesn't want to do it where Marcus can see. So she cries in the bathroom, then washes her face off and walks back into that study with a smile on her face. And she makes him laugh, even through the pain. His and hers.

They're both laughing now as I peek inside with a knock on the doorframe. Marcus is gray and drawn. So thin he's skeletal. But he's laughing with a weak wheeze. Clarissa is grinning. And propped in Marcus's arm is a large pink stuffed toy.

Marcus lifts his free arm, the one with the IV taped to the back of his hand, and gestures weakly for me to come inside.

"Clare thinks I need a little buddy to hug. What do you think?" His eyes crinkle at the corners.

I smile because Marcus wants me to and say, "Pink is your color."

He closes his eyes, but he smiles in return. "I see... the appeal of your Squishmallow, Clare Bear. Very comfy."

"I told you so."

He doesn't open his eyes, his breathing shallow. "Clare." He reaches for her, letting the pillow toy fall away.

She takes his hand, and I move to stand behind her, my hands cupping her shoulders. "I'm here, Daddy."

"You're going to be okay, honey. You're so strong. So smart."

"Yes I am. I get that from you."

His head bobs in a shallow nod. "You bet you do." He tries to catch his breath, then says, "And you got that sweet heart from your mom. We're both... so proud of you."

Clare chokes back a sob, shuddering. I feel it under my hands, but she doesn't make a sound. Doesn't let Marcus hear.

She squeezes his hand gently and brushes the thin strands of his hair from his forehead. "I'm proud of you, too, Daddy," she says, her voice just an octave higher than it should be. "I don't know if I ever said that to you. You know I love you, but I don't think I ever told you how proud I am of you. And there hasn't been a single moment of my life when I didn't know how much you loved me."

He bobs his head ever so slightly. "That's how it's supposed to be."

Marcus surprises me when he opens his eyes and focuses on me. "I love you, too, son. Proud of you. I should have told you that."

I can't. I can't. I can't.

This man has been my friend, but he has also been my father. Better than my father. His love and pride are the most important words I've ever heard in my life. And I can't fucking bear to hear them like this, when it means he knows he's leaving.

I force the words past my closed-off throat. "I love you, too, Marcus."

He closes his eyes again. "I chose you for my Clare Bear. Found someone good enough for her." His small smile is a little smug. "I'd hoped I'd have more time. That she'd be a little older. That you two would figure it out on your own. But this... works."

"I don't understand."

"Saw you... that first time... in the lobby. Dolores Kirby dropped a big box... of paper. She has arthritis... but great at her job. Papers made... a huge mess. Five people just stood there, but you... came through those doors... and helped her."

"I don't remember that," I admit.

"It wasn't you... picking up papers... that did it," he says. "It was what you said... after she walked away... to the assholes... who ignored her."

I blink. "What did I say?"

"No... clue. But you were... an intern who made a group of seasoned executives... ashamed of themselves. And the next time I saw... Dolores—" He wheezes a laugh. "—she had a promotion... and a PA... to carry the papers."

Marcus passes at 10:04 a.m. the next day, with Clarissa holding his hand. I stand on the other side of his bed, and I shove the pain down where it needs to go so I can be there for Clarissa. I keep my back stiff, my face blank, and my eyes on my wife.

I don't look at Marcus. I can't. When I'm alone, I'll look. Not now. Not yet.

Clarissa sits for a long time, just holding Marcus's hand. Quiet. Unable to let go, though he no longer lives in that body. Finally, she stands, eerily quiet, tucking blankets around him, kissing his forehead.

She walks to the door. "I have to call—"

I catch her just before her knees hit the floor. I sink down next to her and wrap her up tight while she sobs hard enough to make herself gag.

Useless. I'm agonizingly useless. Helpless in the face of her pain and mine.

I know this feeling well: the one where it seems I could just fly off into the ether and evaporate into thin air if I don't find something to tether me to solid ground. With the way she clings, I'd guess Clarissa feels the same.

So I pull her onto my lap and don't let go, ready and willing to be her anchor in the storm. I rock her in my arms until she cries herself out. And if I steal some small comfort while I give it, no one has to know.

10

Carry You

JAMES

I'm not around as much as I'd like to be in the weeks following the funeral. Marcus's illness and passing left a large void at work, regardless of how well he orchestrated the transition. I'm working insane hours, even for me, to keep our stock from taking too much of a hit. Stepping into Marcus Harcourt's shoes is an honor; I can't let his life's work suffer because I'm not good enough or because I didn't work hard enough.

But I also made a promise to be a friend to Clarissa.

I'm failing at that already.

I drop my napkin onto my dinner plate and contemplate the empty seat where Clarissa should be sitting.

She hasn't been down to dinner once since Marcus passed. She takes her meals alone in her bedroom. In fact, she rarely leaves her suite of rooms upstairs at all. When she does come downstairs, she floats through the brownstone, ghostlike, quiet, almost transparent in her frailty. On the occasions when I try to break through her haze of grief, she just blinks at me as though she's not sure I'm speaking English.

It's been weeks since the funeral. And while I'm not trying to put some kind of limitation or end date on her grieving—God knows I'm still in the depths of it myself—I'm deeply concerned for her.

Something has to give.

I reach for the bag with the sporting goods company name on it that I'd set on the floor beside my chair. I wanted to be prepared should she actually come down to dinner. But I needn't have bothered.

Snatching it, I head for the stairs.

There's a muffled sound behind her door when I knock, and then it creeps open just enough for her head and shoulders to peek through.

"Yes?"

"I'm here for our half hour."

"What?"

I hold up my phone with the email version of our marriage plan showing. "It's in the rules. Half an hour of conversation."

"I'm not good company right now."

"Are you refusing to follow the rules?" I shake my head at her teasingly. "You little rebel, you."

"I'm serious, James. I'm no fun to be around."

"Then we're even. I'm shitty company too. How about we renegotiate terms? Half an hour in the same room, no conversation necessary."

She blinks, then moves to shut the door. "Tomorrow."

I stop it with my foot. "Why not now?"

She lifts her shoulders briefly, then swings her door open. "You can come in here. I don't want to go downstairs."

It's progress. I'll take it.

I've never given much thought to Clarissa's bedroom. The first time I'd been in it, I was too distracted by the fact that I'd walked in on her lying on her bed.

The subsequent times were overshadowed by the feel of her in my arms and the odd sort of tunnel vision that comes with functioning in the midst of a crisis.

But now I do, and I'm a little nonplussed by what I see. "This room doesn't look like you."

She'd been headed to a seating area near her cold fireplace. At my words, she turns around, showing some interest. "What isn't me about it?"

"Well, you hate pink and cutesy, for starters. And everything about this room is cute."

She frowns. "How do you know I hate pink?"

"You made this face every time you saw something pink at our wedding reception." I arrange my features into a prissy and mildly disgusted expression.

There's the tiniest spark of humor in her eyes. "I did not."

"I've also never seen you wear pink. Your favorite color is green."

She drops into an overstuffed chair and curls one leg under her. "Who told you that?"

She doesn't invite me to sit, but I do it anyway, making myself comfortable in the other chair and dropping the bag I'm carrying onto the floor by my feet. "No one told me. I have eyes. Your favorite scarf is green, your favorite earrings are jade, and the journal you use to write down your story ideas is green."

She blinks at me, startled. Then she says, "You're right. I don't really like pink. I think it's mostly because I went through a pink phase when I was around ten years old and overdid it until I got sick of it. And green *is* my favorite color. Very observant, Mr. Mellinger."

"Thank you, Mrs. Harcourt-Mellinger."

She lapses into silence and leans back against the chair, staring at nothing. She shivers a little, so I get up and light the gas fireplace. Then I pull a throw blanket off the bench at the end of her bed and drape it over her.

I sit back down and say nothing. I did promise we could sit in silence if she didn't want to talk.

She watches the flames and doesn't look at me when she says, "Your favorite color is blue."

I smile a little. "It used to be. Lately, I prefer green. The mossy kind with flecks of gold."

She looks at me curiously, and I could kick myself for saying that out loud.

I change the subject. "If you hate pink, you should change your room."

"I don't want to hurt Dad's feelings. He picked all of this ou—" She freezes, and then devastation floods her features. For a moment, she'd forgotten that Marcus wasn't alive and well and just downstairs. That he won't care that she's changing a room he obviously had a part in choosing. Because he isn't here to care.

I've done it more than once. I think to myself that I need to tell Marcus something or he'll get a kick out of something. Then I remember. And in that moment, it's like I'm losing my best friend for the first time all over again.

Her shoulders shake, and I think, *Fuck it*. I walk over and pick her up, then sit back down with her, wrapped in the throw blanket, on my lap.

And true to my word, we sit in silence.

At some point, she falls asleep on me. And then I drift off myself.

I ALMOST DO

I haven't been sleeping well at all. Which is par for the course for me, even before Marcus died. I never rest for more than a few hours at a time. And when I do, nightmares plague me.

But her dozing weight in my lap, her breath on my neck, her heartbeat against me—all of it acts as some kind of drug. I sleep, and my dreams don't involve murder or my failed attempt to kill a monster. They're of Clarissa, smiling and biting my lip.

I wake when she stirs, my thigh numb under her weight. I'm not sure how long it's been, but it's well over our assigned half hour.

She stretches and clambers off me with a mumbled "Sorry."

I scratch across the scruff on my chin. "Nothing to be sorry for."

"I'm going to take a shower," she says.

I stand, working out the pins and needles in my legs, and pick up the bag I brought with me. I hold it out, and she eyes it curiously.

"What is that?"

I give the bag a little shake. "Open it and see."

She takes it, peers inside with a tiny frown, then draws the contents out. "Ummm, why did you get me a swimsuit?"

It's a one-piece in a shimmery green-and-gold pattern. Made for competitive swimming, not lounging on a beach.

"I swim at my club every morning before work. If you'd like to join me, meet me downstairs at five thirty sharp, and we'll ride over together."

She screws her face up. "That's not morning. It's still the middle of the night."

"Hey, if you can't keep up with me, just say so," I say and reach to take back the suit.

She snatches it away and holds it to her chest. "I like to swim."

"So I've heard."

"Maybe I'll be there."

I smirk. "I won't hold my breath."

11

Safe Place

Clarissa

I slide my goggles from my eyes to my latex-covered head and look up at James. He's talking to me, crouched at the edge of the pool in a black speedo with a white towel thrown over his glistening shoulders, and I can't hear a word he's saying because my *God*.

I don't even know where to look. I've been swimming with him six mornings a week for three weeks now, and the view never gets old. My gaze travels over the swirling ink of his tattoos, the ridges in his stomach, then lower to the bulge in his shorts, down to those muscular, hair-covered thighs—

"Clarissa."

His voice sounds strained, and I drag my attention back up to his face. "What?"

"I said I'm impressed by how fast you're regaining your speed and endurance. You're a natural."

I pull myself out of the pool and sit next to him, enjoying the sensation of gravity returning and the scent of chlorine. "Thanks. Before high school graduation, Bronwyn helped me apply to Blackwater State University. She took video of me, and we sent my times to the swim coach there. We used a fake name—" I laugh at the memory. "—because I wanted to see if they'd let me swim without knowing who I was."

I shrug a little. "I thought nothing would come of it since Dad never let me swim competitively. I didn't really think I stood a chance of making the team, but a girl can dream."

"What happened?"

"Coach said they definitely had a place for me."

"Why didn't you go?"

"Dad didn't want me moving out of the house or going to a state school in the middle of nowhere. He didn't think it was a real school if it wasn't Ivy League. And he didn't want me swimming competitively. There are crowds at swim meets. And sometimes the press. He was afraid... well, you know how he was."

James stands, and I join him, easing the cap from my head as we walk toward the locker rooms. He hands me a dry towel, his expression disturbed. "You should have told him to fuck off and done what you wanted to do."

I choke in laughing surprise, and he stops walking. I pause there in the short hallway to the locker rooms, turning back to see why he's fallen behind. He's scowling, his jaw tight and flexing.

He moves closer, and at the intensity of his fury, I take a step back, my shoulder blades kissing the wall.

He recoils. "Did you think I was going to hurt you?"

"Of course not."

"You backed away."

"I don't like confrontation. You look angry."

"I'm not angry," he bites out.

"Oh—"

"I'm fucking pissed."

I try to understand where this is coming from. "Why? What did I do?"

"What if I told you I forbid you from coming back to the pool?"

My heart sinks. "But... why?"

"Because you're my wife, and I don't want people seeing you here. What if some douche sees you in a swimsuit and decides he's going to stalk you?"

"I—" My throat clogs. "No one else is here but the staff. You reserve the whole pool. Are you sure—"

"Tell me to fuck off."

I shake my head in disbelief.

"We're having asparagus soup for dinner tonight. I expect you to eat it."

"What?"

He moves closer and braces his forearm on the wall above my head. "You hate asparagus. Tell me to fuck off."

Oh, this asshole. He's doing a Bronwyn, except instead of gently coaching me to stand up for myself, he's goading me. But I'm not afraid of hurting James's feelings the way I was with my dad. James can handle it.

I reach up to grab hold of his thick wrist. I whisper, "Fuck off, James."

He makes a sound in his throat and drops his forehead to mine. His voice is deep and growly when he says, "That's my girl. Say it again."

My nipples go diamond hard, and liquid heat pools low in my pelvis. "Fuck off," I say, a little louder this time.

"I'm having a decorator redo the billiards room in pink."

I snicker. "You are not. Fuck off."

He smiles and clenches my waist through my wet swimsuit. His body presses against mine. It's not the first time. We touch a lot. But they're mostly casual touches—nothing overtly sexual.

This is different. This is wet skin and elevated emotions, and I already want him so badly my nerve endings vibrate with it. His cock is an iron bar against my belly.

"Tell me all the things you never did. Do you want to burn everything pink in your bedroom? We'll do it," he says.

"No."

"You sure about that?"

"I want to donate it to a women's shelter."

"Good girl. What else?"

"I want to learn to drive a car."

"Done."

"I want a pet. Dad didn't like animals inside the house. But I want one." There's heat building behind my words as I begin my list.

"Keep talking," he says, his mouth against the thin skin at my temple.

"I want to travel."

"Do it."

"I don't want to be a librarian. I want to write smutty romance novels that nobody will ever take seriously."

"So fucking hot," he breathes.

"I want to kiss you."

He holds still for a moment and doesn't say a word. Then his mouth is on mine, his large body pinning me to the wall. He tastes of chlorine and toothpaste. And the feel of his tongue stroking against mine, his lips as they explore, his stubble that scrapes against my tender skin, it all ignites a maelstrom of sexual longing inside me.

He eats at my mouth, his hand moving to the back of my head to tilt me first this way, then that. I reach up to stroke across the vaulted expanse of his back, exploring the satin skin with my fingertips, exultant that his mouth is on mine.

The door at the end of the hall swings open. There's a murmur of words, then the sound of the door snicking shut again. It's Sasha keeping some member of the staff away from us. I'd forgotten, for just a moment, where we were. That Sasha is right there at the end of the hall in full view.

James eases back a little, his expression troubled as he says, "This is a slippery slope. We're friends, Clarissa."

Ouch.

He steps away and rubs the back of his neck. "We can't be more than that. Not for a long time."

It's almost worse that his expression is so gentle and kind.

This is his reminder—no catching feelings.

Too damn late.

12

When the Party's Over

JAMES

Clarissa is a torment. She's not even trying. She just is. It's not just that I love the feel of her touching me, it's that she's become necessary for me to function.

Knowing she wants me to touch her too? It's torture.

After the incident outside the locker rooms, I've pulled away from her. I'm sure she thinks it's because I don't want to kiss her or touch her or, in her words, "catch feelings."

The truth is worse. I don't just want to kiss her—I want to own her. I don't just want to touch her—I want to tease her until she begs me to give her an orgasm. I want to watch her wrap that innocent mouth around my cock. I want to rut on her like an animal until she's shaking from how hard she comes.

I need her.

And as soon as I think those words, I hear my father's voice screaming at my mother. "You don't get to leave me. I need you. I love you."

He's in prison now. He'll die there.

And I cannot be that man.

I have to stay the hell away from her. Just until I get these feelings under control. Until I can stop thinking about her and wanting her every damn minute of every damn day.

We still swim every morning. And we have dinner together most evenings unless I have something I have to do for work. But I keep my time with her to a strict schedule, and I've attempted to inject a level of formality back into our interactions.

Clarissa's not having it. She simply refuses to be cowed by my reserve. It's as though she sees me, acting stiff and polite, and is determined to be more affectionate. She just calls me her grump and says she'll be my sunshine—whatever the hell that means.

She trusts me, when what she needs is to be on her guard with me.

She thinks the way I goaded her into telling me to fuck off was some kind of game. It wasn't. She has no boundaries with me. It's not just that I want to own her—it's that I could, and she wouldn't even put up a token resistance.

She has a customized spendthrift trust fund that I control until she's twenty-one. At that point, certain parts of her trust fund will become available in increments until she's twenty-five. I'm not miserly about her money. Marcus's goal wasn't to keep her on some kind of budget. It was to protect her from con artists.

But it's a disgusting level of power over her. One no spouse should have over another. If I refused to allow her to leave me, she would be trapped.

Which is why I started funneling money every week into a "spending account" that's only in her name, plus a savings account for the same purpose. If she ever needs to run from me, I don't want her to be stuck with no way out.

So I keep my distance from her for now. After dinner with Clarissa most nights, I work alone in the downstairs den I've taken over as a home office. I could easily use Marcus's study, but his death is too fresh. Someday I'll sit at that desk and think of him with nostalgia. For now, it simply picks at the scab of my grief.

And every night, when I've finally worked myself to the point of exhaustion, I sneak up to the third floor like some kind of stalker. I can't sleep until I've done it.

The first time I eased open her bedroom door without knocking, I caught her reading her Kindle in bed. She should have told me to get lost and reminded me to knock next time. She should have started locking her door.

She didn't. She patted the bed beside her, smiled, and invited me in.

I didn't go in, of course. I told her I was stopping by to tell her good night and remind her I wouldn't be home for dinner the next night.

But when she's asleep? I'm an absolute weird-ass creep. I don't stand in the doorway. Instead, I sit down beside her on the bed and just let the sight of her bring me peace.

I imagine a future where she's sleeping in *our* bed, and I can climb in beside her and pull her into my arms.

Sometimes I even kick off my shoes and lie beside her, fully dressed on top of the blankets. Never close enough to touch. Sometimes I'll even drift off that way. And when I wake, I find she's rolled toward me in her sleep and put her head on my shoulder and her hand on my chest, right over my beating heart.

She's asleep tonight. I guess she's overheated, because she's pushed her new sage-green comforter off her body. And instead of her usual fuzzy pajama bottoms and T-shirt, she's in a silky black thong and the undershirt I gave her on our wedding night. She's asleep on her stomach, one leg bent up in a way that means I could pull that strip of fabric aside and slide right inside her.

She's left her bathroom door partially open with the light on, so I can see everything. And a good man would turn the hell around and leave.

Instead, I ease her bedroom door shut behind me and move closer. I won't touch. I never, ever touch her. But when I sit beside her on the bed, she shivers, and goose bumps pop up all over her.

Damn it.

"Clarissa," I murmur.

She doesn't move or make a sound, so I reach across and drag the comforter over her. "I know you're awake."

She rolls over and lifts her sooty lashes to peer up at me from her pillow. "How'd you know?"

I lift an eyebrow. "For one, I heard you tell one of your friends that you hate thongs. You call them 'butt floss.' I'm finding it hard to imagine you'd enjoy sleeping in one. How long have you known?"

"That you've been coming in here to check on me?"

That's a very gracious way to put it, but we'll go with that. "Yes."

"I think from the first night." She makes a bit of an apologetic face. "I'm a very light sleeper most of the time."

"And you didn't think maybe you should start locking your door or telling me to stay out?"

Her expression is shocked. "Of course not. Why would I do that? I told you the first night you found me awake that you're welcome here."

"How are you not freaked out?"

She shrugs. "When I was a kid, Dad had nightmares. I'd wake up sometimes in the middle of the night to him taking my pulse. I guess I didn't see this as all that different."

"What?"

"He had nightmares about me dying or something happening to me. He had a routine. Even though we have security here out the wazoo, every night, he had to check every door, lock, and alarm personally. And if he woke up with a nightmare, he couldn't go back to sleep until he made sure I was okay. So he'd sit by my bed and take my pulse."

I'd had no idea it was that bad. My chest aches at the thought of it. For Marcus, yes. But also for that little girl who felt her father's emotional well-being was her responsibility.

"And how is this the same?"

"I assumed maybe you felt lonely or were grieving but didn't want to talk. You always left when I was awake. I was trying to give you time to just... I don't know... find some peace."

"That thong is not giving me peace," I say.

She mutters something under her breath.

"What did you say?"

"I said, 'It wasn't supposed to.' Are you satisfied?"

I'm not. We have years to go before we consummate this marriage.

"I have to be at the Los Angeles office after Christmas. I'll be there for a month." I had no plans to say that. I'd had no plans to *do* that. But I can't keep going like this. I need space and distance.

She jolts into a sitting position. "When do we leave?"

"Not we. Just me. I'll be too busy for anything but work. We'll FaceTime every day. If you need me anytime, day or night, you call. You should probably start back up at school next semester anyway."

"I see." Her expression is shuttered as she lies back down. She rolls on her side away from me and pulls the comforter up to her shoulders. Voice a higher pitch than usual, she says, "Can you turn off the bathroom light when you go, please? I'm tired."

I hesitate. What I want is to crawl into that bed with her, hold her, and beg her to forgive me. Instead, I turn out the light and leave.

13

Good as Hell

Clarissa

"That dick-faced dickwad," Bronwyn seethes, throwing herself against the back seat of the car with a huff.

I shoot a glance up toward the front, where my driver, Dean, sits behind the wheel. The privacy screen is up, thank goodness. "It's not... he's not...."

I want to say James isn't a dick-faced dickwad. But that resentment that started bubbling up in me when I took vows with a man who made us write a stupid rule about not falling in love with each other has reached full boil.

What am I even doing here? I'm in love with my friend. And now he can't even stand to sleep in the same house with me.

Franki shoves her highlighted brown hair behind her ear, then reaches out and takes both my hands in hers. "You know I always look for the bright side."

I nod glumly.

"The bright side here is that you do not have to stay there and suffer," she says in her gentle bubblegum voice.

I lift my head to look into her big brown eyes. Then I look toward Bronwyn, who has her arms crossed over her chest and her lips held tight.

"What I'd like to know," Bronwyn says, "is how James could check out your ass in a thong and not tap that. You're fucking fine. Are we sure he's into women?"

I sigh. "Yes, I'm sure."

"Because if he's not... if he's gay or asexual, then that's a whole different situation."

"Bronwyn, I know he's attracted to me."

"I think he's trying to be noble," Franki says.

I roll my eyes. "He thinks because of how strict this trust fund is and how he controls all of my money, my home, and my education that it would be taking advantage of me to sleep with me."

"Hmmm," Bronwyn says.

"What does that mean?"

She puts both her hands up, all "calm down," and says, "He's not really wrong, is he?"

I reach down and adjust the Christmas packages on the floor. We've been spending the afternoon shopping, and suddenly, I'm tempted to toss James's gifts out the window.

I'd never do that. But even the fact that I've thought it feels strangely empowering.

"I don't care that he's in control of my money. I've never been in control of it. What difference does it make?"

Even Franki's jaw drops. She and Bronwyn share a look I can't decipher.

"What?"

"You just want to go from being under your dad's thumb to another man's? And he doesn't just control your money. He could tell you tomorrow that you're not going back to school, that he won't pay for it. Or he could tell you that the two of you are moving, that he's closing up the house you're living in. And you couldn't do a thing about it. He could sell this car without even discussing it with you first. How does that not bother you?"

"James wouldn't do that."

"But he could. And he knows that. If he's uneasy about it, then I have to say, as much as his rejection of you makes me want to cause him extreme bodily harm... I respect it a little."

I frown and lean back against my seat. I hadn't really thought about it, but she has a point.

I don't want to be angry at my father. I won't be angry at him. Dad had reasons for the things he did.

But why did he create this particular type of trust fund? I understand about protecting assets with a trust fund, but why one so strict? Did he have no faith in me at all? I may as well have been a seven-year-old with a guardian instead of a twenty-year-old woman.

My eyes widen at the realization. "James thinks he's my guardian."

Franki shrugs a little helplessly. "He kind of is."

"No," I breathe, my voice shaking a little with the word.

And something in me shifts, like ice breaking up on the Hudson. She's right.

I sigh. "This will never work if I just sit around and wait for James."

Franki lifts her palms. "What's keeping you in that house?"

Only my own fear of taking charge of my life and a pathetic dream that James will change his mind. But he isn't someone who waffles. If he says he's waiting until I'm twenty-five for us to have a full marriage, he means it.

I will not waste my time sitting alone in that brownstone while he finds excuses to not be there. How soon until he moves back into his Manhattan penthouse because it's "closer to the office"?

And what will I be doing while he does? Finishing out a degree I never wanted at a school I never wanted to go to? I wanted to go to school in Pennsylvania before this marriage.

"I still have my acceptance for next semester at BSU," I say tentatively.

Bronwyn's eyes grow wide. She slaps her hands to my cheeks and lands a loud, smacking kiss right on my lips. I sputter and laugh, shoving her away.

"It's perfect," she says. "If you keep living with him and seeing him day after day, you'll be miserable if he doesn't change his mind about your relationship."

I chew on the inside of my lip.

"Is there any chance he'll change his mind about the sex?" Franki asks.

"I don't think so. He seems pretty determined."

"Come to school with me," Bronwyn urges. "Let your relationship develop slowly without all that pressure of your hormones going crazy around him. We both know there's no way you're going to wait until you're twenty-five, but you can make the next year or so easier on yourself."

I look up at the ceiling and bob my head side to side while I think.

"Come on. You've never done anything without an authority figure hovering over you, telling you where to go and what to do. Live a little."

At those words, my metaphorical spine stiffens a little. The last thing I want or need is for James to act like my boss or my father. I've been pushing back against that from day one.

"I'll do it," I finally say.

Bronwyn throws her hands in the air. "Whoo! Girl, we need to celebrate!"

I don't feel like celebrating. This doesn't feel like a win to me. It feels terrifying.

Franki reaches over and pats my hand. "It's a good idea."

"Think we can get Dean to celebrate with us?" Bronwyn asks as she reaches for the button to lower the privacy screen between us.

I push her hand away. "Don't you dare. Leave the poor man alone."

She throws herself back against the seat and crosses her arms. "You know he likes it when I harass him."

"Dean doesn't like anything or, as far as I can tell, anybody. You're just mad because you can't make a conquest out of him."

Bronwyn's jaw drops in outrage at my words. "Dean's not a conquest. He's the love of my life."

"You don't know a thing about him."

"I know enough."

Bronwyn's upbringing differed from Franki's and mine in more than the obvious ways. Until she was five years old, she lived with her single mother in a trailer in a little town in central Pennsylvania. She still has a huge extended family there and spends a lot of time with them.

When Bronwyn's adoptive father met her mother, it was a whirlwind love-at-first-sight thing. He snatched them both out of their Podunk rural lives and dropped them right into the rarefied air of New York high society.

But the two of them never quite made what I'd consider a full transition. And there are things Bronwyn is positively rabid about that I wouldn't have even considered if she weren't a constant in my life.

One is that there's no such thing as "the help." The very idea of ignoring or not being friends with the people paid to take care of basic services is, in her mind, a symptom of a snob. And snobs are, to Bronwyn's thinking, just the worst.

And that's great if said employee is interested in being friends.

Dean is not. Dad hired him last year, and I'm pretty sure his instructions were along the lines of "Keep those girls safe and out of trouble."

That's what he's done. That and nothing else. And when Bronwyn tried her usual friendly overtures, he met her with a stone wall of deference.

First, it infuriated her. Then she decided Dean was a challenge.

He is anything but just a driver. None of them have ever been. But Dean? He's a cut even above the usual bodyguard/driver. I don't even know where Dad found him.

He's probably only in his early thirties, but Dean is obviously a seasoned veteran. He's built like a linebacker, carries a concealed firearm under his black suit jacket, and his head is on a constant swivel, looking for nonexistent threats to our well-being.

Bronwyn took one look at stoic Dean, with his stoic face and his stoic muscles, and decided she was in love.

She inches her hand back toward the button.

"Bronwyn," I warn. "Leave Dean the fuck alone. Not everyone has to like you."

Her outraged expression morphs into first shock, then delight.

"Why is that funny?" I grouch.

"It's not funny. It's awesome. You never tell anyone off. You don't get mad. Ever. Then you went and drank at your wedding—way more than I would recommend, I might add—and you got mad at James. And now you just sassed me. Right to my face. It's wonderful," she says.

"It's not wonderful. It's awful."

"No." She grabs my hand and gives it a squeeze. "It's not. It's normal. You know I loved your dad—"

"Don't," I say.

"I loved him, but he controlled you way too much. It was a kind of emotional blackmail, whether he meant it to be or not. You thought if you let yourself feel bad things, a meteor was going to fall out of the sky."

"That wasn't my father's fault. And the meteor already fell, so what does it matter now?"

"Okay, that's not quite the life lesson I was going for, but let's roll with it."

She looks back up toward the front of the car wistfully. Then her hand creeps back toward the button. It's obviously an act designed to get a reaction out of me, as evidenced by her slow and flagrant progress.

"Grow up," Franki says to Bronwyn. "You act like a middle schooler with a crush around Clarissa's driver."

Bronwyn smirks, and then her eyes widen. "That's it. Clarissa, there's your compromise with James. Tell him you've been unfairly denied the boyfriend experience."

An incredulous laugh punches out of me. "What?"

She shrugs. "If you two just avoid each other or do the platonic friend thing, how are you supposed to transition later into something else? We all know it's not going to take until you're twenty-five, but for this first little while? You should ask him to be your middle school boyfriend. There's no pressure for sex, then. Just hand-holding. A little light French kissing. A promise that you're going steady and won't hold anyone else's hand. Admit it, it's brilliant."

I roll my eyes. "Just as a reminder, I didn't do any of that in middle school. Sasha would have broken the lips of any boy trying to lay one on me."

Bronwyn snorts in agreement. "Yeah, she would have. That's my point. You never had any of that. There has to be an easing into it, you know? You can't soar in the clouds until you've learned to ride a tricycle, little sparrow."

I laugh, then give her my snootiest expression. "Birds don't ride bikes. Your point is invalid."

"No, you listen to your elders, missy."

"You're four months older than I am," I say.

She nods slowly and repetitively. "And I've got a good twenty years on you in life experience."

"Oh, of course, Wise Woman of Brooklyn Heights. Share with me your infinite knowledge of arranged marriages."

"I will. Moving out and dating him will take some of the pressure off. Living with him when your relationship is so squishy has to suck."

"Squishy?" Franki asks.

"Yes, squishy. They're married. And he cares about her, but she's still way more into him as far as I can see."

Oof.

"Believe me—" She shoots a glance toward the front of the car, then back at me. "—that sucks. Your relationship is already weird."

I speak in the soothing tone I do when I know I am absolutely not going to say or do the thing she wants me to. "I'll think about it."

"Which means you won't. But you are definitely coming to PA for the spring semester?"

"I'm definitely doing that."

We've pulled up to the brownstone, and Dean is coming around to open the door.

"Are you coming inside?" I ask them.

They both shake their heads.

Bronwyn checks her phone. "Can't. I have a shift at the youth center."

"You're a really good person, Bronnie."

She rolls her eyes. "No I'm not. I'm a handful. Ask anyone. But if you come to BSU to be my roommate, I promise not to steal your food unless I'm really, really hungry."

"That's a very low bar," I say.

My car door opens in the middle of my words, but it isn't Dean who's standing there. It's James.

He nods at Franki. "Hey, Franki."

She smiles and gives him a finger wave.

He turns his attention to Bronwyn. "Hello, tequila," he says, voice dry as the desert.

"Hello, James." She twinkles at him, and the dimple in her left cheek pops into place.

Now that she's getting her way, she's decided to skip the name-calling, apparently.

James puts a hand out to help me from the car and says pleasantly, "She terrifies me when she smiles like that."

Bronwyn smiles harder as she hands me my packages. "Good."

I turn back to my blonde friend, who's about to have control of that privacy screen without adequate supervision.

She says, "I'll text you later."

I fake a scowl and whisper, "Back off my driver."

She smirks and mouths back, "Never."

Bronwyn's eyes sparkle as she looks past me to make eye contact with my husband. "By the way, James, ask your wife about middle school."

14

This Is Me Trying

JAMES

Clarissa is not interested in discussing middle school—whatever that's about. In fact, she's not interested in discussing much of anything with me.

I'd planned to ask her to go with me to the animal shelter to find the pet she'd said she wanted. But before I could even fully explain where I was going, she gave me a tight smile and said she wanted to get back to a book she's reading.

She's still grieving, of course. But my entire purpose is supposed to be to make her life better. To protect her and make her happy. Instead, I put that bruised look in her eyes.

Worse, I have no idea how to fix it. But I hope this is a start.

I tap on her bedroom door, pet carrier in my left hand.

When she drags the door open, her eyes widen at the sight.

Without a word, I step inside, set the carrier on the floor, and open its door. A fluffy white cat pokes its head out and yowls at us before hiding back inside.

"I don't know anything about cats, but the shelter said this one was scheduled to be put down at the end of the week, so here you go. It's a cat. For you."

"Oh my God!" She lies on her rug and peers into the carrier. "You are so pretty. Yes you are! What's his name?"

"He was a stray, so the name they gave him was new, just to attract someone to adopt him. They said you can keep calling him Puffy, or you can name him anything you want."

"Puffy?" She grimaces.

"Yes, well." The sudden gleam in her eye makes me suspicious. "Just remember, whatever you name this cat, you have to be the one to tell the vet."

She purses her lips.

I nod and turn to go. "There's a bunch of stuff in the kitchen for him. Litter and food. I'll leave you to sort it out."

She stands and says, "You just handed me a lot of work. What if I didn't want a cat? What if I wanted a gerbil or a snake?"

Please. She definitely wants the cat. I listen when my wife talks. I know exactly what she wants in a pet.

But I turn back and answer truthfully. "Then I'd have to learn how to be a cat dad pretty damn quick."

She stands there, posture defensive, and asks, "How can you be a cat dad if you're in Los Angeles?"

"Are you saying you want me to take him with me?" She has to hear the consternation in my voice, but the timing of this cat was at least partially due to wanting to provide her with company while I'm gone.

"You don't need to bother. Actually... you don't have to go to Los Angeles at all. You can stay here." She crosses to pick up a large white envelope from her desk and passes it to me.

"What's this?"

"It's my acceptance to Blackwater State University. I'm starting the second week of January."

I try to keep my expression neutral while my heart pounds out of control. "This is the school you spoke about at the pool? The one you wanted to go to as a freshman?"

She dips her chin in acknowledgment.

"Do you even know a soul out there in the middle of Pennsylvania?"

"If I didn't, I'd meet them. But I'm rooming with Bronwyn. You'll need to keep Mr. Snufflenuts while I'm at school. I'll be back for the summer. I can't keep him at school, though, until I'm ready to move off-campus."

There's so much to work through in that statement. I start with the easiest one. "I'm not calling the cat Mr. Snufflenuts."

"Fine." She drags the word out with grudging acceptance. Then her natural sense of mischief peeks through. "Mr. Fluffynuts?"

"Hmmm, let me think," I say acidly. "No. And I don't like the idea of you rooming with Tequila Bronwyn. That girl's a menace."

"She is not. She's awesome. We had a lapse in judgment one time. It's ancient history."

"We've been married less than two months," I say incredulously.

"Exactly," she says.

She has it all worked out. I'm proud of her for it, even if the thought of her living so far away is a locomotive in my chest, starting out slow but picking up speed as her plans inexorably sink in.

Why was it different when I planned my trip to Los Angeles? Because I was in control. It meant I could turn around and come back the moment she needed me. It meant if it was too hard to live without her, I could change my mind.

What a dick.

"If it's just that you want to move out, we can find an apartment nearby. My penthouse in Manhattan—"

She shakes her head. "My mind is made up. I'm going to PA."

"You're my wife. We should live together."

The look she gives me is pure, sardonic disbelief. "You were planning to go to the other side of the country for a month at a time. We're not sleeping together. You'll barely notice I'm gone."

She can't possibly believe that's true. "You can't go." It's sheer gut instinct to say those words. They rip out of me against my will.

A hint of irritation seeps into her voice. "I am. You're the one who told me I should have gone in the first place."

"You expect me to write the check for this?"

She looks confused, as if it truly never occurred to her that I might withhold it from her. "That money is for my education. I get to choose where I get my education."

When I say nothing in response, her mouth falls open. "Just because I always did what Dad wanted doesn't mean he'd have kept me a prisoner here against my will."

I'd thought my adrenaline was at peak level before. But that word, it lands a solid blow. I've heard it before—my mother begging, "I'm a prisoner in this house. Let us go. Please. Please let us go."

I choke on my words. "I've never tried to keep you from doing anything or going anywhere."

"Except for the one place I said I want to go," she says gently.

She's right. I can't ask her to stay. But how can I protect her from... what? Four hours away? Five?

She's only twenty years old. I'm twenty-nine. Those nine years will be nothing when she's twenty-five. But right now, the gap in life experience between us is almost criminal. Not just because of the actual years but because she's done next to nothing. Clarissa has been a princess in her third-floor tower.

She wants to experience what most young women experience. She wants freedom and the right to choose her own path. I'd be a controlling monster to hold her back from that.

I did this to both of us when I told her I was leaving. I thought I'd control the situation, maintain emotional distance while also knowing she was right here waiting for me.

Now she's flipping the script. She's taking control of her own life and choices. I recognize that fact with grudging admiration.

I remember her demands on our wedding night. The way she wanted to know if I'd been having sex when I was twenty. Is my refusal leaving her frustrated and wanting to find someone else?

Maybe we should sleep together. If I tell her I changed my mind—that I want a normal marriage with her right now—I know she'd stay.

It would keep her here, safe and away from other guys—but that's exactly my reason for not sleeping with her in the first place. It would be too easy to control her.

I'm already obsessed with her.

The thought of hurting her like that makes me sick. If she goes and screws around with college guys, that isn't the same thing as me manipulating her with money and sex.

But thinking of her out there, surrounded by college guys, the most intense jealousy I've ever experienced in my life is clawing through me.

"Will you pretend you aren't married when you're gone? Hook up with frat boys and football players?" My movements are jerky, my words stiff as I move to the mantle of her fireplace.

She makes a sound of frustration. When I turn to look at her, she rolls her eyes at me.

"Will you?" I insist, and before I realize I've moved, I'm close enough that her breasts skim my chest.

She doesn't back away. Instead, she pushes closer to me. Her skin pebbles beneath her black tank top, nipples perking. And I'm a bad, bad man. Because I like that a hell of a lot.

Those captivating eyes of hers stare up at me intently. She brings her thumb up to rub back and forth across her plump lower lip.

Finally, she says, "It's not like you want to sleep with me." Her expression is a little belligerent and a lot hurt. "It feels a little 'dog in the manger' to me."

"I *want* to. The fact that we're not sleeping together is temporary. Have you changed your mind about that?"

She shows me her left hand, where my rings sparkle on her finger. "Fidelity was my idea in the first place. I'm not a cheater. This might not be a normal marriage, but I still promised to be faithful when I said my vows."

I want to kiss her, so I stomp to her window and stare out at the street below instead. The traffic. The bicyclists and pedestrians. The pretty street with all the brownstones lined up so neat and clean.

It looks nothing like the run-down rental house where my mother died. It looks... perfect. The view from her tower.

I have to give her something. How can I expect her to wait for us to be ready if I give her nothing of myself in the meantime?

Forcing myself to speak, I admit, "Marrying you is the best thing that has ever happened to me."

I turn at her scoff. There's a confused frown on her face.

I move closer and smooth a soft auburn curl behind her ear. It's nothing more than a blatant excuse to touch her; I won't even pretend otherwise to myself.

"I know I'm fucking everything up with you. I'm trying to do what's right. We just need to weather the next few years until we're on more equal footing in terms of this power imbalance."

The cat has made his way out of the carrier and is rubbing against her legs. She leans down to pick him up, and he purrs as she snuggles him against her face. She says nothing at all.

"I broke one of our rules," I confess.

Her whiskey-and-moss-green gaze flies to mine, and her face crumples. It takes me a second to understand.

"I'm not screwing around on you." I don't really care if she can hear how offended I am at the thought of it. "You think I'd let anyone but you near me?"

I reach out for her but then drop my hands. I have no business pulling her into my arms.

"What rule, then?" She looks afraid to hope. And I don't know if I'm doing the right thing by admitting to it.

"It's not good. If you think it is, you're wrong, because all it does is make our lives harder."

"What rule?"

I try to say it, but the words don't want to come.

She puts the cat on the floor and moves closer to me, cupping my face. "James, what rule?"

I shake my head. One sharp movement. Then I shove my hands in my pockets and fiddle with the little satin bow I carry there. "The last one."

"James, I—"

"It doesn't change anything right now. We're not having a sexual relationship while I still have this kind of power over you. But I'm in this thing. I'm so fucking in it. Right there with you.

"And you're right. You absolutely should go to school. You've never had a moment of freedom. Marrying you was...." I almost say "wrong," but I can't say that word about the greatest gift I've ever been given in my life.

But that's part of the problem, isn't it? Even at the time, I saw it as Marcus giving me his daughter. And I suspect she saw it that way too. She married me because her father wanted her to. She didn't feel she had a choice, did she? Not really.

I don't have any experience with relationships, but even I can see that we started on a fucked-up premise. That she was this precious treasure being passed from one man to another instead of a living, breathing person capable of making her own choices.

Five years might be enough time for me to be sure I can trust myself with her. But the passage of years alone is not enough to change the nature of our relationship. Especially if she stays here and caters to my emotional needs the way she did her father's.

"It's better for you to go away and stretch your wings. For both of us. But I don't want you to go feeling... rejected."

The sound she makes is almost a laugh. Then she throws her arms around me. With her voice muffled against my neck, she says, "James?"

I press her closer and speak into her hair. "Yes, sweet girl?"

"I want to talk about middle school."

15

Brave

JAMES

I only have three more nights of living under the same roof with my wife—who is also now, in her words, my girlfriend.

I draw the line at calling myself a *boyfriend*, if only because it's been a damn long time since I was any kind of boy.

I love every second of it... except the parts where our physical contact is limited to "safe zones," our hugs are brief, and I give her a sweet kiss at her bedroom door every night before walking back to my bedroom alone.

Those parts, however, can't be helped.

Her departure for school is looming. No longer weeks away, it's now a question of hours—approximately eighty, by my current calculations.

We only have three more of these dinners at home before she's off living in a dormitory in a different state.

The thought is ridiculous. Her closet is bigger than a dorm room. But she sees it as an adventure, and I haven't fought her on it.

She's never had to share a room with anyone, let alone someone with a personality as forceful as Bronwyn's. Again, I haven't objected. At least not beyond my initial knee-jerk reaction. God knows it'll be a learning experience for her.

In fact, I haven't fought her on anything, mostly because I am entirely too aware of my own power. It's not just that I have the ability to make things go my own way with the careful application (or removal) of funds—it's that all I'd have to do is apply the smallest amount of emotional manipulation, and she'd fold like a cheap card table.

I've been careful not to do that to her.

But this? I'm putting my foot all the way down.

I shake out my napkin and lay down the law. "No."

My answer ticks her off. I'm not even sure how I know that. It's not like she ever says she's angry, or even raises her voice. The closest I've ever heard it was that drunken squeak on our wedding night when I suggested we could have sex when she turned twenty-five.

Even when I goaded her to tell me to fuck off, she did it gently, almost as though she was indulging me.

Occasionally, she'll show irritation—though you have to know her well to recognize the signs of it.

Clarissa Harcourt-Mellinger doesn't slam doors or tell people off. She's great at cajoling and charming people. She's outright gifted at it.

I'd guess it's something she learned watching her father. He took her with him often enough as he schmoozed everyone from heads of industry to world leaders.

But she doesn't have the killer instinct he had. When push comes to shove, she backs off. Every single time.

For once, that's a damn good thing.

She clears her throat. "Could you just think ab—"

"No."

Our personal chef sets the last of our meal on the dining room table. "Is there anything else I can get for you?"

"We're all set," I say.

Clarissa smiles at the woman tightly. "Dinner looks lovely, Carol. Thank you so much."

She pats Clarissa gently on the shoulder. "I made your favorite for dessert: double-chocolate cake."

Clarissa nods and looks at her place setting. "Can't wait," she replies.

I wait until Carol has left the room before I pick up my fork and say, "I've made no objection to any of your other plans, Clarissa. But if you think I'm letting you leave here without your security detail, then you don't know me at all."

She picks up her fork and knife, cuts a small portion of her chicken, chews, swallows, and pats her mouth with her napkin. Then she says, "I like that word, *let*. It's funny coming from you. It's almost like you think I'm one of your employees."

Impressive. And not at all the reaction I expected from her.

This is the same girl who sat at this table and smiled at Marcus while he told her it was too dangerous to join a swim team.

"Where is this coming from?" I question.

She stares at her plate hard, then stiffens her spine. "I don't know." She makes eye contact and holds it. "But I know I'm not sorry. And I know the more you push me, the harder I want to shove back at you."

"This isn't like you," I say, frowning.

Eventually, she huffs. "Everyone thinks I don't have a temper. I used to think I didn't have one too."

"But you do?" I try to put myself in her place: imagine myself sitting at this table and conceding the things I wanted to do and the life I wanted to live. Over and over, she did it with a smile.

I'd never have done it, not even to make Marcus happy. I was the poster child for the moody, rebellious teenager.

She nods and looks down at the linen napkin she's twisting between her fingers. "I do have a temper."

She sets the napkin on the table and keeps her eyes trained on it. "James," she whispers, "I am so fucking angry right now."

I watch her for a long, quiet moment, taking in the stiff set of her shoulders. The way her fingers twitch and a muscle flexes in her jaw. Finally, I say, "There's nothing wrong with that."

Her attention shoots to my face. Then she glares at me, fierce and wild. "You're not my father. You don't get to boss me around or tell me what to do."

It's not often that I'm caught without words, but I don't have a single one.

She mutters something, and I'm not sure I trust my ears. "What did you say?"

Her voice is stronger when she says, "Keep fighting me over this, and you'll suffer my wrath."

I can't help the quirk of my lips at her wording or the stab of pride at her spirit. The majority of her social life has taken place in the pages of her books. I hear it sometimes in her language.

I concede her point with a nod, but I can't back down on this. It's just not happening. The things I'm doing are for her own protection.

Clarissa is naive as hell. She's a baby bird, and I'm trying to let her fly while still giving her the safety net she needs.

"We made promises to each other. I expect you to keep those promises," I say.

"This isn't the 1920's. I never promised to *obey* you," she says incredulously.

I dig my palm into my eye, then drop my hand to the table, clenching it into a fist. "I don't want obedience from my *wife*." The idea of it is revolting.

At her wary expression, I say, "Our promises to each other, Clarissa. Chase your dreams, but don't be reckless."

A dent forms between her brows.

"Even I have a certain amount of security. It would be foolish not to. You're one of the wealthiest women in the world. If you're unprotected, you will be a target. That's a fact."

She presses her lips together, her expression troubled. "I want to know what it's like to be normal."

"I'm sorry I can't give that to you," I say. And I mean it. "If you're more comfortable having your bodyguards masquerade as friends or fellow college students, you go right ahead and do that, but you're not going there without security."

"I'll be in the middle of nowhere. Who's even going to know or care who I am?"

"Don't be naive. It just means you'd be an easier mark."

She doesn't get it. Why would she? Marcus did everything in his power to keep her insulated from anything and everything he deemed unpleasant, let alone dangerous.

But the real world is a nasty place. It's full of evil and violence. She needs to understand that—at least enough to not do stupid shit like ditch her security team.

"I wasn't raised in your nice little world, princess. Ask me what I'd do if someone hurt you."

She swallows. "What would you do?"

I hold her gaze, willing her to understand. "Absolutely anything. Remember that before you deliberately put yourself in harm's way."

She lifts her chin. "I want my name added to those security contracts. I want access to everything. Every report. Every plan. And I want them to know that I'm in charge of myself. I'm not passing over that control from my father to you."

I nod slowly. "Good."

She builds up more steam, and I'll be damned if I don't hear a lifetime of resentment in her next words. "If the guards try to act like babysitters, or if I find out they're reporting my activities back to you like I'm a child they're tending, I'm firing them. They follow my orders, not the other way around."

I lean toward her and narrow my eyes, challenge in my voice. "You stand up for yourself any damn time you need to. If you don't, then I'm the one getting pissed."

"Does that count for standing up to you too?" she demands.

I pick my fork back up. "Sweet girl, it counts twice for me."

16

Fall Into Me

JAMES

Four Months Later

I HAVEN'T SEEN CLARISSA outside FaceTime in two months.

She's gliding down the main staircase of our Brooklyn Heights brownstone, dressed for the Marcus Harcourt Charity Gala. And I'm struggling to keep my tongue in my mouth and my dick in my pants.

Her black evening gown clings all the way down until it flares into a little train near her knees. She has one elegant, freckled shoulder on display, and her body is a roadmap of dips and curves and slender lines. She's wearing her hair up, with constellations of gold and emeralds dangling from her ears.

I keep my expression stoic and my hands in my pockets when I want to launch myself up those steps and put my hands all over her.

I knew when I told her we needed to wait for her to be financially independent that keeping my hands to myself would be difficult. But I could never have fully understood the sheer level of self-control it would take to stick to my word.

It was one thing to tell myself—and her—those words when I barely knew her. When she represented a promise to her father and a vague fantasy for the future.

But I know this woman now. We may not see each other in person for months at a time, but we talk every single day. We text all day long, and sometimes all night long.

I know all her favorites: food, movies, books, and music. I know what makes her laugh, what makes her cry, and what makes her angry.

She's kind, stubborn, intelligent, independent, and hot as fuck. Clarissa Harcourt-Mellinger is so much more than the princess I thought I was marrying.

When I'd admitted to myself that I was halfway in love with her before the wedding, I had no idea how far there was to fall.

I haven't landed yet. I'm just in free fall every minute. Every day. I'm never going to hit the ground. She's going to be eighty years old, poking me with her cane, and I'll still be falling and fantasizing about grabbing her ass.

The way I went into this thinking I could marry her and somehow control that feeling? It was ludicrous.

The only thing I can control is my behavior. That, at least, is something I've managed with an iron will.

Despite our dubious beginnings and my own personal demons, this marriage is working. Our path just looks a little different from other people's.

But holy fuck, I want to put these dirty hands of mine all over her.

Clarissa reaches the bottom step, and I hold out a hand for her to take as she steps down onto the black-and-white marble flooring of the foyer. She gives me a sassy little smirk and does a slow spin, still holding on to my hand. "Do I pass inspection?"

I lean down and put my lips on hers. The kiss is just short enough with just enough tongue to drive me insane.

"You're beautiful. You ready for tonight?" She's been anxious about this gala.

She swipes at my lip with her thumb to remove whatever gloss or color I've stolen from her. "I think so. Maybe."

She gives a small but eloquent shrug. "Everyone is going to want to talk to me about Dad. And I want to do that. He meant a lot to a lot of people. But...."

"It might be too much," I finish for her.

"I still get emotional about losing him. I don't want to do that in public."

"Tell you what," I say, holding her hand and leading her to the waiting car. I wave Dean back to the front when he makes a move to come around to open her door. I do that myself, then help her arrange her skirts before climbing in beside her. "If you feel overwhelmed or just don't want to have a certain conversation, just"—I reach out and tweak her earring—"play with your earring. I'll run defense."

"Do you need me to run defense on anything for you?" she asks.

My first instinct is to say I don't need anything. It's my job to take care of her, not the other way around.

But she looks eager, maybe even hopeful. It matters to her. My heart does a weird roll in my chest at the realization.

I scramble to think of something she could do. I'm vividly aware of how easily I can hurt her feelings without even realizing I'm doing it. I've done it more than once.

I've heard people refer to me as a ruthless asshole—which is absolutely accurate. I'm not exactly known for being sensitive or empathetic. But for Clarissa, I try.

So I say, "I *could* use your help with something. But it's more offense than defense."

"Interesting," she says.

"Franklin Barrett."

"Of the Boston Barretts?"

"Yes. I've been trying to nail him down for a meeting, but rumor has it he's offended on your behalf that you didn't inherit the Harcourt shares."

Clarissa laughs. "Oh, Frank. That's actually really sweet."

"The man's got daddy issues," I grumble.

"Many people do. I'll talk to Frank. Maybe when he realizes I'd rather swim naked in a giant vat of stinging jellyfish than deal with anything to do with Harcourt, he'll come around."

"It couldn't hurt." I squeeze her hand. "You also need to keep an eye out for Lyndsay Roker."

She purses her lips and gives me a narrow-eyed look. "What about her?"

Clarissa looks annoyed, which tells me everything I need to know. She's already heard about Lyndsay Roker and the woman's big mouth. It's a big city but a small world.

It's no secret that people talk about us and our living arrangement. But Lyndsay is the most vocal and, arguably, the most venomous of the bunch.

I don't want Clarissa anywhere near her. My wife makes a point of avoiding social media. The last thing she needs is to come into contact with a woman who's built her entire personality around being as nasty as possible on the internet. "Just avoid her if you can."

I wanted to have her banned from the entire event. But our public relations team felt it would be better to allow her to attend—she did, after all, make the $100,000 per plate donation—and simply give her nothing to work with in terms of our marriage. Refusing to allow her to attend would give her what she wants: more drama.

Clarissa's face is the hardest I've ever seen it. "My poor, deserted husband. Did you know I wouldn't even let you kiss me at our wedding?"

"She's a bitch. Ignore her."

"She wants you. That's why she says the things she does about me."

I flinch back, my lip curling in disgust. Clarissa's flinty expression cracks when she sees my reaction, and she laughs. "She's not your type, huh?"

"Very funny. I only have one type. And I'm married to her," I say with a scowl.

She grins at me and puts her hand on my thigh. "Well, we'll just have to make sure everyone can see we are perfectly and incandescently happy together. Just like our wedding reception."

That hand on my thigh is not within the parameters of our agreed-upon boundaries. At this moment, I couldn't care less.

I pull at the knot of my bow tie, which is way too tight. "You don't have to do that. It's just good PR for people to see us happy together."

I sound like a stuffy ass. But this could easily lead to lines becoming blurred.

"Oh, I'm doing it."

I dip my head casually in agreement, as if I'm not virtually sagging in relief on the inside. But the second I pictured being able to put my hands on her at this gala, the thought of not getting to do it became unbearable.

The idea of slow dancing with her body pressed against mine is now a need. It's right up there with oxygen.

She twinkles at me. "It's not a lie, is it? We are perfectly, incandescently happy together."

My fucking heart.

When we arrive at the gala, we walk the red carpet to the flashing lights of the paparazzi. She smiles, and I keep my arm around her waist every minute.

Inside the ballroom, lights are low, a pop artist is singing her ballads onstage, and the movers and shakers are moving and shaking.

A waiter steps near with a tray of champagne, and Clarissa shoots me a mischievous grin. "Darn. I was hoping for tequila."

I tip my head toward the bar. "Plenty over there, I'm sure. Probably some salt and lime too. You can do body shots."

I laugh at her scandalized expression.

"*James.*" She clutches pearls she isn't wearing. "I'm not twenty-one for three months. Don't encourage me. You don't want to see what happens."

That's exactly what I'm afraid of. And exactly what I crave with everything in me.

She orders club soda and lime.

Then she works the room like she was born to it. Because she was. She may not be interested in running a corporation, but she is her father's daughter, and she has them eating out of her hand.

I see Marcus in her. It's in the way she tips her head and laughs at someone's lame joke. It's in the playful wink and the nudge with her elbow that tells the person she's speaking with "You and I, we're on the same team." It's in the way she has of making every single person she speaks with feel important and special.

"... and then I told Dad, 'Don't you dare try to give that company to me, Marcus Harcourt. I'm not mean enough to own a corporation.'" She twinkles at Franklin Barrett and his cronies as she tells the punchline, and they roar with laughter.

Franklin has to be in his late forties. He's a well-groomed black man with a trimmed beard who has a bit of an Idris Elba look going on. He also, much to my irritation, has an obvious crush on Clarissa.

She looks up at me with a wrinkle-nosed grin, and I wrap my arm around her waist, dropping a quick kiss on her mouth. She melts into me with a little sigh.

Barrett shoots me a look—one that says he's not sure he trusts me with my own wife. "Word is you're plenty mean enough, Mellinger."

He's trying to determine whether my ruthless persona is exclusive to business. It isn't. And Barrett can kiss my ass.

Clarissa scoffs. "My husband is an absolute teddy bear. Don't let anyone tell you any differently."

They're laughing again because everyone knows my reputation is anything but "teddy bear." Barrett gives her a skeptical look.

She pulls her phone out of her clutch and scrolls through her photos to one of me and Mr. Snuffleputz. I don't bother trying to remember his real name because every new iteration we come up with makes Clarissa laugh.

I'm lying on my back in the photo with a put-upon expression on my face. Clarissa had been missing her cat and asked for a photo of him while we were texting. He was sleeping on my chest at the time, so there it is. Photographic evidence of me allowing her cat to use me like a rug.

She shows the photo all around to snickers and grins. "See? Teddy bear."

And just like that, she's shown these men that I'm not just ruthless and efficient in the boardroom. I also have a heart.

My wife is a genius.

Franklin Barrett lifts a single eyebrow. He looks first at me, then at Clarissa... then back at me. I see the exact moment he decides I've won. He's done playing his stupid games.

"That, gentlemen, is our cue to move on," I say with a quirk of my lips.

We begin our exit to the sound of chuckling. But Barrett calls out before we get far, "Mellinger, have your assistant call mine on Monday. We'll talk."

As we walk away, I mutter under my breath, "Yeah, that is not happening."

Clarissa leans into me and tugs me down so I can hear her. "I thought you wanted a meeting with him."

I shoot a look around to make sure no one can hear us, then say, "That's before I realized that old lecher has a thing for my wife."

She sputters out a laugh. "That's ridiculous. He's never said or done a single thing that was the slightest bit inappropriate with me."

"You don't know the things he was thinking."

She smacks my chest with the back of her hand, laughing at me. "And you do?"

I slide my jaw to the side, then ease my hand from her waist to her hip. I nuzzle her ear and gently nip the lobe. "Yesss."

CLARISSA NEVER TUGS HER earring. She seems to enjoy reminiscing about her father. Everyone has a story to tell. We eat, we listen to speeches, and she and I each say a few words about the foundation and about the man who created it.

That's the only time she chokes up. But she isn't the only one. There's hardly a dry eye in the house. I squeeze her hand and lift it to kiss her knuckles. She looks up at me and ends her small speech with a bittersweet smile on her face.

And then we slow dance. I get to put my hands on her. Slide my palms up and down her back. Smell the delicate scent of her. And feel her body moving against mine. She leans up to speak directly into my ear, and I bend down to feel her lips against it.

When I pull back, I can't look away from her eyes.

This feels like a real date. The kind that ends with us ripping each other's clothes off the minute we get home.

That's what it's supposed to look like to the rest of the world. But that's what it *feels* like too.

And I am so stupidly in love with my wife that I can hardly think straight.

As we're making our way back to our table, I see my executive assistant across the way and beckon her over.

I don't think Clarissa has met her yet. Considering how often Rebecca communicates with her through email, providing her my schedule, handling minor requests, etc., the omission feels like an oversight.

Rebecca joins us, and Clarissa stiffens beside me. I glance down at her in confusion.

"Clarissa, this is my executive assistant, Rebecca Adair. Rebecca, my wife."

Rebecca pushes her hand forward for a shake, and I have to nudge Clarissa to take her hand. She's looking at it like it's a snake.

I have no idea where the Clarissa who worked the room earlier has gone. Instead, she looks pale. Upset.

"Have you two met?" I ask.

"I haven't had the pleasure," Rebecca says at the same time Clarissa says, "I've seen her around. I just didn't know who she was."

"It's nice to meet you finally face-to-face, Clare. I've heard so much about you. You must almost be ready for summer break, right?"

Clarissa gives a tight smile. "It's Clarissa. And that's right."

"It must be nice." Rebecca shoots me a commiserating glance. "No summer vacations for us, huh, James? Once you get out in the real world, it's all work all the time. Adulting stinks," she jokes to Clarissa. "Half the time I think we'd be better off just keeping a bed in the corner of the office, we spend so much time there. Enjoy these years," she says with a sigh. "They'll be over too soon."

I'm about to point out that Clarissa hasn't actually taken a full summer off to relax since she started school, but Rebecca is still talking. "I wish James and I had a couple months to just lie around and do nothing. Ooh, you should do a tour of Europe over summer break. There'll never be a better time."

I make a noise of agreement, but I'm not really listening to whatever Rebecca is prattling on about. I'm watching my wife. She looks off. Uncomfortable. She glances at me with annoyance, as if she's waiting for me to say something. But I have no idea what she wants from me.

"Did you like the care package last week?" Rebecca asks Clarissa. "I was worried the chocolate-covered strawberries might have melted, but the company promised me they were packaged very carefully with ice packs. Did they arrive in good condition?"

Clarissa slowly turns her head toward me and glares with unexpected venom. She has never looked at me like that before. This isn't annoyance or irritation. She's furious.

She smiles with her mouth but glares with her eyes, and it's the fakest damn expression I've seen on her face since our wedding photos.

"I thought those were from you, James. I didn't know I should be thanking *Rebecca* for my care packages."

"They were from me. I paid for them."

"Absolutely," Rebecca says. "They're all from James. I'm just the facilitator. He's really too busy to spend time tracking down every little present. And I don't mind at all. I think care packages are so important. I remember what it's like to be a young girl away from home for the first time."

"Rebecca," I snap. "Stop." She is not helping. She makes it sound as though she and I are Clarissa's parents on Christmas morning, and I'm the loser dad who has no clue what Mom has wrapped under the tree from Santa.

I may not have gone through every ordering process, but I sure as hell told Rebecca exactly what to buy and when. I approved every one of those orders when they went through. She may as well have been a warehouse worker, packing boxes.

Rebecca wisely steps back, a placating expression on her face. "I'm sorry. I wasn't trying to upset you," she says to Clarissa.

Rebecca looks at her watch, then raises her brows a little, opening her eyes wide as if the time is a shocking discovery. "Maybe Clarissa is tired. She had to have been on the road pretty early this morning to make it here in time for the gala."

She gives Clarissa a patronizing smile. "You have to be completely tuckered out."

"Are you fucking kidding me right now?" Clarissa doesn't raise her voice, but she doesn't need to. The words crack through the space on an incredulous laugh just the same.

Rebecca startles, and we catch the attention of a few people standing nearby.

"I'm not a child," she tells Rebecca. "I don't need a nap. I don't have a bedtime. Jesus, you're a piece of work."

Clarissa yanks out of my grip, and I move to follow her.

My skin crawls when Rebecca's hand lands lightly on my arm.

She says, "I don't know what that was about, but you might want to talk to her about using that kind of language in public. It's not good for Harcourt's image. I know her father tolerated a lot, but she's representing the company as your wife now."

I look down at her hand on my arm, pure ice in my eyes.

She releases me immediately.

"You don't touch me. Ever. And if you disrespect my wife again... if you even look at her with anything less than the deference she deserves, you'll be finding another job. And it won't be in this city. You and I are not friends. We have never been friends. You do the job I pay you to do. That's it. Talk about my *wife*, offer me *advice* about my marriage, and that MBA won't be worth the paper it's written on. Am I clear?"

The color drains from her face. "Of course. I overstepped. My apologies."

I search the room for Clarissa and freeze when I finally find her. It looks like she intended to head back to our table, but Lyndsay Roker has not only stepped into her path, she's got her phone in Clarissa's face.

Clarissa searches the crowd—I'd guess for me. I try to catch her eye, moving as fast as I can, literally shoving people out of my way to get to her.

Something Lyndsay says has a furious flush sweeping over Clarissa's face in a wash of red.

Then Clarissa Harcourt-Mellinger, the sweet angel who once whispered to me that she was angry, says loudly enough to be heard ten people deep, "Lyndsay, you lying cunt."

17

Dangerous Woman

JAMES

I only catch up to Clarissa before she hails a cab because I virtually sprint through the lobby. When I reach her, I ask, "Are you okay?"

She doesn't say a single word.

"Clarissa, please. What happened?"

I put my arm around her waist, but she jerks away, stiff as a board. I back off in confusion, dropping my arm. "You're not leaving here separately from me in a cab. It's not safe."

She's stiff but looks around at the milling crowd and paparazzi, inclining her head and faking a smile.

"What did Lyndsay say to you?"

She stares straight ahead. "Do you sit around and discuss how immature I am with Rebecca?"

"Don't be ridiculous. Is that what Lyndsay said? You know she literally makes shit up out of thin air."

"I'm not ridiculous. And I am not too young to be a good wife."

"I didn't say you were. You *are* a good wife. And there's no point in being sensitive about your age. It is what it is."

She keeps the fake smile pasted on for the photographers. "God, you're either dense or deliberately provoking me," she says.

Our driver pulls up, and I yank open the door to the back seat. Clarissa clambers in, and when I move to help with her skirts, she grabs them and flicks them out of the way herself.

"For the record, I'm not sensitive about my age," she says when I climb in beside her. "I'm not wishing my life away or wishing I could just wake up older. I'm talking about the way Rebecca was deliberately reinforcing the narrative that I'm your dependent while pointing out that it's the two of you who have things in common with me on the outside."

She nods at the hotel behind us. "She made it clear that you and she are teammates while I'm not even on the field. And if you tell me you don't see that she was trying to make me wonder if the two of you are fucking, then I don't believe you."

"Just what are you accusing me of?" I bite out.

"I don't think you're sleeping with her, James. But I don't appreciate your attitude."

"My attitude? Are you fucking kidding me? You started acting like a brat before Rebecca even opened her mouth."

The look she gives me is scathing. "Don't call me a brat unless you want to be called an asshole."

She lets that sink in, then says, "I overheard her say some things at our wedding. It was obvious she knew more about our arrangement than I did at the time."

"It's not an arrangement. It's a marriage," I snap. "She had no business talking about us. But she didn't *know* a damn thing. She was guessing. Just the same as everybody else. I've never discussed the private details of our marriage with anyone but you or your father. Which is not something you can say, is it?"

Clarissa ignores my question and holds up her hand, ticking items off on her fingers. "She knew my father was leaving you his shares. She knows we're not living together, and she's pretty damn sure we're not sleeping together. She knows my schedule. She's the one ordering my presents." She drops her hand and glares at me. "She's probably the one who deposits money into my bank account every week, all while reminding you she paid my *allowance*."

"*I* choose your gifts. How would my assistant even know what you like? And I pay your allowance, Clarissa. *Me*. It takes two seconds on my phone. She knows your schedule because it's on my calendar."

"It's not an allowance."

I glance toward the front of the car to double-check the privacy screen is up because Clarissa has gotten loud.

"Call it whatever you want. I don't care."

"Words matter, James. That language infantilizes me."

"Spare me the psychobabble. Do me a favor and stay off Reddit," I snap back.

She makes a sound of frustrated rage between clenched teeth. Half growl, half squeal. "It's not an allowance. It's money for cost-of-living expenses."

I lean back and spread my hands in a classic "I rest my case" gesture. "Congratulations, you just gave a textbook definition of 'allowance.'"

"I wouldn't need you to send me an allowance if my father had allowed me to manage my own trust."

"But he didn't. Because your father didn't think you were ready for that. And, frankly, I agree. You don't have any concept of how much anything costs. And you're a bleeding heart for every sob story you hear."

"So I'm a child. That's what you're saying. A child who needs Daddy to send her money every week."

"Aren't you?"

She snaps her head to look out the window, arms crossed defensively against her chest.

Fuck. Fuck. Fuck. Why am I saying this shit to her? I knew we'd fight over money eventually. I knew we would. It was inevitable.

I need to be kind. Sympathetic. Keep my fucking cool. I'm supposed to be de-escalating this scene, not fanning the flames.

But her accusations—her implications that I've been disloyal—they infuriate me.

No, that's not it. The truth is… it hurts to realize she has so little faith in me.

And I'm doing what I always do when something hurts. I burn shit down.

I take a breath and try to lower the tension between us. "Before tonight, I didn't realize Rebecca was a problem. But she was patronizing as hell to you. And that's unacceptable."

"So you did notice that," she says sarcastically.

Yes, but obviously far, far too late. The truth is I simply wasn't listening to Rebecca. She was unimportant.

"Lyndsay has video of the whole thing," she says bitterly.

I pull out my phone and begin texting security.

"What are you doing?"

"I'm having Lyndsay and Rebecca escorted from the gala. And I'm firing Rebecca on Monday morning. You and I are the only *team* that ever matters."

Her eyes fly wide, and she swivels her head toward me. "You'd fire your executive assistant for me?"

Why is this even a question? "Yes, of course I would. I'd fire anyone you wanted me to."

Her mouth pops open. "You can't fire your assistant just because I hate her."

"I can. And I will."

Clarissa puts a hand on my arm to stop me. "Please don't. And don't have them removed from the gala. It'll just make things worse. It's enough to know you would. Just... talk to your assistant about the way she represents the company in public. The things she said at our wedding reception... anyone could have heard her. And considering she works directly for you...." She trails off, then huffs. "Put a letter in her file or something."

There's a certain poetic justice in that. I'd rather fire her. But Clarissa is serious. She's too damn forgiving.

I sigh and reach out to pull her into a hug. "I'm sorry for calling you a child. I don't believe that. And it's okay that you aren't ready to manage your own trust, Clarissa. That's hardly your fault. It doesn't bother me to send you money. I'll always make sure you have anything you need or want. I gave you those credit cards so you never have to feel like you need permission to buy anything you want."

She stiffens in my hold and shoves away from me. So I let her go.

"You still don't get it."

I beat my head back against the black leather seat in one sharp, irritated motion. "Will you fucking stop?"

"I'm glad it doesn't bother you to send me a small part of my own money for popcorn and textbooks. It seems a small price to pay, considering you got a multibillion-dollar corporation and a hell of a lot of your own money out of marrying me," she says.

I'm hanging on to my temper by a thread. "I'm not for sale, Clarissa. Your father didn't buy me."

She braces her hands on the seat, leans in, inches from my face, and enunciates very clearly, "If the shares fit."

I'm breathing hard. The scent of her in my lungs. I'm distracted by her freckled satin skin. Her soft, plump lips. The adrenaline of anger is morphing into something far more dangerous. I've never been pissed off and turned on at the same time. I look from her eyes to her lips, then back again. "Fuck you."

She laughs bitterly. "That would be a nice change."

I glare at her for long seconds. She glares back.

And then her mouth is on mine.

18

Don't Blame Me

CLARISSA

He's kissing me back. It's not tentative or sweet or gentle. It's not practiced or controlled, the way he usually kisses me.

He's devouring me with his lips and teeth and tongue. He's pulling out the bobby pins in my updo and tossing them to the floor, then wrapping my hair in a tight fist.

And I give it right back, gripping his hair with both hands and eating at his mouth. I'm on fire. My body aches for him, and everywhere he's touching just reminds me of all the other places he should be touching but isn't yet. I'm starving, literally starving, for James. If he stops, I'll die.

He's wearing the cologne I got him for his birthday. It's clean and woodsy, and there's a hint of his own salt beneath it.

All of it—his taste, his smell, the silk of his hair—makes me feral.

He releases my curls to put his hands on my waist and hike me onto his lap. I end up sitting sideways, his erection shoving against my hip. This dress is too tight for anything else. It has no give all the way to the knee. The design doesn't even allow me to take full steps when walking, so it sure isn't conducive to straddling a man in the back seat of a car.

I let go of his hair, and he pulls back to eye me warily, breaths ragged.

I can see that he's still pissed off. But he's also desperately turned on.

Well, so am I, James. So am I.

I reach down with both hands to gather the heavy silk skirting and shimmy the thing up until the flounce at the bottom is now around my waist.

Then I straddle James, his cloth-covered erection hot at my center. He wraps his hand around the back of my skull and drags me down to his mouth.

His abdominal muscles clench, and he pushes his hard cock against my center. I grind down, and he makes a low noise in his throat. I can feel his hand working its way up the back of my thigh, and I know the exact second he realizes I'm wearing a thong. His fingers clench convulsively on my butt cheek, pulling and spreading me wide. His fingers play with the ribbon of fabric, tugging and teasing me with it.

He groans as if he's the one being tormented. Then he's sliding me back and forth across the hard heat of him with a rhythm of his own.

It's a little rough. It isn't nice. He takes small bites, nipping across my shoulder. Then he tongues my neck and earlobe. He's creating the most delicious pressure against my clitoris. I want to scream. I want to bite and claw. And I want him inside me in a way I don't even fully understand.

This craving is instinctual. If we existed in a bubble on this planet, had never heard of the existence of sex or any of the mechanics, we would still have arrived right at this moment. Of me knowing James's cock belongs in my pussy.

I am still so mad at him, I could scream.

Oh, I know he didn't marry me for money. It's not even a question in my mind.

But he pushed my buttons. So I shoved back at his. I'll be ashamed of myself for it later. Right now, I'm still too angry to care.

How does he not see that the words he uses keep me his subordinate? His *ward*, not his wife.

"*She's not just young—she's a spoiled little princess. I'd be shocked if he ever lays a finger on her.*" Rebecca's words at our wedding reception still irritate me like a pebble in my shoe. I've tried to forget that overheard conversation in the restroom. Tried to put it behind me. Rebecca doesn't know me. But the memory of it prods at my every insecurity regarding James.

I loosen his tie and undo his shirt. I need his skin under my fingers.

I've just yanked his shirttail from his trousers when he grabs my wrist with one hand and forces my hips to stop moving with the other.

"Clarissa," he says. "The car has stopped."

I hear the clunk of a car door closing and know Dean is coming around to usher us out.

James has me deposited on the seat next to him, using his body to block me, mere seconds before the door opens.

"Give us a minute, Dean," James says.

"Of course, Mr. Mellinger." Then the door thunks closed once more.

James turns to me and grabs the flounce of my skirt, jerking it down over my hips. I help by lifting my butt off the seat to make the slide easier.

His eyes travel over my hair, my lips, my neck. He looks... I don't know that look. Wild? A little unhinged?

I indicate his shirt. "Are you going to put yourself back together?"

He smooths a hand through his hair, then says, "No point. It's not like Dean doesn't know exactly what we've been up to."

Then he opens the door.

He reaches out to assist me from the car, so I grab my clutch with my left hand and place my right in his. I glide out of the car with the dignity of a queen. Like I'm not still breathing hard. Like I'm not wearing a catastrophically wrinkled evening gown, with my lipstick kissed right off my swollen lips, love bruises on my neck, and what must be utterly spectacular sex hair.

I catch Dean's eye as he stands near the front of the car. Hands folded, expression stoic.

I tip my head as we stroll past him, James still holding my hand. "Good night, Dean."

He nods. "Good night, Mrs. Mellinger. Mr. Mellinger."

I don't turn my head, but I sneak a glance at James. His tuxedo shirt is completely unbuttoned, shirttails loose. His tie is half shoved in his jacket pocket. His lips are swollen, there is a smear of my lipstick on his neck, and one unruly piece of hair is sticking straight out on the side of his head.

He catches my look with a smoldering side-eye of his own. Then he's moving fast up the steps to the brownstone, and I'm running to keep up.

The moment we're inside, James has me backed against the front door, hands working the skirts of my gown up over my hips, his mouth on mine.

I shove his jacket and shirt off his shoulders. We get tangled for a hot second, and he has to pull his hands off my body to shake them off. His cuff links clatter across the marble floor.

He reaches a desperate, greedy hand up my back, running his fingers over the seams of my gown, searching. "Jesus, woman. How do I get you out of this dress?"

My heart thrills at his words, not just because they're sexy as hell but because of what he called me. *Woman.* That's what I need from him. It's everything I need.

I twist to expose the side of the gown. "The zipper's here. There's a little hook at the to—"

James rips the catch apart with rough fingers and slides the zipper all the way down. Then the gown is in a puddle on the floor, and I'm kicking it away.

He cups my breasts and rubs his thumbs across my peaked nipples. Then he takes a small step back.

He's looking.

"No bra?" His brows are furrowed, his eyes moving back and forth between my breasts and my face like he can't believe what he's getting to see.

"I didn't need one. The dress has a built-in—ahh." His mouth closes over my nipple, sucking, then flicking with his tongue. First one, then the other.

I squirm and push up toward him, holding his perfect, beautiful head in my hands.

He pulls away to look up at me. Runs a single finger over the crest of my breast, just where a spray of freckles scatter. "I always wondered," he says, "if you had freckles here."

He breathes deeply, in and out. He's visibly trying to bring himself under control.

I can't bear it. I don't want James under control.

I squirm against him as he rises to his full height, pulling his mouth to mine once more. When he leans back again, I nip at his jaw. He groans, moving his mouth to my neck.

I reach for his belt, but he stops me with a hard hand at my wrist and a slow shake of his head. I frown, frustrated.

Then he gathers both of my wrists in one of his hands and pushes them over my head, holding me against the door like some sort of pirate's captive. His free hand trails down the front of my body. Then he reaches into my panties and slides a single finger through the seam of my wet sex.

My abdominal muscles clench, and I close my eyes at the sheer wonder. At the unfamiliar beauty of the contact. "James...."

"Yes, sweetheart. That's it. You're so slippery down here. So hot and slick."

I writhe against him, pushing. Trying to make him move. His fingers work me with small, tight circles against my clit, winding me tighter and tighter into a coiled spring.

When he moves down, away from my clit, I could cry at the loss. At the way my body hovers at that edge with no way back and no way over.

James presses a finger inside, and it's an entirely new sensation. Fullness that *needs* friction. He fucks me with his finger, and I'm still in that place, sprung tight, needing more. More.

I realize I'm chanting the word out loud.

James gives me another finger and mutters, "I am going to hell for this."

I open my eyes to look at his face because his words are registering, and I don't like them. He's my husband. He's not going to hell for loving my body.

His fingers keep working my pussy, but he also rubs my clit in those tight circles again.

The pressure is perfect. The friction is perfect. But more than all of that, it's James. It's James who's giving me this.

I've long forgotten why this started. I've long forgotten anything but how much I love this man. I'm right there. Ready to jump from the cliff, not even caring if I'll land in cool water or on jagged rock.

I follow his tormented gaze down to where his eyes are trained—on the outline of his own hand, moving under the wet black silk of my thong. Every motion is set in bas-relief as he watches his own fingers fuck me, his thumb swirling against me.

His fingers hook inside, pressing against something that makes my knees give way. Only James's body pressed against me and that hand working my pussy keep me from crumbling to the floor.

I cry out in a sort of keening wail because I don't know how not to, and his eyes jerk up to meet mine. The second they do, the tension inside me snaps.

Pleasure courses through me, so acute it's just this side of pain. His fingers don't stop, and my eyes widen in a brief burst of panic because the orgasm isn't stopping either. It's too much. I'm electrified. Existing as an aura that hovers just outside of this body. I don't know if it's ever going to stop. His eyes are the only thing keeping me on this planet as I shudder and shake in his hands.

"Good girl," he says. "Shhhh. Oh, my sweet girl...."

His hands are on my face, wiping away tears. I don't know why I'm crying, because I'm not sad at all. My heart is just spilling out of me like a shaken bottle of champagne. I try to will myself to stop because James isn't going to understand that these tears are a release valve for feelings other than pain or misery.

He carries me into the living room and sits on the sofa with me cradled on his lap, my arms wrapped around his neck.

I'm not cold, but I shiver anyway. He reaches for the cashmere throw blanket on the arm of the sofa and wraps it around the two of us.

He holds me in the dark, naked torso to naked torso, as he strokes my hair and my back. And he speaks quietly, lips pressed into my hair. He tells me how sweet I am. How good. He calls me his angel and promises to protect me and take care of me.

I grow sleepy and sated, and when my body is fully relaxed, he says, "That was a mistake."

19

Say You Love Me

CLARISSA

If I had a single speck of pride, I'd let go of his neck and slide off his lap. Then I'd sit beside him on the sofa, and we'd have a cool, calm, collected conversation in which I would—nicely—tell him to get his head out of his ass.

But I don't have a single speck of pride when it comes to James. So I don't let go. I hold on tighter. "Don't say that. Don't you dare."

He sighs, exhausted frustration in the sound. "I never should have put my hands on you like that."

"I wanted you to touch me. You didn't hurt me."

"We weren't ready for this step."

"I was. I am. I didn't cry because I was upset. They were happy tears."

There is a lump in my throat and a sob crouching in my chest now that has nothing to do with happy tears.

To James's credit, he doesn't pry me off him or push me away. He just sits there and rocks a little in place, stroking my hair.

But he won't stop talking. He won't shut up, and I can't plug my ears and hang on to him at the same time. So I hear every horrible word.

"Nothing has changed from that fight in the car. I still control your money, and therefore, I control everything from where you live to what you wear. And you still resent me for it—"

"I do not."

"Clearly you do, or we wouldn't have had a knock-down, drag-out fight about your allowance."

I guess I still have a little pride after all, because I take my arms from around his neck so I don't strangle him with my bare hands. Sliding off his lap, I move to stand, wrapping the blanket around me as I go.

"I don't care about the money," I say. "What I care about is the way you use it as a barrier between us."

Now he's standing. "How are you not understanding how fucked-up this power imbalance is between us? I *have* everything. I *control* everything. Not just financially, Clarissa. You aren't independent yet. You're a baby bird who's just learning to fly, and I'm your soft place to fall. The way things are right now, how could I ever trust that you want me and don't just need me?"

I suck in a breath so hard it almost hurts. I want James. I do. It's also true that I need him, but so what?

Money is the least of it. I need him as my anchor. He's my family now. My *only* family. He's my port in the storm. He's my shoulder to cry on and my soft place to fall, yes. But isn't that all right? Husbands and wives need each other. I want to be the same for him.

Needing him to manage my money is my father's fault for the way he set up my inheritance. But we can ignore that part. It's no different from couples with one spouse at home and the other employed. It's just a question of trust.

He's watching as the thoughts flicker across my face, and he seems to take them as some kind of confirmation. "You don't know yet yourself. You can't separate the want from the need. It's all mixed up inside. If the only person in the world you have to call home wants to fuck you, you fuck him."

"Give me some credit. This isn't prison, and I'm not your bitch," I say.

His expression is unreadable as he says, "That's not just prison, baby. That's life."

"What if I turn twenty-five and I'm not interested anymore? What if I ask you for a divorce because we lost our chance when we had it?"

He draws my hand up and presses it against the hard strength of his naked chest, where his heart is racing in a staccato rhythm. "There is no part of me that isn't terrified at that thought. If you turn twenty-five and tell me to fuck off—if you meet someone else and decide he makes more sense for you—"

"That will never happen. But if you're scared of losing me, the answer is simple. Nail me down now."

He shakes his head, features grim. "As much as I resisted it at first, going away to school was the right decision for you. The two of us maintaining some physical and sexual distance? That was the right decision for you. Every single day, I see you gaining self-confidence and independence. Gaining happiness. I will never 'nail you down now' at the risk of you giving up the person you want to become."

I press my fist to my stomach to hold myself steady. To keep me from losing myself again in wild emotion.

This night is not going the way it's supposed to. He's not saying the things I need him to.

He's right about my growing confidence and independence. I love the person I'm becoming. I make choices for myself, and I'm not afraid to push back when a situation calls for it anymore.

But he's also right that, if he asked, I would give up every one of my other dreams if it meant I could be his. I'd give up my degree and my career plans. I'd move home in a heartbeat to be with him every day.

When I left for Pennsylvania, I was all about setting boundaries and self-actualization. But if it made James happy, I'd give up anything he asked me to.

And that's... horrible. I was willing to give up my dreams for my father too. What does that say about me? It doesn't matter. James would never ask me to give up anything.

"But I love you." I say it, and as soon as I do, I'm ashamed of myself. Because that is not the way to say "I love you." Not in that needy, demanding voice. Love isn't meant to control or manipulate.

James cups my face, and when he says it, he says it the right way. The way that's about giving, not taking. "Clarissa, I love you. I am so in love with you, your name is tattooed on my soul. Every beat of my heart and breath in my body belongs to you. *I* belong to you. Don't ever doubt it. Not even for a second. I exist for you."

20

Lost Without You

JAMES

After the mess I made the night of the gala, Clarissa finishes out the semester at school and decides to spend most of the summer touring Europe with a few of her friends.

If I thought the idea of her moving four hours away to go to school was bad, it was *nothing* on this. I'm barely sleeping or eating. All I'm doing is swimming laps in the pool to try to settle my mind and obsessively plotting how I'll keep her safe and happy from an ocean away.

Not one member of the staff at the house or the office will even make eye contact with me since she announced her plans for fear of me biting their heads off.

Marcus would never have let her go. He'd have guilted her into staying. He was a great man and an amazing father. But even I can see how sometimes—a lot of times—he rode roughshod over her free will, probably without even realizing he was doing it.

I won't do that.

I wonder if Marcus is looking down and hating me now. He trusted me. And I betrayed that trust in a spectacular fashion. I put my mouth and my hands all over his baby girl on the night of a gala in his memory.

I betrayed *her*. The first orgasm I ever gave her wasn't some romantic, loving moment spent on white sheets with rose petals spread all over her on her twenty-fifth birthday. It was up against a door after I practically tore her dress off during an argument.

I got turned on when I was angry. I know exactly what kind of sick fuck does something like that.

I held her hands down.

She cried afterward. Every time I think of it, I want to rip my heart from my chest.

I never wanted to hurt her. I just wanted her to feel good.

I've apologized to her. She says it isn't necessary, but it's the only thing I know how to do. That and encourage her to do the things she wants to do without fighting her on them or asking her to stay.

I text her a list of travel safety tips. Then I print a hard copy and put it in her carry-on. I share contacts of every phone number of every mutual friend or trustworthy business acquaintance I have on that side of the pond, just in case she gets in a bind. I also print those, in case she loses her phone.

I make sure she has her passport. Make sure she has multiple sources of money, in multiple places, in case she gets pickpocketed. I send her itineraries and make her reservations. Remind her to drink water, not alcohol, on the plane. Stay away from drugs and users. Practice moderation. Cover her drinks. Listen to her bodyguard.

Then I stand in the airport and watch her meet up with a giggling Bronwyn and her girls, before they drag their luggage over to Bag Check. I want to just grab a ticket for myself and go with her. But that's not what this is for.

Clarissa leans over, saying something to Bronwyn when they reach the point where it's about to be passengers only. Bronwyn shoots Clarissa a thumbs-up in response, then wiggles her eyebrows at me. Classic Tequila Bronwyn.

Clarissa runs back to me, puts her hands on my face, and yanks me down for a quick kiss. A little tongue. A little teasing suck. Then she pulls back to search my eyes, her own sparkling with excitement.

"I'll be fine, I promise. I'll come home all cultured and shit." She winks.

She's already cultured by anyone's standards. She grew up surrounded by it. But she's barely been anywhere. She's lived vicariously through her novels long enough.

I nod and try to smile at her joke because that's what she wants from me. But I don't say words. I don't have any that aren't "Don't go" and "I changed my mind" and more versions of "Be safe."

Clarissa starts to run back to her friends, then turns midway, jogging backward while she shouts across the busy airport. "Hey, James!" She makes a goofy heart out of her hands. "I still love you!"

I put my fingers to my lips, then hold them up toward her. I mouth the words back, "Still love you."

※

SHE ANSWERS FACETIME IN a pub in Ireland. All the girls are holding Guinness, and a bunch of good-looking guys with Irish accents are crowding around them. She shouts, "I told you I'm married!" and waves her phone around at the table. The pronouncement is greeted by a chorus of laughing male boos.

She calls me freaked out in Amsterdam when she gets separated from her friends and bodyguard, terrified to walk back to the hotel alone after dark. She stays on the phone with me the entire time, and, though it's less than a two-block walk, I'm pretty sure I don't breathe for three whole days.

When Clarissa locks herself safely behind her hotel room door, I call Sasha and threaten the bodyguard with death and dismemberment. It's not hyperbole.

Clarissa FaceTimes me from a beach in the South of France. Topless. When I freak the fuck out, she laughs and turns the camera around to show topless women everywhere, including Bronwyn in a damn thong—because of course she did.

Bronwyn waves. "Heeeey, big daddy."

Clarissa flips the camera back. "You're not actually mad about this, are you? Literally everyone does it here. Nobody's ogling my boobs."

I clear my throat. "No, I'm not mad. Wear sunblock." I swallow. "A lot of sunblock."

She salutes me with a jaunty hand to her head. "Sir. Yes, sir." And I ogle her perfect, freckled boobs as they bounce with the motion.

"Still love you, James."

"Still love you, Clarissa."

She visits old family friends of her parents in England and stops in at our London office to schmooze on my behalf and attend a few business dinners. Even though she has no official role at Harcourt, she is still Clarissa Harcourt-Mellinger. And she knows it matters.

She does the same at the office in Paris.

She also gets sloppy drunk in a Paris hotel and texts me from the hotel bar, annoyed because her friends ditched her to hook up with hot guys.

Me: Define hook up.

Clarissa: You know was hookup is. Don act innocent u prob did it

Me: Random hookups in strange cities? No, I did not.

Clarissa: Prude

Me: Smart. Where is Sasha?

Clarissa: She s alresfh in bed fir the night. Dint wake her up when we decide 2 com down

Me: I'm calling Sasha. You shouldn't be drinking alone at a hotel bar.

Clarissa: IM not alone my friends r here. Juts all pained up. And I pretty surf there all getting laid 2night by fuckbois

Me: Do not let them bring guys up to your suite.

Clarissa: ...

Me: DO NOT LET THEM BRING GUYS UP TO YOUR ROOMS. ARE THE GIRLS AS DRUNK AS YOU ARE?

Clarissa: ...

Clarissa: ... Prolly

Me: WHAT THE FUCK.

Clarissa: Don swear at me. Theres a bar in Newark with ur pitcher mr. do as I say.

Me: SASHA IS ON HER WAY.

Clarissa: Jerk. Shes going 2 be mad.

Me: You and your friends stay exactly where you are. And stop fucking drinking right now. DO NOT GO ANYWHERE WITH THOSE GUYS.

Clarissa: ...

Me: I'M CALLING SECURITY.

Me: WHEN SASHA GETS THERE, YOU AND THE GIRLS GO TO YOUR ROOMS ALONE AND LOCK THE DOORS.

I contact hotel management and have Sasha and security escort the girls to their rooms and the French fuckboys off the premises. I pull rank and name names. I call Bronwyn's father for backup.

I threaten to buy the hotel and fire every one of their asses if a single hair on those ladies' heads is in danger from a strong wind.

Then I put Dean on a plane to France, because clearly Beth and Sasha aren't enough security to keep my wife safe.

The next day, Clarissa texts me.

Clarissa: Just so you know, no one here is speaking to me. Including Sasha. So thanks for that.

Me: Be pissed at me all you want. I'm pretty fucking angry with you too.

I know this anger well. It's the rage of watching helplessly from the sidelines, unable to do a damn thing to make a difference while the unthinkable happens. It doesn't matter that I got Sasha and security down there before anything happened. It doesn't matter that it was even possible that the men weren't a danger to them.

My gut doesn't care about what did happen. It cares about what could have. Every nightmare scenario plays in my head, over and over on repeat. I remember Mom crying. Gasping. Then not making another single sound.

Yeah, I'm angry.

I don't hear from her for another forty-eight hours.

When my phone rings, I stare at Clarissa's name and photo for a long beat before I pick it up. "You're alive," I say, voice flat.

Her voice is subdued when she says, "Don't act like you haven't been checking in with Sasha and Dean this entire time."

When I say nothing in response, she finally makes a sound like a shuddering sigh. Then she says, "I'm a huge bitch. I'm sorry."

"You're not a bitch. But you were irresponsible, and you—"

I take a breath myself, and if mine shudders, too, there's not a thing I can do about it. "There are evil things in this world. Your security team exists for a reason. You don't—" I blow out a hard breath while I work out the right words. "You don't have to do it for me. But do it for yourself."

Clarissa is quiet for a long moment. Then she says, "I will. I won't ditch security like that again. I didn't think it through first, and then...."

I wait for her to finish her sentence, the silence thick between us.

"It could have ended badly. Thank you for looking out for us. Seriously."

"Always."

Her voice is an octave too high when she says, "I miss you."

"I miss you too. Still love you, sweet girl."

"Still love you, James."

She returns from her trip two weeks before the start of her senior year of college. She's tan, with a new haircut and a different style of makeup that's heavy on the red lipstick and light on everything else.

She left here looking and acting like a nervous twenty-year-old. Seven weeks later, she's striding through JFK like she owns the place.

I watch her face change the moment she sees me. She runs the rest of the way, then throws herself into my arms with wild exuberance. She wraps her legs around me, and I laugh and stagger for a second under her weight, slight though it is, just because of how unexpected it is.

I hold her tight. "You did miss me."

"I always miss you," she says and kisses me sweet and slow.

I have to forcibly pry my hands off her ass to let her slide off me when it's over. I look toward her luggage. "Got everything?"

"Yep. We're good."

I shoulder her bag. "I bought you the house we talked about, so you can move off-campus when the fall semester starts."

"Perfect. Thank you. Bronwyn isn't sure she's going to stay at BSU for our senior year. Her dad keeps pressuring her to transfer to a 'real' school, but I was already planning to reach out to my friend Sydney to see if she wanted to move in too. So whether she stays or goes, it'll all work out. Though I'll miss her like crazy." She grimaces when she repeats Bronwyn's father's comment about transferring to a "real" school, but she has to know that's going to be a pretty typical reaction among our social sphere.

"Do you want to change schools? You could try to come back to Columbia. Or even Barnard or Fordham?"

Columbia will open doors for her that BSU never will. Not because the education is necessarily better but because people assume it is. Not to mention the networking opportunities. There's a building at Columbia with her name on it. Literally.

Initially, when she chose a state school, it was more about her emotional health than any career advantages.

But she changed her major when she transferred. She wants to work in publishing, which makes school here a no-brainer.

She stops in the middle of foot traffic, and New York City shoves and dodges around her, irritated glares thrown her way.

"Do you want me to transfer and move back home?"

I reach for her elbow and urge her to keep moving. "This has nothing to do with my feelings."

She looks a little hurt, and I feel like an ass about that.

She wants me to ask her to move home a year early.

But I can't do that. If she comes home out of her own choice because of school, great. But I'm not derailing her plans because I'm greedy for her.

And once she's living with me full-time, how am I going to keep my hands off her? She's become a nearly irresistible temptation.

And yet, nothing has changed. The idea of touching her makes me feel guilty. As if sex with me would harm her. It's getting worse over time, not better. God knows I feel guilty about the night of the gala.

I'm not doing a deep dive into that, or trying to figure out if my screwed-up past is messing with my present. Or if all the things I owe to Marcus are at the root of my guilt. Because it doesn't matter.

We still have the money issue between us. And it's not going away anytime soon.

She's gaining access to more of her own money this week, per the requirements of the trust. Which is great because I won't be divvying out a weekly allowance for her anymore.

Primarily, I'll be managing her investments, the houses, and the staff. She'll only need to request funds from me if they're in excess of twenty thousand at a time.

She's my responsibility. It's a precious charge, and I cannot fail at that or forget it for a moment.

When I tell her as much, she shakes her head, presses her lips together, a small dent between her eyebrows, and tells me she's returning to Pennsylvania.

We have a week at the brownstone. I work an abbreviated schedule from home so we can see more of each other.

When she's away, I usually stay at my own apartment, as it's a closer commute to the office. But when she's here, I'm here.

I ALMOST DO

Every single time I walk out the front door, I think about that night. About holding her against that door and making her come with my fingers.

I haven't tasted Clarissa yet. The fact that I didn't taste her when I had the chance torments me.

She walks around in a T-shirt and underwear a lot. And I can't decide if she's deliberately tormenting me or if she's just become so comfortable around me that drinking coffee in the kitchen simply no longer requires pants.

She wears these clinging little things that let me see everything: the outline of her sweet little slit, the bounce of her tits and ass.

Sometimes, after we kiss, I can *smell* that I've made her wet. I can see it in the darker patch on her panties. And I remember what she felt like. How her pussy sucked on my fingers, how her walls fluttered when she came. How slick and hot she was.

My dick is going to grow a callous from the number of times I hide in my bathroom and tug one out.

I stay away from her suite upstairs. She stays away from mine.

On her twenty-first birthday, I take her to Crown Shy. It's not my usual scene; if I hadn't asked where she wanted to go first, we'd have ended up at Marea.

But the food at Crown Shy is great. The waitstaff are in jeans and Converse. Snoop Dogg is playing in the background. And, watching her, I realize—even though I'm only thirty—until I married Clarissa, I really was well on my way to being the stuffy old man she teases me about being.

Most of my coworkers are at least ten years older than I am. Clarissa's father, a man in his fifties, was my best friend for years. Despite that, she reminds me that I'm not really old, no matter how heavy the years and responsibility are.

For a long time, dinners out were about making an impression or closing a deal. But when I'm with her, I can stop being that driven, ambitious asshole. I can just be the man who is wildly, desperately in love with my wife.

If I'd taken Clarissa to Marea, she'd have had a great time. She'd have worn a cocktail dress and diamonds, used the right fork, and laughed at exactly the right volume to not draw attention from the other customers.

At Crown Shy, she sings along to Lizzo's "Good as Hell" when the song changes in the background.

Her auburn curls bounce with the beat as she dances in her seat.

When she orders a fifteen-dollar appetizer, I must give away my surprise, because she smiles at me and says, "You've forgotten how the other half lives."

I snort. I haven't forgotten. There was a time when a fifteen-dollar appetizer would have been an impossible luxury. "Don't talk to me about the other half. You're a one-percenter, and you didn't even know what the other half was until you went to a state school."

"This"—she indicates the restaurant at large—"is still bougie food prepared by a Michelin-starred chef. When you come visit me at school, I'm making you eat a fast-food burger with cheese."

She laughs out loud at my slow blink and the deliberately blank expression on my face.

When someone is raised the way I was, bounced around between social workers and extended family members, with most of my belongings stuffed in a trash bag as I moved from aunt to grandparent to cousin and back again, it's easy to think that when someone can provide expensive gifts, they *should* provide expensive gifts.

I want to give her everything. And part of me struggles with the way she doesn't assign value to anything via currency. Money has never been in short supply for her. For her, loving something has nothing to do with a price tag.

Money is power. The acquisition of it was my driving ambition for most of my life. I want to feed her a thousand-dollar dinner. She deserves a $150,000 first edition set of novels that she's never going to read because touching them could damage them.

But when we get home, I give her a first edition of *Pride and Prejudice*—a set of three slim novels she touches with reverent hands.

I also give her a Birkin bag—which she tosses over her shoulder and models for me—and a Squishmallow pillow shaped like an ice cream cone. And it's the fifty-dollar toy that makes her smile, eyes wet and shining, as she thinks of Marcus.

We share a double-chocolate mini cake from the Angelina Bakery on Eighth Ave., and I try not to think about licking frosting off her nipples. Or laying that pillow toy down, bending my wife over it, and fucking her. There's not a moment I spend with her that my mind doesn't find a way to turn into a sexual fantasy.

Then it's move-in day. She takes my cat. And I'm missing my wife.

21

Peer Pressure

Clarissa

Fall Semester Senior Year

Bronwyn won the battle with her father and remained in Pennsylvania. I'm selfishly glad of it. Our friend Sydney also moved in with us, which means, including our cook, Jeanine, every bedroom in this house is spoken for.

I am super excited about that little development. And it's not just because I adore Sydney, though I do.

Mostly it's because when James comes to visit this semester and meet my friends, where is he going to sleep without giving away that we aren't having sex? Oh, hmmm, let me think.... That's right. He's going to be sleeping in my bed.

Sydney's a junior chemical engineering major, and I love her to pieces. She's tall, with tan skin and long brown hair that's usually in a single French braid down her back. She's athletic, blunt, and completely no-nonsense. She and Bronwyn are polar opposites in everything from looks to attitude. But they're both fierce and loyal friends.

Sydney's an uber-serious student. She's also got a lot of financial burdens, which is a sticking point with James. Given his own personal history, I can't help but find that a little hypocritical. But he doesn't seem to see it.

He's convinced Sydney is conning me and manipulated me into letting her live here. He sicced a private investigator on her—who found nothing, of course. And he wants me to charge her rent, on principle, to make her prove she isn't using me.

As if. It's okay not to charge Bronwyn because she can afford it, but I'm supposed to charge Sydney because she can't? Pffft. No.

He thinks I don't know it drives him crazy that he can't *make* me do it. Last semester, he could have yanked the financial reins or made threats to have Sydney evicted because he controlled where I lived.

But I *own* this cute little four-bedroom house. It's in my name, bought with my money, even though James had to approve the purchase initially.

And the expenses here don't even come close to exceeding my financial allowance, even with staffing and security. There's really nothing he can do about Sydney, except complain about her. Poor guy.

So James doesn't trust Sydney. And she can't believe he had the gall to have her investigated.

Then there's the whole thing where I let slip to Sydney that I'm still a virgin. She immediately decided that James isn't really in love with me and is using me for money.

He doesn't realize she knows about our sex life, necessarily—though I think he suspects. However, I did accidentally admit that she believes he married me for the tax break on his inheritance.

In Sydney's defense, when you're talking billions of dollars, it's a hell of a tax break.

To keep the peace, I probably should have kept those tidbits on the down-low from both of them. Now they're both suspicious because they think the other one isn't treating me right. It'd be funny if I didn't want to smack their heads together.

I'm not nearly as gullible as James thinks I am. A lot of people have targeted me, trying to use me. But what he doesn't understand is that I grew up watching my father field sycophants and users my whole life. I know how to read a room.

I don't know how it would have been if I hadn't had James. I might have let in losers or let a con sucker me just out of loneliness or desperation. Maybe.

I'll never know because I do have James. And Bronwyn. And now Sydney and Jeanine.

I don't understand how James and I can be so in sync with each other 99 percent of the time. Then—seemingly out of nowhere—he's laying down the law or making edicts on some of the most ridiculous things, like Sydney paying rent.

I understand that he worries. I grew up with a father who did the same thing. But more often than not, James confuses me with the hills he chooses to die on. His answer to that is always "I promised your father I'd take care of you."

As if that explains anything at all.

Dean is driving this weekend so James loses less time working, since he can work on his laptop and phone in the car. And Bronwyn is almost as excited about this weekend as I am, as evidenced by her repeated confirmation requests that Dean is definitely going to be here.

When I'd first come to school, he was one of my rotating guards. That didn't last long, for multiple reasons. For one, I prefer to have someone who can blend in as part of our friend group. For another, something went down with Bronwyn and Dean.

Bronwyn isn't ready to talk about it yet. And I won't pry.

But they disappeared together one weekend near the end of my junior year.

Then Dean requested a transfer to work for James directly, telling him a woman would be a better fit for my situation. And Bronwyn told us never to mention his name again.

She then promptly forgot about that directive and continued to grill me on every single detail about his employment and where he's been and what he's been doing.

The only difference between the "before that weekend" and "after that weekend" as far as I can tell, is the way she crosses her arms and narrows her eyes as she listens to my completely uneventful reports on the man.

When Dean pulls up on Friday afternoon and James steps out of the car, I rush from the house to greet him.

James is wearing jeans and a dark green henley. Suit James is hot. Tuxedo James is scorching. James in jeans and a henley is... gah, I want to climb the man like a tree.

I affect Dean's usual pose by the front of the car, hands folded in front of me. I tip my head, my expression stoic. "Mr. Mellinger."

His white teeth flash in a grin, the autumn breeze ruffling his dark hair. His blue eyes crinkle at the corners, the way I love best. Then he fast-walks up to me, stopping inches in front of me. He's close enough that I can smell his light cologne, laundry detergent, and pure James.

He assumes a serious expression of his own, quirking an eyebrow. "Mrs. Harcourt-Mellinger."

Then he hauls me over his shoulder and carries me up the porch stairs toward the front door.

Bronwyn passes us on the steps with a brief wave for James and heads straight for Dean. I don't even want to know what new torment she's devised for the man.

Sydney's sitting in a rocker on the front porch, wrapped in a red fuzzy blanket and reading a textbook on her Kindle.

James slows as he passes her, giving her a narrow-eyed glare. His left eye twitches like a gunfighter in a spaghetti western. "Sydney."

She returns the exact same expression. "James."

When we get inside, James sits me on the kitchen island. He's standing between my spread legs, his hands braced on the counter to either side of my hips.

I leave my hands on my thighs, afraid to move. Afraid to even breathe in case he remembers his decision not to do things like this.

I've gotten really good at teasing James. When I'm home, and we're alone in the house, I deliberately walk around in a thin tank top and my underwear, just to watch the flush move across his cheekbones. I've advanced so far past that first giggle and bicep squeeze. So. Far.

And maybe I shouldn't do it, but as I've told him in the past, "If I have to suffer, you have to suffer."

Mostly, that's a joke. But when it comes to trying to get him to break his stupid no-sex rule, I kind of mean it.

This is his rule, not mine. I absolutely disagree with his reasoning at this point. I'm not in crisis or overwhelmed by grief. I'm not too young to know what I want. He obviously won't try to guilt me into quitting school or giving up my career goals. And I'm honestly not worried about the money.

If he tries to control me, we'll fight about it. But it's not as though I allow him to walk all over me.

If he didn't want me, that would be entirely different. But he does. I see his erections and the way his pulse speeds up around me.

So if the sight of me nearly naked gets him worked up and possibly rethinking things, then I can only see that as a good thing. It hasn't worked yet, but hope springs eternal.

The last time I was home, he was working in the study. I walked my butt right in there with a cup of coffee, wearing thin white cotton panties and his white undershirt.

Then I sat cross-legged in a chair directly opposite him and started chatting, as if I had absolutely no idea of the picture I made.

His eyes did this fluttery, unfocused thing, and he let out a short, involuntary noise somewhere between a nearly silent "ha" and a whimper. He looked ready to melt into a puddle. Or maybe just grab me and rail me right there on his desk.

Instead, he stiffened his spine, his eyes trained directly on my hard nipples, as he asked, "Aren't you cold?"

I looked at him with huge, fake-innocent eyes peering over my coffee cup and said, "Nope."

Fifteen seconds later, he stood up. "Excuse me. I need to just...." He gestured vaguely at the door.

I sipped my coffee, then quirked an eyebrow at him over the rim. "You need to just...?"

He palmed his cock, which looked huge and hard as a rock under his clothing, shot me a look midway between smile and scowl, and said, "Woman, you're a witch."

"Still love you, James."

Another evening, I took my red lace bra off under my clothing, sliding it out through one sleeve. Then I gave a huge sigh of relief, cupped the girls, and said, "That is so much better."

I proceeded to drape the bra right next to him on the arm of the sofa. Then I sat down beside him to watch a movie, putting my head on his shoulder and my hand on his thigh.

He watched the entire movie sitting straight up and eyes forward. But he was thinking about something entirely different from what was on that screen. I don't have to be a mind reader to know it.

See, the trick with James is to never attack directly. Direct complaints about our lack of sex life end in a fight that he always, *always* wins.

So my plan is to wear him down. But I have to be smart about it.

Which is why, when he sits me on the counter and stands between my spread thighs, I stay very still, as if he's some wild animal. Best to let him approach.

He kisses me, and I revel in the feel and taste of him, wrapping my fingers in his hair. A hot spiral of lust coils through me, but he doesn't shift his body closer or press into the V of my thighs the way I need him to. He leaves his hands on the counter, and way too soon, he pulls his mouth from mine.

Then, as if he simply can't help himself, he lifts his hands from the counter and shoves them under my sweatshirt, holding them still against the bare skin at my waist. He drops his face to where my neck meets my shoulder, and he *breathes*.

He breathes for a long time. Long enough for the tension to leave my muscles as I absorb the heat of him. Long enough for me to sift my fingers through the silky strands of his hair. Long enough for me to start breathing normally myself and let the familiar scent of my husband ground me. This is comfort, and I didn't realize how desperately I needed it until I felt it.

Sydney walks past us toward the fridge and says, "You two are so frickin' weird."

James lifts his head at last, eyes intense and sincere on mine. "God, I hate that girl."

After dinner, James finally manages to tear himself away from Mr. Snickelnuts, who's been clinging to him from practically the moment of his arrival.

We go to Jack's, my favorite dive bar, which, conveniently enough, is owned by Bronwyn's cousin. Our high school friend, Louis, drove in this weekend from New York to play a gig here and hang out. And he and his band have promised they'll play a couple nineties grunge songs, just so I can tease James about his taste in music.

I'm pretty sure Louis is still carrying a torch for Bronwyn after prom night. But if he is, he seems to have accepted that Bronwyn only sees him as a friend.

The place is crowded and noisy, with sticky floors, cold beer, and more townies than college students.

I tug on James's hand as I drag him back to our usual corner booth. He follows me easily enough, but his head is on a constant swivel, and his fingers are wrapped around my own a little too tightly for comfort.

I pull up short, leaning into him and standing on tiptoe, trying to get close enough to speak in his ear.

He bends down to hear me, but he never looks away from the crowd.

"James, what's wrong?"

"You come here a lot?"

I shrug. "A few times a month. The wings are great. Why?"

"This place is a security nightmare."

"That's why we sit in the corner booth. Jack reserves it for us when he knows we're coming. Besides, hardly anybody even knows who I am here."

He rolls his shoulders, tension bleeding from him. Then he takes a deep breath in and blows it out through his mouth.

"Beth and Dean are right over there and there. Why are you so tense? Nothing has ever happened to me here. Nothing will. We're just here to have a good time and listen to some music."

"It's beer," he mutters. "Just beer."

"What?"

He shakes his head. "Nothing. There's a spill on the floor back there. It's—" He swallows. "—sticky."

I rub his arm, smiling but still confused. "Okay, Mr. Neat Freak. They mop the floors every night."

He cracks his neck to the side, then visibly shakes off whatever's got him in a mood. Bending down, he kisses me lightly, then says, "Introduce me to your friends."

When we reach the big round corner booth, Aimee, another one of Bronwyn's cousins, holds her beer high in the air and shouts, "Mellingeerrrs."

Aimee's boyfriend, Brandon, sticks out a hand. "Good to meet you," he says with a smile on his friendly, open face.

James takes his hand, but his voice isn't exactly warm. I call it his boardroom persona. "You are?"

"Brandon Hart. This is Aimee, Monroe, and Phoebe. You already know Sydney. I think Bronwyn is still grabbing a beer," he says. "And we all know who you are."

Monroe laughs. I bump James with my elbow, rolling my eyes, because I know what's coming.

"You're the imaginary husband."

I scoff and shake my head. "He's not my imaginary husband. He's my dream husband. Pay attention."

Phoebe speaks up. "It's awesome to meet you, dream husband. Grab a beer."

James loosens up slowly after that, a little at a time. We laugh. We slow dance. We sing along to Louis's version of "Blackhole Sun."

I drink one beer, then stick with water. James isn't drinking at all.

And when the booth gets crowded, James pulls me onto his lap. I melt into the feel of him. Hard. Sexy. Solid. Then I lay my head on his shoulder and fiddle with the hair at the nape of his neck.

He keeps his hands on some part of me almost every single second we're out. My waist. My back. Even, at one point, my ass.

A couple hours in, I drop a kiss on his lips. "I'm headed to the ladies' room."

Bronwyn raises her hand. "Ooh, pick me, pick me."

Monroe shakes his head. "Don't know why women think pissing is a group activity."

I nod to Beth, so she knows where we're headed, and we make our way to the short hallway where the ladies' room is housed. Before we reach our destination, we hit a bottleneck of drunk frat boys.

Beth clears the area, but as I make my way past, one of the guys stumbles, or maybe is shoved, straight into me from the sidelines. His entire beer lands on two places: my face and the front of my white shirt.

I freeze. Absolutely motionless with shock.

The entire group of his friends crowds around me, some laughing at their friend, some leering at me. Beth is working crowd control and puts her body between mine and the guys.

But not before the drunk guy who dropped his drink on me laughs, says, "Don't look like a princess now," and grabs my breast with one hand and my ass with the other, yanking me against his body.

Beth pulls him off me, doing something that has him squealing, "Bitch," and inserts her body between the two of us, backing me against the wall. Dean and Jack break up the group of guys.

And James loses his ever-loving mind.

It's not a fair fight. Frat boy is trashed, and James hasn't had a single drink. But even if the other guy were stone-cold sober, I don't think he would have stood a chance against my husband.

I don't know how or when he learned, but James knows how to fight. And he knows how to fight dirty. After a pathetic attempt to retaliate, the asshole is crying. No longer throwing his own punches, he's just holding his arms over his face and leaning against the wall.

"I'm sorry, man. I'm drunk. It's not my fault. I'm drunk."

The words are gasoline poured on an already-roaring fire, and James goes back at him, punch after punch.

I clutch the back of Beth's shirt and try to get out from behind her.

That prick isn't fighting back anymore, but James isn't stopping. And for a terrifying moment, I think he has no intention of stopping until the guy's unconscious... or maybe dead.

Jack and Dean are trying to pull him away. They're big guys. Between them, they should be able to get James off him. But they're having no effect at all.

Finally, Jack says something that must sink in. James lifts his head, and his eyes shoot to mine. He stands there, breathing hard, one hand still wrapped in the guy's shirt and the other clenched in a tight fist. His blue eyes are on fire.

I can't hear what Dean is saying to him. I can barely see what's happening because Beth physically keeps me behind her with my back to the wall. But whatever Dean says gets through to him, because James flinches and drops the frat boy with a shove as I manage to push my way out from behind my bodyguard.

James reaches me in three seconds flat. He runs his eyes over me, from my head down to my wet blouse. Then he takes off his henley and gently pulls it over my head.

When I'm covered in his shirt, he pulls me against him. "I'm going to kill him for this."

I shiver and hold on to him. "Just get me out of here."

Jack, with a firm grip on the belligerent drunk, shouts over, "Clarissa, are you pressing charges against this asshole?"

James and I both speak at once.

"No," I say.

"Yes," James says.

"Hey, wait. Don't call the cops. Just forget it, right? I'll forget it. You forget it," the guy whines, smearing blood across his chin with his forearm.

Nobody is forgetting this anytime soon. There's no way video of James Mellinger, beating the shit out of a drunk guy and accusing him of sexually assaulting his wife, isn't popping up all over the internet. I give it three hours before it's viral. Tops.

22

I See Red

JAMES

I haven't lost control like that in years. Before Clarissa, I'd have said the part of me that could kill a man and not lose a minute's sleep over it was dead. I'd have been wrong. That rage is still in me, crouching and waiting.

That bar had me on edge from the moment I walked inside. It smelled way too familiar.

That sticky floor *felt* too familiar. The way my shoes clung with every step.

My sneakers did the same thing when I walked out of our kitchen that night. The drying blood on my shoes tried to anchor me to the floor with every step I took. When the monster killed my mother, I waited too long to fight. I spent most of my teens proving I'd never hesitate again.

As a kid, I used my fists. As an adult, I use power. Tonight I'm using both.

When that prick threw his beer on Clarissa and assaulted her, the entire world tunneled to one purpose.

Protect.

And he did throw it on her deliberately. I saw it happen. Saw the leering looks the guys gave each other. Saw the jerked chin of one to the other and the deliberate pretense.

They think it's over because my wife was cold and shaking and wanted to go home. They think it's over because Clarissa agreed not to press charges. It's not over. It won't be over for a long, long time.

I got my shots in with my fists. Now I'm going to destroy them. When I'm done, every one of those punks will regret this night for the rest of their lives.

Sasha called in the rest of Clarissa's regular security rotation, including those off-duty, to deal with this mess.

I'm sitting on the edge of her bed, looking at my phone, when she walks into the room. She's wrapped in a white towel, water still clinging to her shoulders, as she sinks to her knees in front of me and reaches for my hands.

I hold up the phone. "They think they got to everyone with video. We'll know for sure tomorrow. But it looks good."

She just nods, reaches for my phone and tosses it on the bed beside us. "I don't want to talk about other people right now."

Then she takes my hands in hers and turns them over to look at the swollen and torn-up knuckles on the right one. The left isn't great, but the knuckles aren't split.

She brushes a finger gently just next to a particularly raw area. "Are you okay?" she asks.

I shake my head. I'm not surprised she's worried about me, but I wish she wouldn't. I'm not the one who was assaulted. "That's my line. You're the one I'm worried about."

Her shoulders are high, living somewhere near her jawline, and she brushes her thumb back and forth across her lower lip. "I'll be all right."

She stands and, without a word, guides me into her bathroom, where she cleans my knuckles before covering them with antibiotic ointment.

When we return to the bedroom, she drops her towel and pulls on a pair of panties and a tank top. She's not even trying to be sexual. The fact that my adrenaline is still up and I want to fuck her right now is sick.

I disappear into the bathroom to brush my teeth and throw on sleep pants and a T-shirt. When I get back to the bedroom, she's under her white comforter, curled on her side and lying against her pillows. She looks so fragile. I want to wrap her up and hide her from the world.

She lifts the blanket in invitation, and some part of my brain reminds me of my original plan to sleep on the floor. That part of me is an idiot.

My wife is in that bed, and I'm holding her. Nothing on earth could stop me.

23

Waking up Slow

CLARISSA

WAKING IS SLOW TO come. I rise to the surface in gentle awareness of warmth and comfort and the wet heat of rampant arousal curling through me.

When I finally blink my eyes open to the early morning light filtering through my bedroom curtains, I'm lying on my side with my back to James. He's plastered against me, his left hand not only under my tank top but cupping my breast. His erection is hot and hard as steel as it lies heavy between my thighs.

He's still asleep. I feel the deep, consistent rise and fall of his chest against my back, the loose weight of his limbs.

And I'm so torn. Because part of me wants to freeze like a deer in headlights and enjoy every single second of this moment before he wakes up and leaves this bed. But another part, an almost primal creature inside me, absolutely can't help rubbing back against him and trying for more. I'm so damn greedy for my husband.

Experimentally, I give my butt a little wiggle. Push back just a bit.

James's hand tightens on my breast, squeezes. Our lower bodies are covered by my panties and his pajama bottoms, but I still feel the delicious flex of his cock against me.

My body starts the tiniest little rhythm, and I feel James's breathing change. He responds, meeting me micro-thrust for micro-thrust.

He brings his face into my hair, nuzzling my ear. Then his breath skates hot against me as his cock grinds harder. The decadent thrill of it makes me want to purr.

I'm still a little groggy, my limbs still warm and loose and relaxed from sleep. My body is pure honey sliding off a hot spoon as James moves against me.

I lift my upper leg and rest it on the outside of his. I don't know what I'm doing. It's instinct to give him better access. But when I do it, suddenly his cock is making contact with my clit on every push forward.

We're still covered. Still dressed. I desperately wish we weren't.

"We shouldn't be doing this," James says gruffly, his words skimming past the shell of my ear on warm breath that raises goose bumps on my skin.

I don't say a word to that. I just freeze, barely breathing, heart sinking.

But James doesn't pull away. He stays there, wrapped around me, almost clutching me against him, while his erection presses hot and heavy between my thighs.

I can't stay still. Without thought or will, I move against him once more, seeking friction.

"Okay," he says. "Okay. We can do this much. Just this much."

24

Falling Like the Stars

IT WOULD TAKE AN act of God to pull me away from Clarissa right now.

When I woke up and realized what I'd done, I tried to stop. To regain control and common sense.

But she wants this. She's as needy and frustrated as I am. I can hear her panting little breaths and feel her damp heat even through our clothing.

If we were home in New York... well, we wouldn't have slept in the same bed for starters. And when things get too hot and heavy there, I go to my room. She goes to hers. And we take care of ourselves.

But if I get up right now and go to the bathroom to jack off in the shower—and she stays in here to give herself some relief—does it really hurt anything if we both just stay here?

If I don't touch her, if we just take care of ourselves, then I'm not actually doing anything to her. It's the same thing she'd do if I weren't in the room.

So I pull my hand from under her tank top. And if I give it a gentle squeeze and brush my thumb across her nipple as I do it... these things happen.

She whimpers at the loss, but I reach for her hand. "There's something we could try," I say.

She looks at me, brows furrowed in confusion.

"We could take care of ourselves, together," I say.

Determination chases the doubtful expression from her face, and she nods.

She rolls to her back to look up at me.

When we were plastered against each other, it felt like a natural progression. But now, that moment of introspection and discussion has changed the tone. Turned this moment from some spur-of-the-moment sexual exploration into a conscious choice. It's a decision we've made. And it feels heavy and significant: a deliberate step onto that slippery slope instead of an accidental slide.

This will change things for us. There won't be any going back from it.

Clarissa is lying against her pillow. Everything on this bed is white. Fluffy pillows. Down comforter. Crisp cotton sheets.

I draw the comforter away from her body, and now she's lying exposed on those pristine sheets, wearing her little white cotton panties and white tank top. I know I'm being stupid, but she looks like a real-life angel. Those auburn curls are spread out in a wild halo, and her gorgeous whiskey and moss-green eyes glitter in the weak early morning light.

I have a flash of memory. Our wedding night. Clarissa spread out on the bed in that sparkling white gown, offering herself to me.

She's nervous now, where she wasn't before. I can see that in the way her hands clench and unclench the bedding. I can see it in the fluttering pulse at the base of her throat, where I want to lick her.

But like me, she's more excited than nervous. Her nipples are hard little peaks under her tank. The divot at the base of her throat contracts tight with every breath, and her hips move in a subtle rhythm.

I tip my chin and hold her eyes. "You're sure?"

She nods eagerly.

I sit up and take off my shirt. Then I stand up and walk to the side of the bed. Running my hands down her smooth, bare leg, I touch her from her thigh to her ankle.

When I lift her right foot, she gives me that smile I know and love so well. The one that quirks up on only one side of her face and says *"Now, what are you up to, James Mellinger?"*

Then I give her purple-polished toes a fat, noisy kiss.

She squeals in laughter and jerks her foot back.

So I do the other leg. And I kiss those toes, too, just to watch her giggle and see the nervous tension leave her clenching hands.

I tug gently at the hemline of her tank top. "Do you think you should take this off? Or do you want to stay wrapped up like a pretty little package? There's no wrong answer," I say quietly, sitting on the bed beside her. "If you aren't comfortable...."

She sits up and pulls the tank over her head in a wild rush, tossing it to the floor. "I'm comfortable," she says with a cheeky grin.

I fight a smile, then swallow at the view. There are my favorite freckles, perched just above her rosy nipples. Damn, she's beautiful.

"Are your breasts sensitive? Did you like it when I touched them? When I licked them?" I know she did. She practically came out of her skin that night. But I want her to remember.

Clarissa shivers, though it's not even a little cold. Red flags burn across her cheeks, but she doesn't look embarrassed. She looks turned on as hell. "Yes," she whispers.

"Lie back and give me your hand, sweet girl," I say.

She reclines against the pillows and holds out her hand as if I'm about to shake it. And I'm suddenly reminded how innocent she is.

She's been deliberately tormenting me for months with innuendos, flirting, kisses, trailing fingers, and, yes, near nudity.

I admit, at first, I wasn't sure if the teasing was on purpose. But it became obvious pretty fast. She loves getting a reaction out of me and watching me fight the need to touch her. And I love it too. I live for it.

Because she's become so adept at teasing me, it's easy to forget that the only sexual experience she has happened with me. And we haven't done much, though what we have done feels world-shattering to me.

When she sits across from me in damp panties and pretends to want to chat about how wet the weather is, it's hard to remember my wife is a virgin. Until she's lying here in bed and holds her shaking hand out to me like I'm about to introduce myself.

The two of us could just go at it and masturbate beside each other. But if this moment is going to carry the weight it should, she deserves more. And God knows I want to give it. As long as I keep my cock to myself, it's safe to do that for her.

I draw her fingers up and into my mouth, sucking the first two. First one, then the other, swirling my tongue over the digits.

She gasps at the sensation, a surprised, breathy "Oh" falling from her lips.

"Close your eyes. Don't think about coming. I just want you to relax and let yourself feel good."

She huffs out a laugh, but she closes her eyes, and I guide her hand back to her breast, placing her own wet fingers over the nipple.

"When I'm not here, you can suck your own fingers," I say quietly. "It feels nice when it's wet, doesn't it?"

She makes a tiny sound. Her thighs clench together.

"Play a little, baby girl. Make yourself feel good."

Her fingers pinch and swirl.

"Mmmm. That's nice. I'll remember you like that when it's my turn."

She shudders at my words. And I think it's my voice as much as her own touch that's driving her up. Every sound—every squirming reaction—is happening at the sound of my words.

I reach for her other hand and pull it up to her poor neglected breast. "Don't leave this one out. Feel the weight? Feel how satiny soft your skin is? Your breasts are gorgeous. You have the prettiest pink nipples."

She squeezes and arches her back. "James...."

"Are you ready to move lower?"

"Yes." Another whisper.

"Bottoms off or bottoms on?" I ask. "You can do it either way. You can slide your wet fingers right down under your panties. Do you remember that? When I touched you under your panties?"

She nods frantically, eyes closed.

"You can touch yourself like that, under your panties, or you can take them off and let me see that pretty pussy when you work it."

Her abdominal muscles visibly clench at my words, and she blows out a rough breath. There's a beat where she hesitates. Builds up her nerve. "I want to take them off," she whispers.

"Go ahead."

She nods, flutters her hands down to her waistband, then stalls there. "I want to," she says. "But I'm—"

I make an indistinct sound in my throat and gently take her earlobe between my teeth before I whisper, "Is my sweet girl shy? I've seen you almost bare lots of times. Why is this different?"

"It just is."

She's right. It is. This is about emotional vulnerability, not physical exposure. "Would it help if I took my clothes off now too?"

Her eyes fly open, and I pull back to look at her. She goes for her panties so fast, I almost laugh. But I don't. Because I'm working off my drawstring pants and boxer briefs, and I am way too busy looking at that pretty bare pussy she's just revealed.

I didn't see that part of her last spring. I felt it with my fingers, but it was hidden, always hidden, under those black silk panties.

I didn't taste her then either, and the lack of it has tormented me ever since.

I look up to see her eyes are on my hard cock, wide and every bit as enthralled with me as I am with her. In more than a year of marriage, she's never seen me like this either.

I haven't even touched myself yet, but a bead of precum pearls at the tip of my cock. She reaches out her thumb and swipes across it, then brings it to her mouth, her pretty pink tongue licking it off.

Jesus. My abdominal muscles clench as I resist the urge to push forward. To give her more to taste.

She looks up at me with mischief in her grin, and I shake my head, mock scolding. "Witch," I say, then tip my head back, close my eyes, and try to get it together. The point of this is to take care of ourselves.

When I've gotten the urge to take more than we agreed to under control, I climb on the bed beside her, not touching, careful to leave a few inches between us. I take her hand and use it to run the backs of her fingers between her breasts, down her belly, to rest at the apex of her thighs.

"Touch here now. Slide a finger. Right. There," I say. "You can close your eyes if it makes it easier to concentrate on the way you feel. Or you can leave them open and watch yourself."

Her gaze leaves my face and moves down to where I hold her hand as she slides a finger through the slick folds of her pussy.

"I like to watch too," I admit. "But I bet you remember that."

Her gaze flies to mine, then down to my aching cock. "I want to watch you," she says.

Her breathing has picked up, ragged and raw. I feel her hand flex under mine, her fingers circling faster. Her movements are frantic, brows furrowed. She looks frustrated. Poor thing.

"Are you trying to come?" I scold her gently.

"Yes."

I make a small tsk sound. "I told you not to think about coming."

"So bossy," she grumbles, but her lips quirk in a smile when she says it.

I am bossy. I'm a domineering asshole. I don't know what Marcus was thinking when he asked me to be her husband.

I pull her hand back up to my mouth, suck on those fingers again. For her. But also for me.

And I was dead right to be tormented by the lack of her taste in my mouth, because Clarissa Harcourt-Mellinger's flavor is decadent. She's delicate, clean, a bit salty. And that little taste is almost worse than having had none at all because now I know what I'm missing.

I move her hand back down, guide her fingers to her clit. When she begins to move them again, copying the rhythm I used last year, I breathe out long and slow. Then I wrap my free hand around my cock and work it leisurely. No hurry.

She makes a sound of annoyance. I remove my hand from hers and brush her hair off her forehead. I watch her face as she works her clit.

Her eyes are closed, a little dent is drawn between her eyebrows, and she has her bottom lip clamped between her teeth. She works and works, concentration written on her face.

"Good girl. Move your fingers down. Explore. Do you feel how swollen and wet you are?"

I reach down with one hand and gently spread the lips of her vulva. "Look, Clarissa. Look how swollen and wet and pretty you are."

She looks down, and her hips squirm up in an involuntary thrust.

"Yes. Slide the tip of your finger inside."

She does, thrusting up against her own hand, then stares up at me, demand in her eyes. She wants me to touch her. I want that too. She's water in the desert. She's the promise of salvation.

But when I look at my fingers as they separate the lips of her pussy, I see swollen knuckles, the skin torn from an act of violence. And it isn't my own hand I see against her skin. So I give her my words instead. "I want to lick and suck your pretty breasts. I want to trace the firework sparks of your freckles with the tips of my fingers. I want to taste your orgasm on my tongue. I want to slide my cock into your snug wet heat and ride you until we're both shaking from it."

She cries out, her lower body twisting and thrusting. But it's not an orgasm. Not yet.

I release her vulva, and the outer lips of her sex close over her fingers, playing peekaboo. "Are you ready to play with your clit again? Bring all that honey on up. Feel how it makes your finger glide over your hard little button? I can't see your sweet little hole anymore, Clarissa. I can't see your clit. You're covering it all up. But all I have to do is close my eyes, and I'll remember it for the rest of my life."

Clarissa makes a keening sound, her eyes on mine, her fingers swirling. I work my own hand faster. The muscles of my forearm are tensing and flexing. My thumb swipes over the sensitive head of my cock.

Her fingers keep moving on her clit, but her attention is on my cock now, on the way I work it. She probably thinks it looks rough. I bet she's wondering how it would feel if I fucked her like this.

There's a solid flush of heat on her chest, up her neck, and on her cheeks. Those gorgeous, ethereal eyes are fever bright.

"This is yours, sweet girl. I can't wait to fill you up. I'm going to ride you until you scream from how good it feels. I love you so fucking much."

Clarissa comes with an inarticulate wail forced through clenched teeth, her entire body seizing and her eyes on my cock.

In two more strokes, I let go, ropes of my semen gushing over my fingers and landing on her soft belly.

25

Incomplete

JAMES

I kiss her temple in the aftermath and hold her hand until her breathing slows and the aftershocks stop. Then I move to her attached bathroom and bring back a warm cloth and a soft towel to clean her.

She pulls the comforter back over her, and I throw my sleep pants on and lie beside her on top of the covers. I've still got plenty left in me to go another round. Postcoital cuddling with both of us naked is a recipe for a disaster, but I hold her like this while I try not to think too hard about why this may have been a mistake.

Reaching out, she drags her finger across the swirling path of my latest tattoo. Her name, worked into the existing design. Hidden until you know where to look, and then it's all you see. Every other bit of ink on my body is now just about paying homage to Clarissa. I knew she didn't notice in the chaos last night.

"James," she says, tears thick in her voice.

It wasn't supposed to make her cry. "You don't like it."

"I love it," she says, her voice fierce. And there's my tigress who likes to threaten me with her wrath.

She traces a finger over one of the circular burn scars on my chest. Her voice is curious as she asks, "What caused these?"

Cigarettes. But she doesn't need to hear about something that ugly. "Accident. Not a big deal."

"Okay," she says, "then what's wrong? You're brooding."

"I don't brood. Don't make me sound like some emo kid with black eyeliner and an earring listening to depressing music and writing bad poetry about how pointless life is."

She bursts out in a laugh, then sucks in a breath and turns toward me, a look of realization on her face. "*James.*"

I pull back, a little wary. "What?"

"That was an oddly specific description of brooding."

I brazen it out. "Isn't that everyone's idea of brooding?"

"I was initially thinking more along the lines of Mr. Rochester. But you went straight to guyliner."

She leans over and touches my earlobe, right where a small scar remains from when I, very briefly, wore an earring.

"It was a phase. I was fourteen."

"How does an emo rocker turn into"—she runs a displaying hand Vanna White style up and down my body—"this?"

"I was living at my cousin's house at the time. But then she had a baby, and they needed the extra room, so I moved back to my grandmother's place. My mother's mother," I explain.

"Your grandmother didn't let you keep the eyeliner and earring?"

"No, that wasn't it at all. My grandmother never said a word about it. She just asked me what I planned to do with my life. And when I told her that someday I was going to have more money than God, and people were going to call me 'sir,' she said that was a fine dream. But she didn't want to know about my dreams. She wanted to know what I was going to do to make the life I wanted."

"Wow," she says.

"If I'd told her I was going to play in a band and sell out concerts, she'd have made the T-shirts for me. But I decided on a future in finance. I became pretty single-minded about it, actually." My grandmother reminded me that, regardless of my past, and even regardless of an unsure present, I did have the ability to shape the life I would have as an adult.

"I've never met your grandmother."

"I only lived with her for six months before she passed," I say. "Aneurysm." I shove down any emotion the memory might provoke.

"I'm so sorry," she whispers, hugging me.

I wrap my arms around her. "You deal and move on." In this case, I moved on to live with an aunt, uncle, and three cousins.

"Your mother died when you were very young?" she asks.

"I was seven." I need to change this subject. I don't want to talk about my parents. I don't want to talk about my childhood at all. It's best left in the past, where it belongs.

"So," I say, "masturbation."

She looks up at me, thrown for a moment by the conversational pivot, then laughs.

"Yes?" She drags the word out questioningly.

I shrug. "I'm just curious if we're going to try this on a regular basis or if you were thinking it might be a one-off."

Curious, my ass. I'm dying for confirmation that what we did worked for her.

"We should definitely be doing this on a regular basis."

I lean over her and indicate her nightstand. "What do you have in the drawer? Anything fun?"

Her eyes go wide in delighted shock. "*James.*"

"Don't be shy now," I say. "What's in the drawer?"

She narrows her eyes at me, then reaches over and pulls it open.

I peer inside in expectation. I can't wait to see what she uses on herself.

What I see is a phone charging station, a small jewelry box, a jumbo bottle of Advil, and a Kindle.

I squint. Look at her. Look back at the drawer. Look back at her. "Where do you keep them?"

"Them?" she asks with exaggerated innocence.

"Your toys, you tease."

She laughs at me. "I don't have any."

I'm horrified. Legitimately horrified. "Why?" I ask.

"I don't know. I just never bought anything."

"You might like the way a vibrator feels."

"I guess," she says. "Do you have toys?"

And now I see why she felt embarrassed at my question. "I'm an adult man in my prime who is not having intercourse with my wife. So, yes, I have something to make the situation easier."

She nods at me sagely. "Blow-up doll."

"No, not a blow-up doll. My life isn't a nineties screwball comedy." I reach for my phone, do a quick search, and pull up an image. "This."

"It looks like a flashlight. If I saw that in your drawer, I would legitimately think, 'Wow, James really must be afraid of a power outage,'" she says.

I pinch the bridge of my nose and close my eyes, but I'm grinning.

"Do you think I should order something?" she asks.

"Oh, yes. When they arrive, you can call me to test them out while we're on the phone."

There's a hot flush of color on her cheekbones when she says. "I will absolutely call you."

"Good girl."

I run a finger up her arm. "Do you watch porn?" Yeah, we opened this door. And I am walking right through it.

"Mellinger, you are all up in my personal business today," she says. But her voice is breathy, and she's rubbing that thumb over her bottom lip.

"Hmmm," I say, looking deeply into her eyes and speculating whether that nonanswer means she does or doesn't.

"I prefer to listen to romance audiobooks rather than watch porn with real people in it. It's easier for me to imagine myself or you as the characters in the book. And I need it to be loving, not just about sex."

Ah. "What kinds of books do you listen to?" I ask curiously.

She reaches down, pulls out her Kindle, and shows me the library there.

"You just told me you picture me when you listen to these."

"Yes," she says. "Sometimes."

I scroll through. Orcs, minotaurs, aliens.

I click on one with a giant blue alien who has his arms around a woman in a fur bikini. The book is called *Barbarian's Treasure* by Ruby Dixon.

I raise an eyebrow and turn the book to face her. "This? You picture me in this?"

"Are you *judging* me right now? You ask me all these intrusive questions, encourage me to share my vulnerable side, and then you—"

"Of course not." I say, horrified.

She nudges me. "Totally screwing with you. But you should try it. Maybe you'll like it."

Then she reaches for her earbuds and hands the left one to me. She puts the right one in her own ear. "Listen."

When I put the earbud in, she clicks on the narration, which begins on Chapter Seven. And... I get it. It's hot. But there's also a vulnerability to it.

When the blue alien sucks on the woman's toes, I scoff. "Totally unrealistic. When I kiss your toes, you try to kick me in the head."

"Oh, sure. It's the toe sucking that's unrealistic in alien romance," she quips.

She scrolls through and shows me a cover with a half-naked dude with photoshopped abs on it.

"I like non-aliens too," she says. "This narrator has the hottest voice." She clicks on the audiobook, and a guy with a raspy voice starts reading a book about a hockey player in love.

His voice is not that hot.

Just then the narrator says, "Fuuuck," in my earhole. I have no idea what my expression looks like, but Clarissa pokes at me with a finger.

"You are not jealous of an audiobook narrator," she says. "Stop it."

"Absolutely not jealous," I say.

I absolutely am jealous. Which is stupid. I couldn't care less if she watches some random guy nut in a porn vid, but this guy talking into her earbuds and turning her on makes me... weird. Not that I will ever, ever admit to being that big of a douche.

She takes the Kindle back and shows me a bunch of novellas. "I just read these because they don't have audiobooks," she says with a sigh. "Maybe someday."

"You could tell me which ones you want, and I could read them," I say in a rush, "on an audio file for you." I trail off, a little embarrassed by my offer. I'm not a narrator. I'm good at public speaking. Did some theater in college, just because I thought it would help me gain some skills handling a room. But I'm not that guy.

"Are you serious right now? Yes! Yes! A thousand times, yes!"

My lips twitch.

That's right. Jason Clarke can suck it.

She wants *my* voice in her earholes.

26

Naked

Clarissa

Spring Semester Senior Year

SYDNEY WALKS PAST THE living room, where I'm lying on the sofa with a heating pack on my lower stomach, a bottle of Advil clutched in one fist, and Mr. Fluffernuts in the crook of my other arm. She skids to a stop in the doorway and glares at me with her hands on her hips.

"Nuh-uh. Girl, no," she says. Then she hollers, "Jeanine! Come talk sense into this idiot!"

I glare back at her, because, honestly, who yells at a person when they're in pain?

Jeanine joins Sydney at the casement opening and peers in at me, her brown eyes sparking with outrage.

I know they're both concerned, but neither of them is exactly the mothering sort. Or, well, not what I think the mothering sort is. I barely remember mine. Maybe all mothers are bossy and call you a dumbass when you won't go to the doctor.

Bronwyn can be the hovering, nurturing sort. But she also loses patience if she thinks someone needs to get their head out of their ass. And she's definitely used the phrase "Get your head out of your ass" to me about my current situation.

To be fair, I did go to urgent care a few months ago. But they said, "See your gynecologist," which I do not have. Now Sydney and Jeanine call me names, Bronwyn tells me to remove my cranium from my anus, and absolutely nobody says, "Aw, let me get you a heating pack," anymore, unless it is also accompanied by a lecture or name-calling.

"This is nonsense," Jeanine says. "Make a doctor's appointment. First it was the periods from hell. Now it's all the time. When was the last time you didn't need to take handfuls of Advil just to get through the day?"

"You're not the boss of me," I mumble under my breath.

Sydney's eyes pop. Straight up bug out of her head like a cartoon character. She shoots Jeanine a wary glance and takes a step back. Mr. Pooterfutz scrambles out of my arms and takes off out of the room with a yowl.

Jeanine is five foot nothing, and she insists she's "in shape," then winks and says, "Round is a shape." She looks soft and sweet. But absolutely nobody sasses Jeanine unless they have a death wish. The woman used to run a kitchen in Manhattan where underlings yelled, "Yes, chef!" the second she opened her mouth.

"What did you just say to me," she says. No question mark. She knows what I said. She's daring me to say it again.

"You're a chef, Jeanine. You're not my nanny," I return.

"Holy. Shit," Sydney breathes. "Shut up."

"I will not shut up," I screech at Sydney, and I know this feels like a random outburst out of nowhere to them. Because it feels like one to me too. But I hurt. All the time. I'm not sleeping because of it. And I just need them to get off my back. It's honestly such a good thing I took all those extra credits my first couple years of college, because if I were trying to carry a full course load this semester, I'd have crashed and burned.

"Everybody wants to tell me what to do," I continue. "And I'm sick of it. If I want to skip class and lie on the sofa with a heating pack, I'm allowed to skip class and lie on the sofa with a heating pack." And then I burst into tears.

Sydney and Jeanine share a shocked look, then, as one, surround me on the sofa with their arms wrapped around me.

"Honey, this is not normal. There's something wrong. Your hormones are all messed up. You're in pain all the time. You have to go to the doctor," Jeanine says.

"I don't have one," I whine.

"Oh my God." Frustration bleeds into her voice, despite the fact that she's got her arms wrapped around me in a comforting hug. "I love you, but stop. Get on your phone, find one, and go."

"I can't," I say. And I know exactly how stupid that sounds. Of course I can. All I have to do is pick my phone up off the coffee table and search for a gynecologist.

But I can't. Because I don't want to know what's wrong with me.

It's absolute cowardice. My father would be so, so angry at me if he were here. Probably my mother would too. But they're not here. Because they both died of cancer.

If I go to the doctor, I have to stop pretending I just started having "bad periods." And if I stop pretending, I have to face the fact that I'm scared to death.

"That's it," Sydney says and snatches my phone off the coffee table. She shoves the screen in my face, and I blink back, startled, not realizing at first that she's using my own face against me to unlock my phone.

She walks across the room while tapping buttons. I think she's looking for doctors at first, but then I hear James's voice mail message play over the speaker. I try to lunge off the sofa after her, but those hugging arms of Jeanine's have become iron bands. I holler, "Traitor!"

Then Sydney's talking over the sounds of me cussing her out. "Hey, surprise. It's not your celibate little love muffin after all," she says. "It's Sydney. I stole her phone to tell you to make your wife go to the doctor. She's been lying to you."

I flat-out screech, "I have not been lying."

Sydney looks at me from across the room and pinches her finger and thumb together in that measuring thing that says, "Eh, just a little."

She keeps speaking. "Okay, maybe not lying. But she has been hiding something big. So call her. Thanks. Bye."

Sydney comes back and drops the phone onto the coffee table, then crosses her arms over her chest. "Go ahead," she says. "Kick me out of the house now. Tell me what a terrible friend I am. But I love you. So if kicking me out means you go get whatever this is fixed, then so be it."

"I'm not kicking you out," I snap. "But James is not my boss any more than you are. He can't make me go to the doctor, and it's fucking sexist of you to try to get him to."

"You did not just call me sexist," she seethes. "I'd have called your spouse if you were married to a woman too. Your spouse is supposed to be your partner. The person you are married to is your support system.

And if you won't take care of yourself, then James is the only person I can think of who might talk sense into you."

"Well, you shouldn't have. James is busy. He just got back from London two days ago. I don't like to worry him. He freaks out if I stub my toe."

"We," Sydney says, indicating Jeanine, herself, and me, "are worried. So why shouldn't your husband join in the fun?"

I just shake my head. "You don't understand. He's going to kill me."

James calls me five minutes later. Palms sweaty, I head to my bedroom and shut the door before I answer.

"Hello?"

"What the fuck is going on?" he bites out.

"Hello, Clarissa! How is your day?" I imitate his deep voice. "Why, it's just fine, James. Thanks for asking."

"Do not fuck with me right now, Clarissa. I will haul your ass out of that backwater town before you can say 'college dropout.'"

I actually pull the phone away from my face to stare at it before I rally and snap back, "*Please*. You are not pulling me out of school with one week left to go. You're the one who's always freaked out at the idea of me quitting school, not me, so don't threaten me with a good time."

That's not an entirely accurate statement, but it is guaranteed to get a rise out of him.

I can hear him gritting his teeth through the speaker.

"Clarissa," he says slowly, with obvious forced patience, "please tell me why you need a doctor."

I flop on my bed, then groan because it made the cramps so much worse. "Sydney's being dramatic."

"She's not dramatic," he says. "She's blunt. There's a difference."

Huh. Wow, I think Sydney just earned a little respect from James. And it only took turning traitor to get it.

"It's just uterus-owner stuff," I say. "I've been getting bad period cramps lately, so I need to see a gynecologist. They'll probably put me on birth control to regulate my schedule."

I don't tell him that in the last month, the cramps are now 24-7. Or that it's not just cramps. I'm bleeding intermittently all month long now. This week, the pain around my left ovary has become nauseating in its intensity.

"Okay, how long has this been going on?" he asks.

I think back. "The period cramping started last summer, while I was in Europe, and then it's just slowly gotten worse."

James doesn't say anything for a long moment. I clear my throat.

His control snaps. "Almost eleven months. Are you kidding me?"

"It's not something for you to get worked up over. A lot of women have cramps. It's part of getting older. It's just lately it's getting to be a bit more of an issue." I'm gaslighting. I'm a *gaslighter*.

"We talk to each other or text every single day, and this is the first time I'm hearing about this."

I'm.... What *is that* in his voice? I have never heard that tone from him.

"I didn't want to worry you."

"It's not your job to protect me. It's my job to protect you, and I can't do that when you're lying to me and hiding things from me."

I want to unpack all that because it makes no sense at all. I'm not his child. He's not my parent. We should be protecting each other. Helping each other.

And though I admit keeping this from him was stupid, it's not an excuse for him to treat me like I'm a child.

So I have a hang-up about the doctor. Yes, it's bad. But I watched my mother die when I was four and my father die when I was barely twenty. *They both died*. Of cancer. I'm entitled to have an occasional issue to work through.

James loves me. I know that.

But sometimes he acts like a parent who's sent a child off to college. I'm his wife, not his kid. Why does everyone seem to be forgetting that today?

"Why didn't you go to the doctor?"

"I have an issue with doctors," I admit. "Because of my mom and dad."

He's quiet for a moment, then says, "I'll schedule you for right after graduation. I'll go with you if you want me to. You have finals next week. Are you okay with that, or do you need to see someone right now?"

"It's been going on for close to a year. I hardly think a week or two makes a difference at this point. I need to get these finals over with first."

"Okay."

"Thank you for making the appointment and coming with me. Seriously, James. I should have done it myself, but I just get a little... panicky when I think of it."

James is quiet again. And honestly, it's strange the way he keeps sitting in silence so much of this conversation. "Don't thank me. This is my fault," he finally says.

"How do you figure that?"

"I promised Marcus I'd take care of you. That means making sure you go for your checkups. I didn't do that."

"I'm an adult. I'm supposed to take care of doctor visits myself."

The silence now is pregnant. He doesn't say it, but I hear it anyway. *"But you didn't."*

27

If You Need Me

JAMES

Three Days Later

Sasha calls on Monday morning. Four minutes later, I'm in the car.

I almost take the jet, but when Dean hears me telling Rebecca to take care of it, he interrupts in a very un-Dean-like moment.

"I can do it faster," he says.

At my quick look, he says, "Traffic into JFK is crawling right now. Construction. I can get us there faster by car if I break a few traffic laws."

Dean breaks more than a few traffic laws. And I'd have had him break more if I'd thought of any he missed. He screeches to a stop in the ambulance parking spot two hours and twelve minutes after I answered that call.

When I step into the waiting room for surgery, Jeanine, Bronwyn, Sydney, four of Clarissa's other friends, a hospital administrator, and a sweating middle-aged man in a cheap suit all jump to their feet. Two of her security team are already standing.

The man is pushing forward, extending a hand to shake. "Mr. Mellinger, Dean Rosen. It's an honor."

I ignore him. "Which one of you knows what's happening with her right now?"

They all start talking. Every single one.

I put a hand up. "Quiet."

I point at the administrator. "You. Come with me."

I'll give her credit. The administrator seems prepared for this moment. She'd better be.

She has brown skin, short-cropped iron-gray hair, and an attitude that says absolutely nothing will phase her.

We'll see about that.

She guides me to a small room for privacy and shuts the door.

"I'll cut to the basics, and we'll fill in the rest after. I'm assuming you'd prefer that."

I just do the "get on with it" wave. My ability to pretend not to be an asshole is nonexistent in this moment.

"Your wife is currently in exploratory surgery for suspected ovarian torsion." She passes me a sheaf of papers. Like I'm supposed to be able to sift through this shit right now.

"You couldn't Life Flight her out of this place to a hospital that specializes in this surgery?" I demand.

"I assure you, we are well qualified to perform this type of surgery, Mr. Mellinger. And your wife was experiencing a true medical emergency. She required immediate care. It was in her best interest for the surgery to be performed here."

"Do you know who she is?" I snap out.

The administrator, whose name I've already forgotten, drops her chin and gives me the kind of look a fourth-grade teacher gives an unruly student. "Mr. Mellinger, I am well aware of who Clarissa Harcourt-Mellinger *is*."

The woman puts her hands on me. Sticks her hands right on my biceps, like we're buddies or she's my Little League coach, telling me to swing for the stands.

"She's a young woman surrounded by people who love her. That tells me all I need to know about who she *is*."

There's a knock on the door, and a sturdy brown-haired woman in scrubs enters. "She's in recovery."

Am I supposed to just trust that some ob/gyn in the middle of nowhere PA did everything exactly as it should have been done? Fuck that. I've already had Rebecca organize a surgeon from Brigham and Women's Hospital to come in to consult. I wouldn't even send a report past my desk that hasn't been double-checked by a second set of eyes for errors. I'm sure as hell not just trusting that this doctor knew what she was doing when she cut into my wife.

The Boston surgeon's not here yet, of course, because nobody else is as big of a lunatic as Dean and I were. But when she arrives, and she confirms everything was done exactly as it should have been, and takes over her follow-up care, then *maybe* I'll be able to breathe again.

The gist of all this was that Clarissa had a large cyst on her ovary that eventually caused the ovary to twist and cut off blood flow.

According to Jeanine and Bronwyn, she'd started vomiting and running a fever this morning. She'd insisted it was a stomach bug and attempted to take one of her finals this morning anyway—until she promptly passed right out in class from pain and blood loss from internal bleeding.

The ovary and fallopian tube are both gone now. They were starved of blood flow for too long to save. They couldn't do the laparoscopic version of the surgery on her, so she has a large incision under her belly button and will take close to two months to recover, just from the surgery. That's not including follow-up to determine whether she has any cysts on the remaining ovary.

The only silver linings I can find are that she hasn't gone septic, the cyst appears to have been benign, though we're still waiting on official results, and she does still have one ovary remaining, which means future fertility, while diminished, is still a possibility.

Three days ago, I had the opportunity to take her to a hospital immediately. Three days ago, they probably could have saved her ovary. They could have prevented infection and blood loss.

Three days ago, I said, "I'll schedule you for after graduation." And she said she didn't see what difference a week or two would make.

She's lucky she's alive.

I'm epically failing to care for the greatest gift in my life. I've never deserved her, and I've always known it. When Marcus said, "I need you to marry her," I thought it then. I thought the very idea of marrying Clarissa Harcourt was like flying too close to the sun. I'd crash and burn, and my greatest fear was that she'd burn with me.

She's so pale in that hospital bed. The only color anywhere is her hair, where the auburn highlights glimmer in a halo as she rests against the pillow.

When I entered her room, a nurse handed me a small ziplock bag with her wedding rings inside. Something about that, having a sympathetic-looking woman in hospital scrubs pass me a plastic bag with my wife's wedding rings in it, gutted me.

I'm sitting in a green Naugahyde chair, pulled up next to her bed, forearms resting on my knees, hands and head hanging loose, when

I hear her shift on the bed. I look up as her eyelashes flutter, and she turns her head. She's looking for me. I know because her whole expression relaxes when she sees me.

"You're here," she says.

I brush her hair back from her forehead. "Sweet girl, make no mistake. When you need me, I will always be here."

She takes me in, and I'm not sure what it is she sees, but she gives me a gentle smile and says, "You look like shit."

My words are like gravel. "Don't make a joke of this."

She reaches for me, holding on to my hand. "Hey. I'm okay."

She doesn't understand. "Nothing can happen to you, Clarissa," I grind out. "Not ever. I couldn't take it."

28

I Don't Want to Lose You

CLARISSA

JAMES IS ANGRY. AT himself. If I thought he was overprotective before surgery... well, all I can say is I was a sweet summer child who knew nothing.

It's awful. I don't mean awful in that kind of humble-brag I occasionally experienced in the past. I'd get irritated when he tried to boss me around, of course. But 99 percent of the time, his fussing didn't feel truly intrusive. I just felt loved.

Then it was "Oh, you know how he worries about me." And what it really meant was he loved me. Because I'd been taught that love equaled worry my entire life.

It's not that I don't still feel loved. But his love now is tempered by an equal measure of his own self-hatred, and I don't have a single clue what to do about it. Or if there even is anything I can do about it.

I could always fight James when he tried to tell me what to do. If he said, "Wear a jacket," I'd just shrug. And if I didn't need a jacket, I'd say, "No."

Compared to my father's need to keep me rolled in metaphorical bubble wrap, James's "orders" to drink more water or wear sunblock are a breath of fresh air.

I get a little thrill out of refusing to do something he tells me to do. I don't refuse for the sake of it, but if I'm not thirsty or cold or needing to rest, I'm not the least bit afraid to do what I want.

But I don't know how to fight the way he feels about himself.

When James looks at me, he sees his own failures. And what a god-awful feeling that is, to know he looks at me and hates himself.

I recovered from the surgery just fine. James worked out something with the dean so I could take my finals online. The university mailed me my diploma. My remaining ovary looks great. The cyst wasn't cancerous. So the day the doctor released me to regular activities should have been a happy one.

Instead, I feel lost.

My relationship with James has always been complicated. It started out as a crush, moved into hero worship, and eventually into bone-deep love.

And I have also always considered James to be this wise, infallible god. Even when I was frustrated and arguing with him, he never quite fell from that pedestal.

Even when I recognized he wasn't technically *perfect*, I still always believed he must have some insight I didn't have. He's older than I am, has more life experience.

Even with the lack of intercourse between us, the way he'll only allow mutual masturbation, and the way he won't let us sleep in the same bed since I came home, I convinced myself his reasons regarding my trust fund held validity for him. That he just didn't understand that I didn't care about the money or "needing" him.

But now that I'm here, really here, every single day, I realize James has blinders about a lot of things. And most of those things have to do with me.

I was juvenile to put him on that pedestal in the first place. There are some things in this world that I'm actually *wiser* about than my husband, despite the nine years and vast difference in experience between us.

He carries a tremendous amount of guilt and responsibility that was never his to pick up in the first place. And if he can blame himself for my choices and failures, then he is clearly not always right.

He also puts weight on my shoulders that doesn't belong to me. He says things like "We're not ready for intercourse" and blames my trust fund. He's implied many times that I am simply too young or incapable of knowing my own mind, when what he really means is *he's* not ready.

And while he just happened to be right about me not being ready in those earliest days, the simple truth is he can only decide what *he's* ready for. He doesn't get to decide what *I'm* ready for.

I can't regret a moment of the time it took to get me to where I am now. I learned so much about myself as a result of those experiences.

I'd have learned those lessons regardless of whether we'd been sleeping together. But the lesson, particularly on our wedding night, might have been more painful.

And I was drunk that night. Drunk and grieving my father, though he hadn't passed just yet. Taking every single other thing out of the equation, what kind of man sleeps with a woman under those circumstances? Not my husband, thank God.

If we'd slept together on our wedding night, how long would it have taken me to realize I was trying to win his affection and comfort my own grief through sex? I have no idea. But we didn't, and I didn't.

And I learned to recognize that insecurity in myself and squash the fuck out of it. Because I deserve better than that.

When it came to the gala, while I'd already started to learn to establish my boundaries, those boundaries weren't rock-solid yet. But I don't believe sex would have torn down the ones I'd already built, even for a minute. And I would have continued to get stronger, regardless of whether we were sleeping together.

Our wedding and the gala, and any of the other times James refused when I tried to coax him into intercourse, were never about my boundaries or my readiness.

I didn't understand that at first. I'd believed his words and not his eyes. And so I'd set about trying to lure him to me. To convince him I was ready. But it was never about me in the first place.

So I've backed off on my torment of the man. I don't tease him anymore. I don't walk around half naked. It was never my intention to actually torture him. I just wanted him to recognize that I was more than ready for that part of our lives.

In my mind, I'd built up graduating and moving home into not just a physical milestone in terms of location but a relationship milestone.

I'd move back after my degree, James would recognize my adulthood and independence, and boom! We'd be married in truth.

But it was never about my adulthood or my independence, no matter what he says. So instead of beginning a new phase of our married lives, it's just limbo.

I made decisions about my career and started working on a business plan. And I'm writing. Trying to build up a catalog for a series of lighthearted romance novels. I'm really excited about that.

But James and I? Nothing is happening there. We're in an incredibly painful holding pattern. And the only thing I can think to do is start pushing his buttons and see if I can get any reaction out of him that isn't a tight smile, a cool kiss on the cheek, and a "Whatever you want."

I'm done walking around half naked. Now I just want him to talk to me about his feelings. And if I thought enticing him into sex was hard, it was nothing on trying to get James Mellinger to say something—*anything*—real.

When I tell him I want to eat dinners in the kitchen most nights and cut back on our regular personal chef's hours, his eyebrows rise, and then he shrugs and says, "You can do whatever you want."

The next night, I make him sit at the kitchen island, then present him with his dinner.

He looks intrigued and pleased. "Is this beef stew?"

I shake out my napkin and pick up my spoon. "It is." I shove a cutting board holding a loaf of fresh Italian bread toward him. "Have some bread. It's good together."

"This isn't Carol's usual fare."

"That's because Carol didn't make it. I did."

He looks back down at the bowl, then at me. "You?"

I smirk because if anything calls for smirking, it's his dumbfounded expression. "I made the bread too. I told you I was learning to cook."

He takes a bite, and his eyes widen. "This is really good." He takes another bite. "Really, really good."

I shrug, but I'm pleased. "I know all kinds of crazy life skills now. Laundry, dishwashers, vacuum cleaners."

He frowns. "They aren't life skills necessary for you. You don't need to do those things."

"I'm aware. But cooking is fun for me. Especially since someone else does most of the cleanup. Besides, I like knowing I can take care of myself."

His expression is doubtful. It irritates me. But before I can address it, his phone dings. He pulls it out of his pocket, reads something with a frown, and spends the next twenty minutes taking distracted bites of his dinner while working on his phone.

When he finally puts it away, I say, "You work too much."

"Your father left big shoes to fill."

He says that all the time.

Time to push those buttons. I say, "Wearing someone else's shoes is a good way to give yourself blisters or fall flat on your face."

He pushes his bowl away. "What's your point?"

"My father trusted you and loved you. When you worked for him, did he micromanage you or trust you to do your own thing?"

I know the answer. My father always talked about finding the right person to do the job, then trusting them to do it. He was never afraid to defer to experts. It was a huge part of his success.

James just frowns.

"Do you honestly believe you're supposed to try to recreate my father or second-guess whether every choice you make is the same one he would have made? You're stressed out all the time about not letting my father down, but he isn't even here to let down. And I don't believe he'd have wanted that for you, even if he were."

He pushes away from the counter, rises, and brushes a kiss across my cheek before he heads for the door. "I'll be in my office."

"Hey, James," I say. When he pauses and looks at me, I say, "Still love you."

He frowns, gives a brief nod, then says "I still love you too."

J AMES LOSES HIS OWN father the next day. He texts me in the middle of the afternoon.

James: I'll be headed out of town for a few days.
Me: This is unexpected. Everything ok?
James: My father died. I have to go make the arrangements.
Me: I'm so sorry. Are you okay?
James: Of course.

James hasn't seen his father since he was seven years old. He has a handful of half-siblings through his father whom I've never met. Some of them, *James* has never met.

The fact that James is the only one willing to make the man's funeral arrangements says volumes about who he was. Though James rarely speaks of him, and never in more than monosyllabic grunts, it's clear the man was an asshole.

Me: I'll go with you.
James: No need.

No need to have your wife there to support you at your father's funeral.

Me: I want to go. I want to be there for you. I can hold your hand, and you can wiggle your earring if you need me to run defense.

James: Lol. Thanks. But I'm fine. I'm not broken up over his passing. He was a bastard.

Me: That almost makes it worse. It means you have to grieve the father he should have been. Let me come hold your hand.

James: He's not getting a funeral. I'm only going to check on my half-siblings. And to deal with paperwork. I'm taking Rebecca to handle that part. So I really don't need any help.

I take a second to absorb that body blow. His father died, and instead of leaning on me, he's taking Rebecca.

Oh, I know he's not cheating with her. James is nothing if not loyal. He looks at Rebecca like a piece of office equipment. To him, he may as well have said, "I'm taking my laptop." But reminding myself of that doesn't fix the pit of confused feelings churning inside me.

Me: I want to be there for you

James: I don't need that. I just need to know you're safe at home.

I don't text back, and after a few moments, he texts again.

James: Still love you.

I sigh and text back.

Me: Still love you.

He comes home after a few days looking drawn and tired. When he walks in the door, I wrap my arms around him and hold on. He puts his face in my hair and breathes, grounding himself in me.

Then he pushes away, smiles, and says, "Did your text say chicken pot pie for dinner?"

And so it continues. Days and weeks of it. James smiling tightly. James working constantly. James avoiding my eyes. He kisses me when I kiss him. But following my surgery, we've never gone back to the intimacy we established before it.

In early August, I decide to try a new tactic. But I plan to butter him up with Italian food first. When I present him with lasagna for dinner, his eyes practically roll back in his head with pleasure at his first bite. "That's it. Carol's fired. It's all Clarissa, all the time."

I laugh, but I feel a hum of pride inside.

Now for something completely different. "What would you say about the idea of a vacation?" I ask. He needs it. James is nothing if not stressed out right now. And time away together without the distraction of work is a luxury we've never had.

There's a hitch in his movements before he recovers. "Where do you want to go?"

I shrug. "It doesn't really matter. I just think it would be good to take some time away."

He nods, but his mouth is tight. "Are you sure you're up to traveling?"

That makes me laugh. "I'm fully recovered. I promise. Right as rain."

Again with the doubtful eyes. Then he opens his stupid mouth and says, "You should take Sydney with you. Tequila Bronwyn is a menace. The two of them can balance each other out."

I set down my fork and push away from the counter. My feelings are hurt. Maybe when I analyze it all later, I'll decide I'm overreacting. That this isn't another rejection.

But I am *tired* of him sending me away with other people.

He watches me with a frown as I clear my place setting with jerky movements.

When I finish, I see him still watching me, wary-eyed, but also... torn. Like he'd give me what I wanted if he only knew what that was.

He swivels his seat toward me as I approach. So I scooch right up to him, in between the V of his thighs. I sigh inwardly at the sensation of just being close to James. I'm touch-starved right now. And even the heat from his body and the smell of his cologne are enough to make me want to just fall into him and hang on.

At my approach, James somehow tenses and relaxes at the same time.

He brings his hands under my shirt to rest against the bare skin of my waist. And just that—just his hands—stirs the most intense yearning inside me. It's not just a longing for sex; it's the need to feel close. To love him and be loved.

I cup his face and kiss him. He hesitates for long moments, not kissing me back but actively receiving mine. His hands clench tight against my skin. And when I start to pull away, he hauls me back against him, lifts one of his hands to wrap around the back of my skull, and devours me.

29

Only Love Can Hurt Like This

CLARISSA

I CLUTCH AT HIS shoulders as he drags me closer. His hands are moving now, not content to remain where they started. He lifts me so I'm straddling him, dragging my T-shirt over my head and tossing it to the floor. Then his mouth is back on mine.

I can taste the wine he was drinking with dinner. The spice of his cologne and the clean, masculine scent of his shampoo fill my senses.

He showered after working out, so he's dressed in a gray T-shirt and black track pants. I slide my hands down and then up under his shirt, pressing against the hot silk of his skin. I drag my palms up, reveling in the differences between us. The hardness of him. The way that line of hair below his belly button *beckons* me.

James has my bra off before I even realize what he's doing. Then his mouth is on my breast, teasing and tormenting. I prop myself up by standing on the rung of the kitchen stool so I can reach between us and palm his cock through his track pants. Even through the fabric, I can feel his length, hot and thick, and I want it anywhere and any way I can have it.

"Pull these down," I say, trying to tug at his waistband.

He shudders and stiffens, freezing. He's fighting with himself. I can see it.

So I don't say a word. I don't move. I wait for his decision patiently, quietly, as if this moment doesn't mean everything.

He stands, holding me up by my ass. Then he turns and, using one arm to shove the remainder of our meal aside, lays me down on the counter. My eyes flare with giddy arousal, and I burst out in a surprised peal of laughter when he drags my shorts and panties down my legs, *smells* my panties, and then stuffs them in his pocket.

But James doesn't smile back. His expression is dead serious when he yanks his pants down, revealing his rock-hard cock. The head is almost purple, a bead of clear liquid pearling at the tip.

I reach for him, but he takes my hand and sucks my fingers into his mouth. And my heart sinks, even as the swirl of his tongue ramps up my arousal. Because I know what this is. It's just a variation—a sexy variation, but still, it's the same thing we'd already been doing before my surgery.

He guides my fingers to my own pussy, then jacks his cock over me. And I can't do it. I don't want to touch myself when he's right here.

So I sit up and grab fistfuls of his T-shirt, pulling him closer. He props one hand on the counter while he grips his cock with the other and stops moving. He stands there, breathing hard, blue eyes on fire.

I move my hands to his face, pulling his mouth toward mine. "No, it's okay. Keep going. We don't have to.... Just kiss me. I just need you to kiss me."

He does. He stands between my spread thighs and kisses me with a raw carnality that both owns and cherishes while he pumps his own cock, never, ever letting it touch my body. He comes on my stomach and breasts with a grunt, and I mutter against his mouth, over and over, "I love you. I love you. I love you."

When he's finished, he stays there, his forehead pressed against mine, his chest rising and falling like bellows as his semen dries on my skin. Finally, he draws back, pulls up his pants, and moves to the kitchen sink. He returns in moments with a warm, wet paper towel and begins to wipe me clean.

I try to catch his eyes, but he won't meet my gaze. "Hey," I say. "What's wrong?"

He grimaces. "I shouldn't have done that to you."

Whoa. *Whoa*. Now he's going to backtrack on masturbating too?

"Yes, you should have. We both wanted it, so why shouldn't you?"

"Did we? Because you didn't get a damn thing out of that. It was just me being selfish."

"I got being close to you out of it."

"Yeah. Okay." He picks up my T-shirt and shorts and hands them to me. I've barely gotten my shirt over my head when he's headed for the door. "I have some work I need to get to in my office," he says.

"James...."

He stops with a white-knuckled grip on the doorframe. He doesn't turn his head back when he asks, "Yes?"

"The vacation. I want to go somewhere with *you*. We've never done that. We never even took a honeymoon." Of course we didn't. When would there have been an appropriate time for that?

After a beat, he says, "We can do that. Any requests?"

I shrug. "Anywhere you want is fine. Somewhere you'll have fun. Surprise me."

He raps the doorframe with a double tap of his knuckles. And then he's gone.

JAMES BECOMES EVEN MORE standoffish after that night in the kitchen.

He's never unkind. If I reach for his hand, he holds it for a few brief moments, then kisses my knuckles and finds a reason to drop it. If I kiss him, he keeps his hands at his sides, gently returns my kiss, then hurries away. And he always, *always* reminds me he loves me.

Then he surprises me with a trip to Hawaii.

It's a vacation, not a honeymoon. Not that I'd ever had any confusion there. James books us a suite with two bedrooms, and at first, this trip feels like it's going to be more of the same cold kindness.

However, his veneer begins to crack on the very first day when I ask him to apply sunscreen to my back. He's efficient about it. But I've got pale, freckled skin. I need a lot of sunscreen, and it has to be reapplied often. The very act of touching me repeatedly seems to break down some wall inside him. It's as though every time he touches me and nothing horrible happens, he gets a little more comfortable doing so the next time.

But the day James sees me slip-slapping my way across the deck in snorkel gear is the day the knot in my chest finally begins to unwind.

Those blue eyes of his sparkle, and his grin is real.

I ALMOST DO

When we're preparing to do a tandem zipline, he laughs and pats my butt when I clutch him like a spider monkey. And when I turn to him from our seats in the helicopter to point out something in excitement, he smiles and reaches to hold my hand.

By the end of our vacation, he no longer rushes through applying my sunscreen and lets me do the same for him. He puts his arm around me or his hand on my back again. He drops random kisses on my forehead and temple again. When he catches me rubbing my lip, he takes over and does it for me.

His smiles come easier, his shoulders are relaxed, and, while he's with me, he doesn't answer a single work email.

He's almost back to the James from before my health crisis.

And then we're home, and he's tan and, yes, working a lot, but he's still smiling easier. And that knot I carry loosens a little more.

It's as though our vacation worked as some kind of mental reset button for him. We're not intimate with each other. We're not even intimate *near* each other. But the trip still seems to have been a change for the better for him, and it gives me hope.

The next week, he tells me he's taking me to a trendy club for my twenty-second birthday. I haven't seen that particular expression on his face in a long time. Part adult calculation and part mischievous boy. It says he's up to something. And it fills me with hopeful excitement.

When we arrive, the VIP lounge is full of my friends, both the New Yorkers and the Pennsylvania crowd, who road-tripped here to surprise me.

"Somebody has to keep Tequila Bronwyn in check," James says about Sydney's invitation. He can be as grumpy as he wants. He doesn't fool me. He loves my friends.

Bronwyn makes me wear a tiara and a hot pink pageant sash that says "Birthday Girl" on it. We didn't really celebrate my twenty-first the way a lot of people do—Bronwyn was out of town, and Sydney wasn't twenty-one yet—so I'm honestly ridiculously happy and surprised by the whole thing this year.

James organizing this feels significant to me. I can't help but feel it's a sign he's reconsidering his twenty-fifth-birthday timeline.

I am a twenty-two-year-old college graduate. No one in his right mind would still consider me a child or immature. And I have access to plenty of my own assets, even if he does still control the majority.

James gets absolutely hammered. And not the fun hammered. The brooding, "sitting in a corner throwing back bourbon like it's water" hammered.

After a while, I leave my girls—and the guys who have flocked around them—on the dance floor, flag down some water from the waitstaff, and sidle up to James. I pluck his tumbler from his hand, replacing it with water. "Have some," I say. "Someone once told me water and moderation were the key to drinking alcohol."

He looks up at me with bleary eyes, then pulls me down onto his lap. "You," he slurs against my temple, "are so smart. You're so hot and smart. And hot."

My lips quirk, and I nod to the water. "Drink."

He chugs the water, throwing it back like he's at a kegger. Then he slams the bottle onto the tabletop and says, "I want to fuck you."

Joy. Relief. Excitement. All of it bubbles up inside me like a geyser. I knew tonight was special. I'd been almost afraid to hope. But some part of me knew it was coming. And, God, I've waited so long, but for this moment, every bit of it was worth it. I wish he hadn't felt like he needed to get drunk to tell me, because he didn't have anything to be nervous about. Of course, the answer is ye—

He laughs, low and bitter. "I'm not *going* to fuck you. I'm going to fuck my own hand." He gives a slow blink, then holds up his hand and looks at it with disgust. "Going to close my eyes, remember what you taste like, fuck my hand, and pretend it's you."

What? This isn't— "You can fuck me. When you're sober, we can make love any time you want."

"I'm not defiling Marcus's daughter," he says. "He *trusted* me with his baby."

I frown as something like horror twists in my gut. "Making love with me isn't defiling me. And I'm nobody's baby."

"You're my respon-sability," he slurs. "I promised. You need me to take care of you and protect you. Especially from me. That's my job, and I'm shit at it."

"No," I bite out, "I don't. I am not your responsibility."

His brows are lowered in an exaggerated frown, and he bobs his head in a repetitive nod. "You are. You're my own little baby bird."

He pats my head. *Pats my fucking head*I jerk away from his hand and stand up. "I'm not a baby bird."

He shrugs drunkenly. Sadly. "You'll always be my baby bird."

"I thought tonight was… I thought you were going to tell me you realized that twenty-two was… *why* were you so excited about tonight?"

He looks at me blearily, grouchy and slow to understand. "It was a surprise party. Thought you'd be happy to see your friends."

30

Hurts Like Hell

CLARISSA

THE NEXT AFTERNOON, JAMES is sitting at the kitchen counter with a cup of coffee and nursing a hangover. I pass him a plate with peanut butter toast, then hand him a bottle of Advil and a glass of water. He grunts his thanks.

Then I say, "I'm moving to the house in the Hamptons."

His face shows first surprise, then slowly dawning horror. "What? Why? You need to be here."

I sigh in defeat. "What's the point? We aren't married, James. Not really. You don't see me as your wife—"

"Of course, you're my wife," he says, irritated.

"On paper, not in practice."

He rubs his forehead, then pinches the bridge of his nose. Pushing away from the counter, he stands there in the kitchen, looking stressed and exhausted. "This is about sex, then. We're not married because we're not fucking?"

I shake my head, but he nods his, as if he were expecting this conversation all along. As if the events of the night before were already front and center in his mind.

He closes his eyes in a long blink, and when he opens them, he says, "If you want sex, you can have it."

I stare at him, trying to remember the words I rehearsed for this moment. They're all gone. All my cool, collected arguments and evidence. Poof. On the wind.

If I hadn't heard the words he said last night when he was trashed on bourbon, I'd throw myself in his arms right now and pretend this is enough.

Instead, my gut churns with unexpected anger.

"How incredibly romantic, James. Thank you for that."

He scrubs at his face with his hands and then looks up at me with bleary eyes. "I love you. I *love* you. So much it actually hurts to stay away from you. That's not hyperbole. I feel it right here." He pounds his chest with his fist, and I know what he's saying, because the hollow aching he feels is the same one I feel. "Living with you like this is impossible. I'm not doing you a favor by agreeing to it. I'm giving in to what I want to do."

"But you'll feel guilty for doing it," I say. "You'll make love to me, then lie there and feel like you defiled me or hurt me by having sex with me."

He doesn't say a word.

I move closer to him and put my hands on his face. "You recognize that's messed-up, right? The way you see me is not healthy."

He holds my wrists and pulls my hands down to his chest. He still doesn't say a word.

He's going to make me say it.

"You have some emotional work to do. You have to untangle all this crap you have mixed up in your head about my dad, and what you owe him, and this guilt you have about me. I don't know where it comes from, but you need to figure it out and sort it if we're ever going to be together as man and wife."

He steps back and shakes his head. "That's ridiculous. Your father was a good man. I'm just trying to do what he would want me to do."

"Why? I am your wife! Why would you care more about what my father may or may not have wanted than what you and I have together right now? Besides, I can tell you, my dad would have just looked the other way and pretended he didn't know I slept with my own husband, the way pretty much every other dad of an adult woman does."

"You don't know that. You said yourself he sheltered you before we were married."

I wave my hand in the air. "It doesn't matter. If my father did object to a woman having sex with her husband, so what? It's not his choice. It's yours and mine. I'm an adult. I don't need a guardian. If you can't recognize that when I'm twenty-two years old, you never will."

"So it's about the money. You want control of the rest of your money."

I scream, "*Goddammit,* it's not about the *fucking* money." I step back and take a deep breath. When I'm ready to speak more calmly, I say, "It's about how you see me. I'm not your partner. You want to take care of me, but when I try to do the same for you, you tell me that's not my job."

"I don't—"

"You don't need me. That's my point." I shake my head. "I want a husband, not a father who's hell-bent on protecting me. You don't get to make my choices for me, or decide what's good for me or what's not good for me. You don't get to beat yourself up over my choices, as if I'm a toddler you allowed to go to bed without brushing her teeth."

I cross to the french doors to look out at the pretty little patio and lawn. All sheltered and protected and cozy, hidden by a fence and trying to pretend the city isn't looming over it.

"My dad used to eat breakfast with my mother out there." I nod toward the patio. "In the summer. He never left for work without kissing her goodbye."

I turn to James. He watches me, bleeding tension and frustration.

"Did you know my mother was twenty when I was born?"

He blinks rapidly. This is new information to him. I've thrown him off, disturbed him.

I nod. "My mother died at twenty-four years old. How old was your mother?"

James flinches, and I'm sorry for it. But I don't stop. "Twenty-five isn't a magic number where I'm suddenly an adult who makes adult choices. Twenty-five doesn't suddenly make us able to have an equal relationship because you no longer happen to be managing some investments for me."

"The cyst wasn't cancerous. You're fine." His words are reassuring, but his tone is panicked.

I frown. "You're not listening to me. I'm not telling you I'm going to die young. I'm telling you I don't want to wait to live. Nothing extraordinary happens on my twenty-fifth birthday besides the fact that I'll manage some investments, which I'll probably continue to consult you about anyway. We're wasting the time we have with unnecessary guilt."

James reaches out to hold me, but I back away. Because that would be too easy. I could let him wrap me in his arms and soothe me, and then tomorrow absolutely nothing will have changed.

He shakes his head. "It doesn't matter. We can start sleeping together now. We'll share a bedroom now."

"And are you happy about that? Because, I have to be honest, you don't look happy."

He says nothing.

"If I stay, could we talk about this? If not me, then a professional maybe?" I hold my breath, waiting. Hopeful. I can't bear to see him so unhappy.

"Jesus Christ, I don't need a therapist. I'm fine. We're fine," he spits.

I close my eyes. And I rest there in the dark, with my heart in my fist. When I open my eyes, James's fly wide, and he gives a violent shake of his head.

"I'm leaving," I say, "and you're going to work through your issues. Or you're not. That's up to you."

"You can't," he says, head still shaking. "You've never lived alone. You'd be on your own out there."

"I am."

His brows are furrowed, and his jaw is tight. His blue eyes burn me from beneath a thunderous scowl. "Don't you fucking do this."

The words are a warning. But this is James; he'd never make me stay.

I'm scaring him right now. I'm hurting him. And I don't ever, ever want to do that. I want to fix everything. Smile and say I'm happy with whatever he thinks is best.

But I can't.

If he won't get help, there's no version where I stay and we don't hurt.

My heart is bleeding through my fingers. I tore it out of my chest all by myself. "I still love you. I'll always love you. I promise," I say.

The movers arrive the next day. I don't take much, really—mostly just clothing and personal items. I take every present James ever gave

I ALMOST DO

me, except Mr. Flootlepus. I leave him with James. He loves that cat, and I can't bear to see him alone.

At the front door, James stops me as I'm about to go. "Text me when you get there."

I've thought about this. A lot. "I don't think that's a good idea. We'll keep in touch on an as-needed basis for a while."

"What the fuck, Clarissa?" The words are almost a whisper.

I don't answer, I just lean up to kiss his cheek. And then I go.

31

If the World Was Ending

Clarissa

I miss James. It's a dull, aching pain that never leaves. Sometimes it spills over into agony, and for a while, I can't breathe.

But I carry on. I've had lots of practice leaving him. What I haven't had is practice living without him.

Every day, I almost text him. Sometimes about something silly. Sometimes something serious. It's almost muscle memory at this point. I'll catch myself with my phone in my hands and his contact pulled up before it registers that I'm supposed to be giving him space.

I hope time and distance will allow him to separate the Clarissa he loves from the Clarissa he feels responsible for.

He tries to text every few days at first, but I ask him to give me more time. So we settle into a monthly check-in. Every month, he texts.

James: Do you need anything?

Me: Nope. I'm good. Do you need anything?

James: I'm good. Still love you.

And my heart seizes in my chest, my eyes fill with tears, and I text back, **Still love you too.**

On our anniversary, he has a package delivered. It's a twelve-pack of bottled water and a case of Clase Azul tequila. The bottles are gorgeous. Hand painted. Out of curiosity, I google the collection and realize my husband just sent me $450,000 worth of tequila. Because of course he did.

I call Bronwyn. We make margaritas, spill our guts to each other, and cry in our shaved ice.

I drunk text him that night.

Me: Thanks u for my pressed

James: You're welcome. You're not drinking alone, are you?

Me: Nah. Brown is spending the night

James: Good. Happy anniversary, sweet girl.

Me: Happy anniversary. I still love you.

James: I still love you too.

I KEEP WORKING ON my novels. I also contact James about accessing a lump sum of my inheritance well above my $20,000 daily allowance.

James: That's a lot of money.

Me: Check your inbox for my business plan. Get back to me with any questions you may have.

James texts me a couple hours later. He has a few questions, for which, thankfully, I have the answers. Then he replies, **Looks solid. I'm impressed.**

There is an adage that it takes money to make money. I know for a fact that I wouldn't have been able to start my business without it—not on the scale I have planned, anyway.

I'm not about to pretend this thing is about pulling myself up by my bootstraps. It's not. I was born already pulled up. Way, way up.

I'm able to accomplish what I do so quickly partially because I dump cash into it, and partially because I was raised by Marcus Harcourt, who talked to me about scent profiles, and public image, and management, and a hundred other little things that give me a leg up in simply understanding what things can drive success.

I've known I wanted to do this for the last two years, so I geared as many of my college courses around my future plans as I could at the time. But classroom experience is just not comparable to actually working with real money, real resources, and real people. It's more than a little terrifying, and I take ruthless advantage of advice from my father's business connections.

I hire a small, experienced staff and pay the necessary consultants. Then I create an online resource connecting independent authors with vetted professionals, like editors, writing coaches, cover designers, marketing experts, etc. We have everything from paid education resources to basic referral services to lots and lots of free articles and YouTube education videos.

At its heart, my business is about connecting people with each other. It's a niche. But it's one I love.

In the beginning, I work hours like what James would call "a Victorian coal miner." But it's intensely satisfying. The business is still growing and expanding, but it's off to a healthy start.

Christmas sucks. Until James texts, and it doesn't.

James: Merry Christmas. I miss you.

Me: I miss you too. What are you up to today?

He sends a pic of Mr. Snickelputz sleeping on a red stocking with what appears to be a stuffed felt mouse clutched in his paws.

James: Watching the cat turn into an absolute demon with a catnip-stuffed mouse until he passes out. That's it. Might get some work done in the home office later.

Me: Did you get my present?

James: Yes. Thank you.

Me: What did you think?

James: I didn't open it yet. I was saving it until we texted. Did you like your present?

I hit the FaceTime button. James picks up immediately, a smile on his face. "Look at you, gorgeous."

I smile back, the pang in my chest painful at the sight of him. "Merry Christmas."

I hold up the unopened package he sent me. "I didn't open the present you sent yet either. Do you want to—"

It belatedly occurs to me this might be a bad idea. This is putting a lot of pressure on the man. It also might make things awkward if he thinks this is me trying to tell him I'm ready to come home. Because we're definitely not there yet. I just miss him so much. And it's Christmas.

James shuffles around a bit on his end, and I get a view of the ceiling of his apartment. Then he's back with a small smile on his face, holding up the package I sent. "So, how do we do this? One at a time or together?"

"Umm, can I go first and you open yours second?" If his reaction to my gift doesn't go well, then we won't have to awkwardly hang out on FaceTime while I open his gift afterward.

He nods, clears his throat, then says, "Go ahead. Just—" He scratches his head and looks a little sheepish. "It's probably stupid. It was a lot harder than I thought it would be. I had to hire someone to teach me how to do it. And, yeah—"

"Now, I'm incredibly intrigued," I say. I pick up the small box and give it a little shake near my ear. Then I prop up my phone and pull off the wrapping.

Inside is a pretty wooden box, and inside the box is a classy crystal USB. I hold it up between my fingers and shoot him a questioning look. "Photos?"

He shakes his head, and there's a splash of color on his cheekbones. "Audio files. There are five novellas on there. Do you remember I offered to read for you? But then...."

Ah, yes. Then he'd never needed to because we'd started having phone sex when we were apart and mutual masturbation sessions when we were together instead. His slippery slope and all that.

"Anyway," he says, scratching his neck, "I thought you might still like... but if it's stupid, you don't have to...."

I clutch the USB against my chest, and I know my eyes are shining. "James. I *love* it. It's the best gift I've ever received in my life. I can't wait to listen."

He shrugs and looks away, but there's a small smile on his face. "Good."

He holds up the gift I sent. It's larger and heavier than his. "Shall I?"

I nod, and now I'm the one who's nervous.

James has always encouraged my writing, always reading my projects and raving about them. He's the one who gave me the initial confidence boost to allow myself to write the types of things I enjoy reading. And he never scoffed that it wasn't literary enough or that my stories were silly pulp fiction romance, even though they are.

He props the phone against something on the coffee table so he can use both hands, sits down on the floor in front of the sofa, and unwraps the book I sent, holding it up with a questioning look on his face.

"Good book?" he asks. "I haven't read this author before."

"I hope it's good," I say, rubbing my lip with my thumb. "And you've definitely read this author. That's my pen name."

His eyes grow wide. Then he looks down at the trade-size paperback in his hands. It has a matte cover, with gloss title text on a pale blue background. A single purple gerbera daisy, its stem long and green, curls up the right edge, with the text *Waiting for Sunshine* in magenta block text to the left of it. The edges are deckled, and it's just so pretty.

James's smile is incandescent. "You did it."

I nod, briefly pulling my sweater up over my nose and mouth, and smile. Dropping the sweater, I say, "I did. The release is scheduled for next month. And there are two more in the series coming after that."

He looks down at the book again, reading the back blurb. "Did you sign it for me? You better have signed it," he says. "This will be worth a lot of money someday."

I laugh because he's so ridiculous, but I'm inordinately pleased by his reaction. "Maybe you should look and see."

He flips the book open and grins at my inscription that reads "Yes, James, I signed it for you." Then he begins to page through the beginning. I can tell the moment he finds the dedication: "For James. Still and Always. I promise."

He freezes solid, a dent between his eyebrows. He blinks rapidly, swallows, and his lips press tight. He looks back at me through the camera lens. "I love you too. God, I hope you know how much I love you."

My chin wobbles, and I can't speak for a moment. I manage a tight nod.

He sets the book on his lap. "I know why you left. I understand," he says. "I was fucked-up. I still am. But I took your advice. I'm talking to someone about... everything. I'm not where I need to be. I can't talk about it yet. But I'm working on it. I wanted you to know that."

My voice is barely a whisper, but I manage to say, "I'm glad."

I hear the cat yowl in the background and the sound of something crashing to the floor. The tense moment between us is broken as James looks off-camera. "He's awake and losing his mind over the catnip again," he says.

"It sounds like you need to go take care of whatever he broke," I say.

He nods. "Yes."

I hold up my USB. "Thank you for this. I'll be listening as soon as we hang up."

He holds up my book. "No office for me today after all. I can't wait to read it."

"Merry Christmas, James."

"Merry Christmas, sweet girl."

32

I Will Be

JAMES

Previously in September

THE MIDDLE-AGED WOMAN WITH the blonde, feathery hair and practical shoes ushers me into her office and indicates the sofa and chairs placed comfortably in the corner.

"Have a seat anywhere you like."

I choose a chair, and she makes herself comfortable in another one, set a comfortable distance away, with the length of a small coffee table between us. She's close enough for conversation but not so close as to encroach on my personal bubble. Right now, my bubble is huge.

Dr. Carlson gives me a small smile and says, "I'm pleased to meet you, James. What brings you to my office today?"

I'm leaning forward in the armchair, both feet planted firmly on the floor, hands on my thighs. I probably look ready to bolt. So I take a few breaths in through my nose, blow them out through my mouth. I straighten my spine and let my hands rest on the arms of the chair.

I use my boardroom voice and say, "I want to remind you that our conversation is confidential. None of what I say here leaves this room."

She doesn't look intimidated by me or the tone of my voice at all. She just nods and continues with her reassuring smile, some new lines crinkling around her eyes behind the clear plastic frames of her glasses.

"You have my word. It's my professional responsibility, but also something I believe in implicitly."

I grunt and nod, then say, "I'm here because my wife thinks I need a therapist."

"What do you think?"

"I think I hate therapists, but she's not coming home until I work my *issues* out. So here I am."

She looks down at the reMarkable tablet in her hand, makes a brief notation. "What do you believe you need to work out?"

"I can't have sex with her without feeling guilty about it."

"I see. That must be difficult for you."

I give a sarcastic bark of laughter. "You could say that."

"Have you always felt guilty about sex, or is it a new development?"

I laugh, but I don't find a damn thing funny. "Always. There were a few women before my wife, though not... relationships. But Clarissa is different."

She makes another note, then says, "How is Clarissa different?"

"I made a promise to her father to protect her and keep her safe. It feels like a violation of trust."

"What do you feel as though you need to protect your wife from?"

I lean back against the chair. "Everything."

Early October

"I'm thinking about calling these appointments quits," I say.

"Why is that?"

"Because I feel *worse*. You're not helping me. This is exactly what happened last time. Talking about this shit is stirring it all up inside. It used to sit there under the surface. Now I'm thinking about it all the time. I'm fucking falling apart."

"Explain what you mean by falling apart," she says.

I give her an incredulous look. "I'm feeling this stuff. I'm thinking about it constantly."

She sits quietly and allows me to collect myself, then asks, "How are you feeling right now?"

"Angry. Guilty. Sad... afraid," I say.

"Any time you need to take a moment for your breathing exercises, go ahead and do that."

I shoot her an acidic look. "I don't need your permission."

She agrees. "No you don't."

After a moment of silence, she says, "Those feelings—anger, guilt, sadness, fear—they sound a lot like the feelings you mentioned regarding your friend Marcus's death. Do they feel similar?"

Late October

"Tell me about your mother's death," Dr. Carlson says.

"Is this part necessary?" I ask.

"Usually, I would say no. Our immediate goal is to focus on the present and the situations that are currently distressing to you. But intrusive thoughts of the past are something you've said are a current problem, so you may find it helpful."

I swallow, and she continues. "You decide what you're willing to discuss, James. I'm not here to badger you, only guide you. You've mentioned your guilt and the need to protect Clarissa feel similar to the way you feel about your mother. Understanding what happened there can clarify those emotions for you."

In for a penny, in for a pound. "When I was seven, I let my father murder my mother," I say.

"You *let* him? Do you feel his actions were your responsibility?"

"I was capable of stopping him. If I'd fought for her sooner, I could have. He beat us all the time. I don't remember anything about that time except having the shit beaten out of us or worrying about the next time we'd have the shit beaten out of us."

"That's rough," she says.

I shrug. "It's over now." Except it isn't. I relive it every day.

"Why do you believe you were capable of stopping him from hurting your mother?"

"The night he killed her, I tried to kill him. He was... hurting her. In the kitchen."

I stop for a moment, then force myself to say it, my voice as flat and unemotional as I can make it. "He was strangling her and raping her. I stabbed him with a steak knife."

I roll my eyes to the ceiling, then just sit there, trying to get the tension to leave my shoulders and my gut.

Dr. Carlson gives me a moment, patient as she waits.

"I didn't know what I was doing. I just hit him in the back with it. I thought it would be like a movie. That he'd go straight down, and Mom and I would run away. But I was too late. She was already dead, and that asshole survived."

November

"I'M NOT A SOLDIER or a cop. I don't have hallucinations or forget where I am."

"The vast majority of people who deal with PTSD don't experience those things. It can occur after any traumatic event: a car accident, a medical emergency.... Nearly 7 percent of people in this country will have to contend with it at some point in their lives. For many people, it manifests as heightened anxiety. They're always on guard, and many develop unhealthy coping mechanisms."

"I don't have unhealthy coping mechanisms," I say. *Shit, I sound defensive.*

"None?"

I shrug. "I avoid things, I guess."

"Complex PTSD can occur as a result of a series of traumatic events over time or a prolonged event. The symptoms can be—"

"I don't have *symptoms* of anything."

"You mentioned difficulty sleeping."

I grunt.

"You feel sick when something triggers a memory?"

I shrug, then nod.

"You believe the world is a dangerous place, and you're in a constant state of hypervigilance?"

I shake my head. "That's not a symptom. That's just life."

She tilts her head slightly, her expression gentle. "Not for everyone, James. Most people don't think of their daily activities as inherently dangerous."

Some part of me *knows* that, but I can't stop thinking of what could happen. To Clarissa. To me.

"You said you avoid sex with your wife because it causes you to feel guilty and ashamed. It triggers memories of your mother's abuse and murder?"

I let out a long breath before I admit, "I'm afraid of becoming him."

Early December

"He died in prison last summer, and I went to make the arrangements," I say.

Dr. Carlson nods at me encouragingly, so I go on. "I had to see he was dead. I thought if I saw his body, I could put him behind me."

"But it didn't work out that way?"

"Fuck no. That dead man? He didn't look anything like Lee Willis. He was an old, beaten-down, pathetic piece of shit. Do you know who does look like Lee Willis?"

"And yet you're nothing like him."

I look down at the back of my right hand. The knuckles aren't swollen or torn. I'm almost surprised by that. "My grandmother helped me change my name legally when I was fourteen. Before that, I had to listen to teachers and social workers and doctors call me by that bastard's name. I was a 'junior.'"

Something flares in Dr. Carlson's eyes so briefly I almost don't catch it before her professional mask falls back into place. She dips her chin. "How did you decide on your name?"

My lips quirk for the first time today. "My mother's maiden name was Mellinger. And my grandmother had a bunch of James Bond DVDs. I liked James Bond. Still do. He wore a suit. He had money and power. He was the good guy, and I guess I thought that wasn't a bad blueprint."

January

"This is taking too long," I say. "I don't understand why I can't just stop these thoughts. Why do I have to keep catching myself and reframing them? If I know what's real and reasonable, why does my brain keep trying to sabotage me."

It's not a question. I know the answer. It's a lifetime of rutted road that needs smoothing out. It doesn't happen in a few weeks or even a few months.

"You're frustrated with your progress," Dr. Carlson says.

I just give her the no shit look.

"Last week, you seemed pleased with your progress. What's changed?"

"Clarissa is leaving me. I mean, she's already not living with me, you know that. But she always loved me. I always knew she was waiting for me to—" I stop talking because I can't breathe.

"Did she tell you she wasn't waiting anymore?"

"No."

"Did she tell you she doesn't love you anymore?"

"No. Every week she tells me she still loves me. Clarissa is kind. You don't understand. She wouldn't tell me she didn't love me anymore while I was in the middle of fucking therapy."

"Why do you believe she's planning to leave you?"

"Over the last few months, she's been pulling away financially. She sent back the car I gave her and told me to remove her as an insured driver. I received a notification from our health insurance company that she's no longer on our policy as my dependent. I think she's using her own company insurance. She's got her own cell phone account now."

"Did you ask her why she's done those things?"

"She said she doesn't want me taking care of her."

February

"**I**'M TELLING HER I'M ready."

Dr. Carlson gives me her encouraging smile. "That's exciting."

"No it isn't."

She tilts her head slightly, raises her eyebrows. "You've come a long way, James. You've worked really hard."

I shrug, and she continues. "You told me you wanted to have a healthy relationship with your wife. Have you changed your mind?"

I snort in disbelief. "You know I haven't."

"But you're not happy about telling her about your progress?"

"I'm not going to pressure her into coming back to me," I say. "I don't know how to explain that I'm ready to try without also making it sound like I expect it from her."

"You're a very accomplished businessman. You have a lot of experience with negotiations. Could you come at it from that perspective?"

"I don't want to. I know how to manipulate people and pressure people to get what I want, yes. But that's the last thing I want to do here. I want to be an equal partner with her."

Dr. Carlson smiles. "That's lovely. That's a very healthy attitude in a marriage."

"Doesn't fix my problem," I say. "As soon as I start talking, she's going to hear the desperation in my voice. She's going to hear the words I don't say."

"That just sounds like honesty to me. Who are you trying to protect by withholding your feelings from her?"

"Goddammit," I mutter.

"Do you think Clarissa should be given all the facts so she can make her own informed choice about your relationship?"

"Yes," I admit.

Dr. Carlson nods.

"I was thinking of writing her a letter," I say.

"That could work."

I give a bark of laughter. "Now the hard part. I can see it now: 'Dear Clarissa, I'm completely ready to fuck your brains out, and I promise to try not to sink into a pit of self-recrimination if you skip your dental hygienist appointment.'"

Dr. Carlson snorts and briefly covers her eyes with her hand before she looks up with a grin and says, "It's a start, James. A very good start."

33

Roots

JAMES

I sent the letter and waited for a call that never came. She'd have received it yesterday. I think.

It's possible the mail was delayed. Her delivery time is first thing in the morning. So she could still call today, but I'd have expected it a couple of hours ago in that case.

I thought the letter was the best way to know I didn't forget to tell her anything. I also thought a letter would give her time to process what she read without the pressure of me hovering over her.

Now I'm second-guessing that choice.

"Worst-Case"—she doesn't call at all. She's already decided she's done, and this is her cue to exit stage left without feeling guilty about it. Maybe she'll write me her own letter and include divorce papers with it. Maybe she'll just show up one day with a "Glad to hear you're doing better. Sign these papers, and we'll both put this all behind us."

I came into the office early today, thinking it would keep my mind off Clarissa while I wait to hear from her. I've been here since 5:30 a.m. and haven't even bothered to put my tie on yet.

My assistant popped her head in at nine. Then she promptly popped her head back out. She knows I'm about to go on a tear just by looking at my face. I pull up my emails regarding an acquisition in Tokyo and scowl at what I see.

Fucking incompetent....

I drum my fingers on my desk, then throw on the headset I use when I'll be on the phone for any length of time. I hit the intercom and swivel around to glare out at the gray skies and grayer skyline. "Have you made those calls to Lofton yet?"

There's a pause, and then her voice comes through my headset. "Not yet. It's the middle of the night in his time zone."

I grunt. "If he'd done his job yesterday, we wouldn't need to interrupt his beauty sleep now. Call him," I snap.

"Of course. Um, your *wife* is here to see you. In the office. Right—"

I turn back toward the door. And there she is.

"I see that," I manage to choke out. "No interruptions."

I very methodically remove the headset, place it on my desk, and thread my hands together in a single fist.

This is my "Worst-Case" scenario, then. She didn't call. She showed up here, unannounced, looking nervous and with a briefcase over her shoulder. I've never seen Clarissa carry a *briefcase* in her life.

The building may boast her maiden name on the side of it, but she's never even been inside my office before today. She's never been to my apartment either.

Our marriage wasn't normal. She said that to me over and over again. I ignored it, and now it's over.

She closes the door and takes off her jacket, laying it over the back of one of my guest chairs. Then she clears her throat, smooths down nonexistent wrinkles in her skirt, and plays with the lock on the briefcase.

The lock. Because God forbid the press get hold of her divorce petition before my own lawyers have a look at it.

Fuck that. My lawyers aren't going to look at it. I'll sign whatever she wants me to. I won't fight her on anything. Then I'll come up with a plan to win my wife back.

She pulls a manila folder from the briefcase and gives me a small, shaky smile.

I don't smile back. I can't. I'll give her what she wants. God knows she deserves to be happy. But I can't smile at her when she hands me divorce papers. I'm not that big of a person.

I stand and drink her in. She's stunning. She always shakes her head a little when I tell her that. But she's the most beautiful woman I've ever known.

Though I can tell she tried to tame her auburn curls, the wind had its way with her outside. Her lashes are a sooty frame for those gorgeous eyes of hers. Her lips are a natural rose—the exact same color as her nipples. And her freckles... I want to taste every one.

I let my gaze travel down her body. Over those slim curves. She's wearing a silk blouse and a gray pencil skirt, which are not her usual style, and ruby boots that definitely are.

Her breath catches, and I drag my eyes back up to find her expression stricken. The realization that she might be feeling intimidated by me makes me ill.

I wait for her to speak, but she says nothing. So I move to the front of my desk, sit on the edge, and beckon her closer. I hope my more casual stance will relax her a little.

I try again to smile, but I can't. I'm physically incapable of it.

She comes closer… closer… until she stops within touching distance. She's not maintaining a "casual acquaintance" personal distance of two to four feet. Instead, she's moved near enough that I can scent her shampoo. I imagine I can feel her body heat.

But for as close as she's come, she won't look at me. I think she's staring out the window past my shoulder. *God*, the mouth on her. She's close enough to kiss. All I'd have to do is lean forward and close the distance.

I look up and find she's finally ready to make eye contact. I clench my jaw to hold back the words I shouldn't say. Words like "You can burn those fucking papers. I'm not signing them."

Aaand now she's looking past my shoulder again. She acts like she's the one about to get her heart ripped out.

"You traveled all this way, Clarissa. It must be important for an in-person meeting without calling ahead first. What can I do for you?"

She holds out the envelope, and in a gentle voice, she says, "You can sign these papers."

Of course. I knew she wanted a divorce the second she walked through those doors. What else, besides divorce, would be so important she'd show up in person unannounced?

If there is one universal truth, it's that Clarissa Harcourt-Mellinger is pure class. Even in pajamas and a messy bun. Even in a wrinkled evening gown with the lipstick kissed right off her face. Even when she moves out and takes my heart with her.

She'd never tell me she didn't love me anymore over text or a phone call. She'd do it in person, with kind eyes and a squeeze of my hand.

I've known this day was coming for a while. She's spent the last four months pulling away from me. She's not on my insurance anymore.

Not on my cell phone service. She sent back the car I gave her and bought her own.

Even as I worked to get my head out of my ass and move out of my own damn way, she was done. I got my shit together too damn late.

She's talking, but I haven't heard a word since she said, "Sign these."

"James."

I jerk my head to where she's standing. She's moved over by the seating grouping, indicating I should sit on the sofa. She still has that manila envelope in her hand.

I give a disoriented blink, then frown. "I'm sorry. What did you say?"

She pulls a sheaf of papers out of the envelope, and she holds them out to me. "I said, I'm sorry if I misinterpreted your letter. If you meant it to let me know you wanted to move on, I'll"—the distress on her face is clear—"I'll understand."

Wait. What is she saying?

"I was hoping you'd rather sign these papers," she says, letting them hover in her extended hand between us.

I walk over and take them from her. I skim them, from the law firm letterhead to the words written beneath. Then I sit on the sofa. Hard. Just drop right there without a single thought or plan.

I lift my eyes and see her standing there, nervous. One of her hands is clenching and unclenching at her skirt.

I turn my attention back to the papers in my hand. It's a petition to transfer the trustee status of her trust fund from me to a corporate entity owned by Harcourt. The justification is cited as "conflict of interest."

"There's more," she says. Then she sits next to me and opens the briefcase she carried in with her.

She holds up a piece of paper, then places it on the coffee table. "The title of my car." Another paper. "Proof of car insurance." Another. "My health insurance. My quarterly taxes. My credit score."

She reaches for another piece of paper, and I stop her with a hand on her wrist. "Enough," I say, and I don't even know how she understands what I'm saying because my voice is so raw it feels like my vocal cords are shredded.

She lets go of the paper and swallows hard. "I don't need you, James. I can manage my own life just fine. But I want you. I love you so much I—"

I can't breathe. My eyes don't even know quite where to focus. "You're not leaving me."

It's not a question, but she answers anyway. "*No*. You said—you *told* me that as long as I needed you, you couldn't trust that I really wanted you. So, I was showing you—"

She's shaking, her wet eyes just on the verge of spilling over. Then she reaches out and punches me on the arm.

I laugh. It's watery, and giddy, and I know she can see the tears in my eyes, but for once in my life, I don't care. I yank her into my arms. And I kiss my wife. I haven't touched her in six months. I thought I never would again. And suddenly she's here. And she's still mine. She will always be mine.

I kiss her like I want to be inside her, because I do.

She kisses me back with the same desperation, and she's pulling my hair, and I'm ripping at her shirt.

Then she leans back. Stops me with a hard hold on my hair. "James."

When I try to kiss her again, she holds me still.

When I make eye contact, she says, "Is that a yes?"

"Yes, that's a fucking yes. All those stupid things I said about you needing me... sweet girl, that was all on me. Every bit of it was just me rationalizing. You don't have to prove yourself to me. Not a damn thing."

And then my mouth is back on hers, and I'm smoothing her blouse over her shoulders and tossing it onto the floor. I undo the zip on her skirt and slide it down past her hips. She kicks it off, and she's shoving my jacket off me.

"Are you sure about letting someone else handle the trust fund?" she asks against my mouth.

"I have never been more sure of anything in my life," I say.

I lower her onto the sofa and follow her down. She tries to yank my shirt off, and we're both frustrated when we realize it won't come off over my hands because I forgot to release the cufflinks. I let her fuss with the left one while I use my right hand to hold her pretty little breast. I thumb her nipple through the lace. Then I suck right through the fabric. When that's not enough, I yank the cups down and groan as I feast.

She's done with the left sleeve, and now she's pulling on the right. I let her hold my arm captive while I work my way down her body, open mouth dragging down her belly. I stop to kiss the scar from her surgery. Then I'm pulling her panties down her legs, and for the first time, my mouth is on my wife's pussy. It only took two and a half years to get here. And it's everything.

She's everything.

34

River

CLARISSA

James Mellinger is a god. I thought it the first time he kissed me, and I wasn't wrong. He eats my pussy like he's starving, and I'm the most delicious thing he's ever tasted. Never, in any of my frenzied imaginings, did I do justice to what James would do to me with his mouth.

He works me up that cliff so fast, it's ridiculous. If I were even capable of thinking at all, I suppose I'd be embarrassed at how quickly I go off. But I'm not embarrassed. I'm just coming and calling his name. My legs are shaking, and I'm clutching at his head. Then he's kissing my inner thighs, and he's sliding up my body. I reach for his belt buckle. And I feel the hot length of him in my hand.

Previously, I'd only touched James's cock directly that one time. I'd reached out with my thumb and swiped the bead of fluid from the tip to see what he tasted like.

Wrapping my fingers around his cock now is entirely different. He feels so solid, not a tease or a torment but everything I need. His cock is hot and silky, and when I pump my hand the way I remember James did to himself, the satin skin glides over a core of iron, flexing in my grip, so alive and real.

He groans, then holds my hand by my wrist. "Clarissa," he grits out against my ear, "that feels incredible, but if you keep it up, I'm going to come before I get inside you."

Just those words make my thighs clench together, the fever inside me rising again, burning me from the inside out.

There's a wild desperation bleeding from both of us. Neither of us has any patience. Neither of us can get close enough to the other.

I wrap one leg up and around him. "Now," I say.

He moves against me, watches himself as he presses against my opening, and then freezes, eyes closed. "Oh shit," he groans. "This is not happening right now. Clarissa. Baby."

I hold still. "It's okay. If you're not ready, it's fine. It might take time for us to work up to—"

James's eyes go huge. "I am *ready*. Trust me. But I don't have any condoms."

Oh, that. I push back up against him. "I'm on the pill. So get in there."

Someday, I'm going to look back on those words, and I'm going to laugh about the way I demanded he take my virginity. But not today. Today I'm just desperate.

James's entire being collapses in relief. He tips his head down, resting his forehead against mine, and says, "Oh thank God," at the same time he pushes that gorgeous, perfect cock into my pussy in one slow, unrelenting glide. The sensation is overwhelming. It's nothing like the toys he bought me. I'm so full, I feel him everywhere. He's in my *throat*.

When he's fully seated, he stops. Holds still. I'm looking down our bodies, taking in the sight of his cock inside me. He puts a long-fingered hand on my jaw and uses it to gently push my head back to look into his eyes.

"You okay?" he asks.

A single ecstatic burst of joy punches out of me. "God, yes. You?"

He grins and drops his face against my neck. "Oh yes," he says, the words vibrating against my skin and into my heart.

Then he rides me hard and fast, the way he promised he would.

He pushes his thumb into my mouth. "Suck."

I do, curling my tongue over the digit. He pulls it out with a pop of suction. Then he slides that hand down between us, swirling his thumb over my clit as he works me on his dick.

"I'm going to take you over fast this time," he rasps. "I have to. I'll go slow next time. I swear it."

I don't even know if I say anything to that. I'm just pushing up against him. Crying out. This isn't even my body. I'm just a halo of pleasure and need that hovers over the person I used to be.

James has his face pressed into my hair, his mouth inches from my ear. "That's my girl. That's my strong, smart, amazing girl. Clarissa, I love you. I love you so fucking much. You are never leaving me again. I won't survive it. God, your pussy feels so fucking good. Do you feel that? Do you feel how hard you make me? How good you make me feel?"

I don't even think James knows what he's saying. It's just stream of consciousness pouring out of his mouth, but I love every word.

I'm practically sobbing from pleasure, so twisted up inside, so coiled with tension, I feel frantic with it.

He keeps moving, swirling and pumping, while he talks into my ear. Taking me higher and higher.

"You have no idea how often I dream of this. Holding you in my arms, fucking into your sweet little pussy with your taste on my tongue."

I jerk and shudder silently as I come, pleasure robbing me of breath and voice.

I'm still coming when his cock jerks inside me. With a gush of liquid heat, James orgasms with a groan, his ass clenched, a slick film of sweat on his skin.

"I love you," I say, tears choking my words. "I will never not love you."

James didn't lie when he said we'd go slow the second time. He kisses me everywhere, from his gentle touch against my temple to his goofy slurp on my big toe that makes me shriek and laugh.

His hands glide over my skin with a leisurely, exploratory touch, both of them moving in firm sweeping motions over my back, down my arms. His hands weigh my breasts and trail over my abdomen. He slides a hand from my butt to my knee and back again.

When he sits and pulls me on his lap to straddle him, he teaches me how to ride. And while I ride, he works my clit so slowly, I could scream in frustration. I give him a seething look, and he laughs, then sucks my fingers into his mouth, guiding them to my clit to let me set the pace.

And we come together, wrapped in each other's arms and holding on for dear life.

An hour later, we're standing near the door to James's office. His eyes travel over my hair, my lips, my neck. He looks satisfied with himself. Maybe a little smug.

I indicate his gaping shirt. "Are you going to put yourself back together?"

He tries to smooth a hand through his wildly ruffled hair, then says, "I can't. My wife ripped three buttons off my shirt."

Then James opens his office door. He reaches out a hand for me, so I tuck my briefcase strap onto my left shoulder and put my right hand in his. I glide out of his office with the dignity of a queen. Like I'm not wearing a catastrophically wrinkled pencil skirt and blouse, with my lipstick kissed right off my swollen lips, whisker burns on my neck, and what must be utterly spectacular sex hair.

I make inadvertent eye contact with Rebecca as she sits at her desk, a blush heating her cheeks as she fans her face with a sheaf of papers.

I nod as we stroll past her. "Have a good day, Rebecca."

She dips hers in acknowledgment, her lips tipping into a grin. "You, too, Clarissa. James."

I don't turn my head, but I sneak a glance at James. His lips are swollen, there's a smear of lipstick on his collar, and his hair is an emo rocker's wet dream.

He catches my look with a side-eye of his own. Our lips quirk at exactly the same time. And we race for the elevator.

Epilogue

YOU MAKE MY DREAMS

James

Two Weeks Later

Clarissa is practically vibrating in the seat next to me on our private jet. She typically flies commercial. As do I, unless I've got an entire team in the air, purely for environmental reasons.

But her plans for our honeymoon included me having not a single clue where we were going.

I squint at her and quote her words back to her in mock complaint, "You say I won't need clothing. And I'm just saying that it seems like something I should question. Who knows what you plan to do with me once you have me naked and alone in a foreign locale?"

I turn to Jerome, our flight attendant, as he returns with a shot each of Mezcal for Clarissa and me. "I'm a suspicious person, Jerome. Where could my wife possibly have planned to take me that involves no clothing? And what could we possibly be doing there?"

Jerome grins and says, "I'd love to tell you, Mr. Mellinger, but my boss has forbidden me from mentioning it."

Clarissa presents an exaggerated face of innocence. I lift an eyebrow first at her, then Jerome. "Your boss, huh? I thought I was your boss."

He smiles benignly. "Did you, sir?"

Clarissa snickers and lifts the shot glass to her lips.

When Jerome walks away, I toast her with the Mezcal, then place my hand on her knee, sliding it just under the skirt she's wearing. I inch my hand higher and higher, until it rests exactly where I want it, with my pinky finger pushing gently and rhythmically against the silky fabric covering her pussy.

Her eyes fly wide. "*James*," she says breathlessly.

It's my turn to look innocent. "Yes?"

She squirms beside me, then frantically rubs her thumb over her bottom lip. Finally, she throws her arms straight up in the air as though she's stretching. Then she yawns and announces quite loudly, "You know it's going to be a long flight. I'm going to take a nap. In the bedroom. Because I'm sleepy."

She's the worst liar I've ever seen in my life. No finesse, whatsoever. "So it's a long flight, is it?"

She represses a grin. "Yes."

She stands, and I join her. "The bed sounds like a good idea, then. Since it's a long flight."

She turns her head back toward the security detail at the front of the plane, then smiles at me, clears her throat and says, "That's what we need. A nap. You must be tired."

"Not even a little," I say, leading her by the hand back to the bedroom where I have absolutely no intention of sleeping.

"New Zealand, huh?"

"Have you been? It's supposed to be beautiful and February is still the warmest part of summer here," she asks.

I take in the luxurious and, most importantly, private home she's rented for the next two weeks. There are floor to ceiling windows enabling us to enjoy the view. A wall of accordion-style glass doors retract to provide access to a patio space that includes everything from a fire pit surrounded by plush cushions to a sparkling salt water infinity pool. All of which overlooks a pristine private beach.

"I have been to New Zealand," I admit.

She looks a little anxious now that we're here... worried her surprise could fall flat. As if that's even possible. We could stay in a leaky shed somewhere, and as long as she was with me, I'd be having the time of my life.

"I've never been here to have fun, though. And I've never been here with you," I say.

"I did actually pack you clothing, you know. I didn't want to give away the weather. But you won't be naked."

I pull her close and rub my nose across hers. "We don't really need it while we're here, though. Do we?"

I suck on her bottom lip, and she shivers in response.

"The gates are locked tight. The guards have their own space and orders to give us privacy." I loosen the buttons on her shirt, one by one.

She reaches out to work my belt buckle free. We're not frantic. It's a slow burn. Teasing. Gentle.

Until we're down to our skin, and I'm just about to haul her to the first horizontal surface I can find. She stops me with a hand in my hair and locks eye contact, mischief sparkling in her eyes. "Do you remember our wedding?"

I brush her hair from her forehead. "I remember all kinds of things about our wedding. You'll have to be specific."

"There was a moment. It was the first time I had the nerve to tease you. I messed your hair all up. Do you remember that?"

"Sweet girl, it's a core memory for me."

"You had this look in your eyes after I did it," she says. "I couldn't wait to see what you were going to do next. I almost ran from you, just to see if you'd chase me."

"I'd have wanted to."

She wrinkles her nose. Grins. Then gently bites my lip.

When she pulls away, she wiggles her eyebrows. Then she bolts, naked, straight for the patio.

For half a heartbeat I stand there, stunned stupid, just like I was at our wedding reception. Then I give chase. She's got a small head start, but I'm not worried about overtaking her too quickly. I'm enjoying the view too much.

She turns her head back, laughing, and I catch her in my arms. Then we both suck in a deep breath, and I take the last flying leap with her straight into the deep end of the pool.

She wraps her legs around my waist, her arms around my neck, and she kisses me.

I hold on, both of my arms wrapped tight around her middle as my feet hit the bottom. She pulls her face from mine, gripping my hair in tight fists. When I open my eyes, she's looking back. Water muffles the sounds of nature. There's no hum of insects or birdsong down here. It's just the two of us in the quiet shelter of crystal clear salt water.

Then I push hard against the pool bottom, propelling us both with my legs, aiming straight up. She releases my hair, just long enough to use her arms to move us faster through the water.

We break the surface, water streaming from hair and skin. Then I slide my hands down to cup her sexy, freckled ass. And I kiss my wife.

Twenty-Five Years Later

Marc says, "Okay, Dad. Do not freak out."

I look up from my dinner with a frown on my face. Because any time I hear "do not freak out," I know something is definitely about to freak me out.

I shoot a glance at Clarissa, but she's just sitting there, smiling encouragingly at him. Which tells me she already knows what he's going to say, and it's not that bad. Surely it's not that bad.

Marc reaches in his pocket and shoves a folded-up letter at me. I can tell the thing has been folded and refolded many times. He's been carrying this around with him, trying to get up the nerve to share it with me.

I pick up the letter and read the contents. My gaze flies to Marc, sitting there, tense and nervous, and looking so much like the perfect blend of his mother and me. My height and build. Her eyes and hair and freckles.

His hand clenches and unclenches on the table. There's a spark of defiance in his eyes.

"You want to go to an art school in London," I say.

"Yes?"

I glance at Clarissa again, and she just smiles and nods at him.

"Art school," I repeat.

"Yes?"

"In London."

"Yes?"

I shake my head, and his shoulders slump.

But I say, "Don't say 'yes' like it's a question. Is this what you want to do?"

He straightens his shoulders, and in his firm, newly deep voice, he says, "Yes, and I'm sorry if you're disappointed that I don't want to go to business school. But it's just not what I want to do. I want to work in fashion design."

My brows knit in confusion. "Marc, I'm not disappointed. I want you to do something that makes you happy."

"But Harcourt is supposed to be this family legacy."

I remember something Clarissa once said to me and give Marc my wise and benevolent parent look. The one Clarissa says makes me look like a stuffy old man, but she always tries to rip my shirt off afterward, so....

"You don't need to live your life trying to fill someone else's shoes," I say. "Wear your own shoes, Marcus Mellinger. They're a lot more comfortable."

Marc lifts his foot out from beneath the table and gives it a shake. "These boots are gorgeous."

I grin at him. The kid does have style in spades. He'll be a hell of a fashion designer.

"Don't worry, Dad," Ellie says. "I'm going to business school."

Our daughter inherited more than my dark hair and blue eyes. She's only fifteen, but she's already very driven. And she spends an awful lot of time in my office. I swear sometimes she's sizing the place up. The look in her eyes when she walks in the building is pure Marcus Harcourt.

Marc snorts. "Shocked. I'm shocked."

I shoot her finger guns. "Got a summer job in the mailroom with your name on it, if you want it."

She grins. "Perfect."

Before bed, Clarissa stands in the bathroom doorway and watches me as I brush my teeth. She's leaning against the doorframe in panties and one of my T-shirts.

She's got blonde highlights in her hair now. She says it's to disguise the gray, but I love when the silver strands sparkle through. The same way I love the laugh lines at the corners of her eyes. They're evidence of a life well lived, and she's living it with me.

Her arms are crossed. She wears a small grin on her face and a speculative gleam in her eye.

I rinse, put my toothbrush away, then make eye contact with her in the mirror. "What?"

She sidles up and wraps her arms around me from behind. I turn, lean against the counter, and pull her into the V of my thighs. She brushes a lock of steel-threaded hair off my forehead, then rests her hand on my cheek. "You handled that really well."

I give her a confused smile. "You know I don't care what the kids want to do with their careers as long as it makes them happy."

She laughs. "I know that. But you didn't even freak out over the fact that he wants to go to London."

"Mmmm, that part actually was hard for me," I say, rubbing my thumb across her bottom lip.

"I know."

"Parsons is right *here*. He could even commute from home."

She raises her eyebrows, and her eyes sparkle at me with amusement. "I *know*."

I look at her in suspicion. "Clarissa Harcourt-Mellinger, you are totally freaked out by this, aren't you?"

She collapses against me in helpless laughter. "Completely. Totally. Oh my God, if he doesn't text me every day, I will absolutely kill him."

I run my hands under her shirt, just to feel her skin. Then I kiss her, sweet and slow.

When I pull back, I say in my wise, I-know-everything voice, "No you won't. We're going to let him fly."

She grins as she reaches for the waistband of my boxer briefs and says, "Still love you, James."

I smile against her mouth as I answer back as I always will, "Still love you, Clarissa." Then my wife squeaks and giggles as I haul her over my shoulder and carry her to our bed.

Afterword

Thank you for reading *I Almost Do*. I hope you loved Clarissa and James.

Would you like to keep up with all the tea (and be the first to find out what Bronwyn and Dean were up to on that crazy weekend)? Sign up for my newsletter here. You'll be the first to receive sneak peeks of upcoming releases, access to freebies when they're available, and even occasional bonus content and deleted scenes. Hope to see you there!

www.evangelinewilliams.com

Acknowledgments

It really does take an entire team to bring a novel to life, and I am eternally grateful for everyone who had a hand in the creation of *I Almost Do*. I absolutely could not have done it without each and every one of you:

The one and only Ruby Dixon. I still can't believe I had the audacity to ask you for permission to reference "Barbarian's Treasure" in my debut novel. Or that you were so incredibly kind as to agree. From the bottom of my heart, thank you. My sister, alpha reader, and biggest cheerleader, Trish Alexander. You're the reason this novel ever saw the light of day. Thank you for your endless patience and feedback as I bounced ideas off of you. My daughter, Annalisa S., thank you for both your emotional support and for sharing your professional expertise and experience in wealth management and Cognitive Behavioral Therapy. Any mistakes are mine. My editors at Hot Tree, Kristin Scearce and Jamee Thumm, you're both absolute rock stars. Thank you to the designers at GetCovers for a beautiful cover. Kurt, Megan, and Ben, thank you for tolerating both my distraction and my incessant need to bounce ideas off of you and "read just one more scene" to you. Your support means everything. Dad. What can I say? Thank for raising a reader, your belief in me, and your invaluable feedback (and for skipping the sex scenes). LOL. My beta readers: Bill C., Megan S., Kurt S., Sandy M., Beth T., Shannon J., Dori A.M., Donna R., Lindsay Murray, Kimberly Rose, and Annie S. Thank you. This book is better because of your contributions and support.

Printed in Great Britain
by Amazon